# LAST RESORT

# SISTERS IN CRIME/LOS ANGELES PRESENTS

# LAST RESORT

### EDITED BY
## MATT COYLE, MARY MARKS
## AND PATRICIA SMILEY

### INTRODUCTION BY MICHAEL CONNELLY

Down & Out Books
3959 Van Dyke Rd, Ste. 265
Lutz, FL 33558
www.DownAndOutBooks.com

The characters and events in this book are fictitious. Any similarity to real persons, living or dead, is coincidental and not intended by the author.

Cover design by JT Lindroos

ISBN: 1-943402-62-0
ISBN-13: 978-1-943402-62-5

# CONTENTS

# CONTENTS

# Introduction
## Michael Connelly

L.A. is Suitcase City, everybody here seems to come from someplace else. It's what makes the place vibrant and lonely, all at the same time. It makes it full of opportunity and danger, all at the same time. People leave home because there is something wrong, something that doesn't work. They come here to get it all fixed.

They are all running from something when they come to the last resort. Blue-steel ocean, soft-edged sunshine, green mountains and white desert. A land of seemingly boundless change and opportunity. They come here because it's a place to start again. That is what is folded so nicely and packed so gently in the suitcase: hope—the life blood of the second chance.

But what they find here is that the ground is unsteady. It shakes and slides. Not everybody is lucky. Not everybody sees their hopes realized. There are those who disappear and those who despair. There are the haves and the have-nots—as visible as the traffic that jams every freeway. Look out the window to the left, then look out the window to the right. Look at the cars that surround you and the score is clear. Those who have had the dream come true; those who haven't. And between them is a thin dark line as fragile and tense as the line between the tectonic plates beneath them. Friction builds and at any moment the big one could hit. At any moment there could be tremors in the fabric below and above the ground. Here is a collection of tremors; stories where the ground in some way is shifting. This is a collection of stories that sit on the unsteady ground of the last resort. In the zone where anything can happen.

—Michael Connelly
Los Angeles

# EGGS OVER DEAD
## Wendall Thomas

Tweedledum is off his meds again.

I can see him through the "tasteful" cast iron security bars on my apartment window, pressing his naked potbelly, thick and lop-sided as a bean bag chair, against the balcony railing next door.

He's been yelling for his cat, Portia, every five seconds for a solid fifteen minutes, occasionally alternating the cat's name with the phrase "Check the phone records! Check the phone records!" This kind of outburst happens about once a week. It's five a.m.

The "phone records" mantra is a holdover from a fight he had with his freakishly identical lover around midnight. One of them has apparently been caught sexting, with photos. As Holly Golightly would say, "The mind reels."

I reach for my new glasses, hipper than I can afford—courtesy of a three-hour line at the annual l.a. Eyeworks sale—then down a cup of Trader Joe's blend, grab my black T-shirt, jeans, and apron, and head to work.

I cover the weekday breakfast shift at Summer/Winter/Fall. The "of the moment" restaurant is not where I thought I would wind up when I drove cross-country ten years ago, but waitressing pays better than a development job, and I'm in a bills situation. I should be working the more lucrative weekend brunch—the mecca for all fedora-wearers—but I'm afraid

I'll eventually lose it, stab the fifth lead in a streaming sitcom, and wind up on TMZ.

The restaurant reeks of kale chips, and the phone is already ringing.

It's a customer frantic to know if we have his gold teeth. After searching the lost and found box and register, I finally locate the crescent of gold Chiclets swept under the bar, entwined in a tuft of "emotional support dog" hair. I shake them off and put them in a take-out bag for pick-up.

I'm filling the artisanal salts when I hear a mad *click click click* on the glass door. Outside, a lanky forty-year-old, still dressed in his mid-life clubbing clothes, waves and points to his mouth. I let him in and hand him the bag.

"Thought I was gonna have to call my jeweler in Jersey. I owe you one."

Literally one, I guess. He hands me a dollar bill. He takes the glittering brace out of the bag and pops it straight in. If he'd given me a twenty, I might have told him he should rinse it first.

I check the clock. It's seven minutes to eight and a few regulars are already hovering outside. I take my last chance to sneak out into the alley for a smoke. I look down the street of one-bedroom pseudo-Spanish, Deco, and Tudor bungalows, all listing for well over a million. Not for the first time, I consider moving back to North Carolina where the mortgage payment on a three-bedroom ranch house would be less than the rent on my current hovel. Still, I prefer Jerry Brown to Republican bathroom monitors, so I decide to stay put until I can afford a better fate.

Bang. Bang.

In another L.A. neighborhood, it might be a gunshot, but in Beverly Grove, it's more likely a Prius with muffler issues. I grind out my American Spirit, swear on general principle, and go back inside.

I bring my two starving writer regulars tap water and steel

myself for the dreaded Thursday Guy, usually expecting to be let in early. Maybe I dodged a bullet today. I ask Ashley, our model/hostess/half-wit, not to seat him in my section if he shows up. I'm not in the mood.

Half an hour later, a BMW 7-series tears around the corner and parks on the street-cleaning side of the road. The vanity plate reads BGSHOT on its bumper, or should I say BUMPR. I guess big shots can afford the seventy-eight-dollar ticket that waitresses can't.

The next time I emerge from the kitchen, Ashley is leading the Thursday Guy to my prime four-top. She puts two menus down. She's either evil, or twenty-five years of Ritalin have left her with the attention span of a gnat. I'll get my revenge later by asking if she's gaining weight for a part.

I swear, specifically, then approach my nemesis, already spewing self-importance at full volume into a Bluetooth. I notice the Etch A Sketch scattering of pattern baldness stubble on his usually smooth head. He's got his current uniform on: Armani suit, overstated silk tie, a wave of choke-worthy cologne. I'm sure it's expensive, but honestly, anything smells cheap if you use too much of it.

For all his designer trappings, he's a cheapskate, with his breakfast meetings (cheapest of the day) and ten percent tips (before taxes). He talks with his mouth full, he doesn't stand up when his guests arrive, and his gestures are limited to pokes across the table and jerky, insistent snaps of his hairy, manicured fingers when he wants something. Like now.

He gives me a snap which means "Get me my fucking coffee."

I come back with a large French press and a fresh cup, which he takes without acknowledgement. For once, I can't hear his conversation. I check back five minutes later, while he pummels his iPad.

"Would you like to order?"

He points at the second menu across the table. "Can't you see I'm waiting for someone?"

"Of course, sir. Just let me know when you're ready." I can hardly wait.

Half an hour later, I'm on the other side of restaurant when I hear a grating "Hey!" and see him, curling his finger in a "Get over here now" gesture.

There's murder in my heart, but a smile on my face, as I move to the table. I wait while he licks his napkin and smears a fleck of red off his turquoise tie. Finally, he raises his head and shoves one of his two menus at me.

"Yes, sir?"

"The man I was meeting is dead. I've just been on the phone with the police. I'd like to order now."

Wow. A new low in human decency, even for him.

"I'm sorry to hear that," I say, after a few seconds of silence. "What would you like?" An egg white omelet with a side of E. coli? Roasted Brussels sprouts with a belladonna foam?

"Eggs over hard. Turkey sausage. Hash browns, well done. Tell them not to fuck it up this time."

While I contemplate what kind of bacteria I can release into his potatoes, I go to turn in his order. Who's dead? Someone famous? Someone I've waited on? I do a mental flip through the faces that usually sit opposite him, most of them are indistinguishable from each other, with their Beverly Hills haircuts and too-tight dress shirts. There's only one face I remember—a mousy man with an optimistic comb-over and manners. He always insists on paying for their breakfast, tips twenty-five percent, and never sends anything back, which puts him in the customer Hall of Fame as far as I'm concerned. As I put in the order, I hope it isn't him.

It is.

The next morning, I find a small article and photo in the California Section of the restaurant's *Los Angeles Times*, complete with comb-over: Henry Costa, father, husband, CPA, found shot in his driveway in the Fairfax district in the early morning hours. Anyone with information should contact the LAPD.

I shove the paper into my backpack and head back onto the restaurant floor. My talent agency screamer is about to blow: someone has "taken" her Equal. The woman, who carries a vintage handbag worth more than my car, offers references to "Bob" Redford, "Tommy" Cruise, and "Jimmy" Woods as part of her introductory spiel, followed by the refrain that she discovered Charlize Theron at Du-par's. I find it a little hard to imagine Charlize shoveling down a short stack, but what do I know?

Given the poor quality of both her recent face work and her breakfast partners, Ms. Equal is losing her grip. I can almost see her disappearing. In this town, failure equals invisibility. Even people who've known you well for years just manage to miss your eye or walk right past you.

Still, she's trying—I have to give her that—with her leopard skin prints, asymmetrical haircut, and Jimmy Choo mules, which reveal her unfortunate heels, pressed into three bulging layers like an undercooked panini.

She always orders hot water with lemon, then proceeds to empty eleven Equals into her mug. Yes, eleven. I know this because we are ordered to fill the containers with twelve, and after she leaves there's always just one sad aqua packet left. I want to hate her, but if ten years in Hollywood has taught me anything, it's that no matter where we buy our luggage, what berth we're assigned, or how big the gift basket is in our cabin, we're all on the *Titanic*. The freezing waters of oblivion are just an iceberg away.

I'm refilling her Equals when I spot two men in bad ties decline Ashley's offer of menus. She points them in my direction with what a bad actress might consider undisguised glee. On her, it looks like constipation.

The men introduce themselves as Detectives Ivy and Tanaka. They'd like a word.

What could they want? Has something happened to my family? I'm up to date with my parking tickets, and it's my understanding that four cars going left after a red light is now L.A. standard. Though I have the urge to kill Tweedledum and Tweedledee daily, they were still alive enough to be having make-up sex by the outdoor washing machine when I left the house.

"Is everything all right?" I ask as I seat them at the bar.

"Just routine," Detective Tanaka says, looking with longing at the shiny silver French presses going by. I ask them if they'd like some coffee. They hesitate, then agree.

I ask Taylor, my fellow waiter/bass player, to take my tables and return with the pot and sit sideways while I ease down the plunger and divide the tarry liquid between them. "How can I help you?"

"We're just following up on one of our inquiries," Detective Ivy says, pouring all the half and half into his cup, provoking a glare from his partner. "Were you working yesterday morning?"

"I was."

Detective Tanaka pulls out what appears to be an old photo of the Thursday Guy, when he had hair. It's probably the one he still uses on OKCupid.

"Do you recognize this man?"

I squint at the photo, then back at their cards, which read *Robbery-Homicide*. "Is he dead?" Could I be that lucky?

"No, no," Detective Tanaka says. "We're just verifying his whereabouts. He said you could confirm that he was here yesterday from just before eight until ten in the morning."

"He said I could? He gave you my name?"

Detective Ivy pulls out an old-fashioned notebook and flips it open.

"He said 'the middle-aged waitress with the frizzy hair.' The hostess said that was you."

Middle-aged? I'm thirty-two. Oh God. Is that middle-aged? I glare at Ashley, who's twirling her hair and looking down at her phone, while three people stand in line, waiting to be seated.

I assess the situation before I answer. It appears the Thursday Guy is using me as an alibi with L.A. Robbery/Homicide. For what? A burglary? Then I remember the whole "the man I was meeting is dead" comment and the news about Henry Costa, who died blocks from here. I think about the "bangs" and the spot that looked like blood on the Thursday Guy's tie. I think about his snapping fingers. And then I think about the five minutes I spent in his office that ruined my life.

It was six years ago. My agent said a meeting with Norman Steinberg could make my career. The producer was looking for "something fun." His credits included a great movie twenty years ago and a mediocre one, *Spanish Fly*, the previous summer. I spent weeks preparing the fifteen-minute pitch Steinberg's office required. I arrived at a Century City high-rise ready to meet the great man, only to find myself pitching instead to his head "d-girl," Stokely, a twenty-something executive with bangs that swung like a beaded curtain over her waxed eyebrows.

She explained that my pitch was far too long and proceeded to tell me what I needed to take out of it, which was basically everything that made sense. After my repeated objections, she said that if I went over two minutes, Mr. Steinberg would just walk out. Or start screaming. Or fire someone, probably her.

She insisted I come back for two more meetings to practice, where she and her three underlings, also sporting metronome hair, chopped more and more away from my story until it was "ready for Mr. Steinberg." At this point, I offered to email what was essentially a phrase to Mr. Steinberg, but Stokely insisted that I make the rush-hour drive for the fourth time, as Norm wanted "the human connection."

I'll never forget entering the massive office, the burnt orange, L-shaped couch aimed at the floor to ceiling television in the corner. There was Steinberg, facing the other way, complete with the classic "aging (i.e., balding) producer" baseball cap and running shoes, glued to what appeared to be porn. Only in the movie business would someone fail to acknowledge that five women had entered the room. We all stood there for a full minute and a half, trying to ignore the orgasmic moans.

Finally, the producer clicked off the TV and shifted towards us.

I held out my hand, ready to introduce myself. He ignored it. Instead he pointed his remote control at my breasts, and said, "Okay, go."

A remote? Seriously? What did he use if you actually got the job? A Taser? This stupefying level of rudeness threw my story completely out of my head. As I tried to collect myself, the other women sat down. Stokely elbowed me in the thigh, sending her bangs into overdrive. Finally, I remembered that this was my big chance and lowered myself onto the couch. I launched into my abridged presentation, complete with the rehearsed gestures the women had demanded. Somehow, I got through it in the requisite two minutes, ignoring Norm's repeated attempts to fast-forward me with the remote.

When I was done, he patted me on the knee. "Hmmph. I kinda like it. Almost. It feels like there's something missing."

There was, Norm. It was the other ten minutes of the pitch.

"I did tell her it was full of holes," Stokely said. I repressed my urge to elbow her back. In the eye.

"Still, there's some potential. Maybe we can work something out," Steinberg said.

What the hell did that mean, I wondered, as his development executives disappeared as if on cue, leaving me and the producer alone.

Norman's potential "solution" to my story problems made a back-alley blow job seem dignified.

A smart writer would have said a gracious, ego-saving "I'm so flattered but no thank you," congratulated him on his sexist summer sleeper, and lived to meet another day. I was a stupid writer. I stood up and removed his hand.

"Actually, I only do that kind of thing with men who have a full head of hair. And more than a two-inch penis," I said.

Norman Steinberg rose for the first time. I understood why he had remained seated. He was about five-two.

"Lifts might help," I offered, looking down at him.

"Jesus, you're not even a five. I was taking pity on you." He pointed a hairy finger at me. Apparently he had hair somewhere. "Do you really think you're going to get a chance like this again? From someone like me? No one is ever going to hire you for your idea. Your idea sucked. You're just another cunt screenwriter with no gratitude and no talent. There are thousands of you. Women can't write."

"And you couldn't even sell *Spanish Fly* to Canada. You should ask Ted Danson where he gets his piece. You must know him, right?"

I didn't breathe until I made the elevator. I thought it was worth it until I realized I hadn't gotten my parking validated.

By the time I got home, my agent had already fired me by voicemail. He'd gotten a call from Steinberg's office saying I was just another "unprofessional girl (read: bitch) screenwriter," and how could he waste Norm's time this way? The agency had decided "it just wasn't working out, but we all wish you the best."

At that point, it had been five years since Sony optioned

my novella, ruined it, and put it in turnaround. I'd had one horrific job and written three scripts that had "fans," but hadn't sold. There was no going back to serious fiction or academia—abandoning graduate school on my agent's recommendation and my credit on *Cartel Wives: Lipstick and Blood* pretty much took care of that.

So, now, this is my life: I bring extra tahini and take back overcooked mahi-mahi; I try to drown out the petty, *Through the Looking Glass* squabbles next door, and I hold onto the standard screenwriter's delusion that one script sale will clear my debts in one fell swoop. So far, no swoop, just the hope that the new article in *Westways* about our blueberry-ricotta pancakes will bring in enough tourists to cover my Visa bill.

If Norman Steinberg had ever acknowledged that we'd met before, even a modest "You're that bitch!" on any of the one hundred Thursdays I had brought his eggs over hard, I might not lay the disaster of my life at his feet. But every time he snaps his fingers, I see that remote and hear my agent wishing me "the best in your future endeavors."

Detective Ivy is staring at me.

"Sorry. I'm just trying to remember." I nod at Ashley, who's taking a selfie of her and her iced green tea. "Did you ask her?"

He rolls his eyes. "Millennials. Not the most reliable witnesses."

"They're always looking down."

He smiles. "Exactly."

I think about yesterday. Did Steinberg pay with a credit card? No. He left a twenty on an eighteen dollar check. We only have security cameras on the alley. So I'm it: the only thing between Norman "Thursday Guy" Steinberg and a possible homicide investigation.

I look at my fellow servers/somethings and know most of us will either head back east or make sad marriages and go into direct sales. I think about how, despite the current outbreak of hot yoga and meditation studios on La Brea, karma is hard to find in this town, or anywhere. It's always the most awful people who get rich, who get their movies made, and it's the loveliest people who lose their husbands or get cancer. If you wreck your car trying to avoid a raccoon, your rates fly up. If you ask someone politely to stop talking in a movie, they tell you to go to hell. Or shoot you. I know there's nothing I can do about Tweedledum and Tweedledee—they have rent control and aren't going anywhere—or about my failed screenwriting career, or about all the Bob's Big Boys disappearing. But I can do something about this.

"Look. I wait on a hundred people a day. Most of them are wearing either expensive suits or baseball caps." I gesture around the room, proving my case. "I'm a waitress. To be honest, I really only remember the ones who tip well. I really can't verify that he was here. You can check the security cameras if you'd like. Just ask for the manager."

As they head towards the back office, the Thursday Guy walks in. On a Friday.

The great Norman Steinberg tries to catch my eye, waves and fake-smiles, the bastard, then takes a menu and heads to my section. I'm guessing on his lawyer's recommendation.

Taylor heads towards him, but Norm waves him off. Then gestures to me with his signature snap.

When I make it to his table, his newly shaved head looks a bit pale.

"Hi!" he says. "How's it going?" Honestly?

"Busy," I say. "The LAPD is here. We have gluten-free pumpkin pancakes on special today, if you're interested."

"The LAPD?" he says, looking around the restaurant. "What do they want?"

We look at each other for a minute. I make it a minute and a half, for old time's sake. "I believe it's about the dead guy you were meeting? The one you always yell at. I was just going to tell the Detectives that," I say.

13

"I yell, so what? Just as long as they know I was here yesterday."

"But I don't remember your being here yesterday. Norm."

At the sound of his name, his grip tightens on the menu. His hirsute knuckles turn white; he considers me.

"Maybe we can work something out," I say.

I make sure Ivy and Tanaka are still in the back when I bring his check. It's for coffee and what he should have paid me for my pitch, adjusted for inflation. I include my checking account information. He frowns. As I said, he's cheap. Then he sees the detectives walk towards the bar.

I point my pen at Norm's bald head. "Okay, go."

"You'll say I was here?"

"I'll say you were here. That's it? That's all you want? Just that you were here?"

"Think you can handle it?" As he punches numbers into his phone I go to get his "over hard" eggs. I've told the cook to make them runny.

By the time they shiver onto his table, sloshing against his turkey sausage, I've verified the money's in my checking account and moved it to savings, so he can't cancel the transfer.

He looks at the eggs in disgust as I walk back with coffee for Detectives Ivy and Tanaka, who are still facing away from their suspect.

"Any luck with the cameras?"

"Nope. Just a lot of cigarette butts. Can we show you one more picture?"

"Of course."

Norm tries to watch me, while keeping his face turned away from the cops.

"Do you recognize this man?" Detective Ivy hands me a photo of Henry Costa, dead CPA. Norm watches me take the photo. I stare at it.

I smile at Detective Tanaka and nod several times, sending Norm a subtle thumbs up behind my back. "Yes. Him, I remember. He's a generous tipper. He usually comes in with another guy I think, but he wasn't here yesterday."

"No, he wasn't," Detective Ivy says, taking back the photo and shaking my hand. "Thanks for your help."

I see Norm head for the exit, anxious to get out before the cops do.

Detective Tanaka turns back. "One last thing. Is this the man he comes in with?" He hands me the photo of Steinberg again.

"Wait a minute, I think he is the guy that comes in with my big tipper. He's bald now, though. Yeah. I remember, last time they were here, they were arguing. Sorry about that."

"No problem. Was he in here yesterday morning, the bald guy?"

"Yes, yes I think he was."

I see the valets give Norman Steinberg a BMW 7-series with the license plate BGSHOT.

"Before eight?" I look at the photo of Steinberg's air-brushed ponytail. I consider the semantics of our deal. I hesitate for a long second.

"No. I don't think he came in until nine, nine-thirty."

They thank me for the coffee and leave.

Karma's a bitch, Norm, I think as I hand in my notice. I keep the apron, though, in case of icebergs.

# The Ride of Your Life
## Laurie Stevens

"Get over!"

A stranger, a man, yanked open Mary Fitzpatrick's car door. He waved the blade of an open pocketknife in the woman's face.

"Get the hell over!" he yelled. He thudded into the driver's seat and shoved Mary aside. In one rapid and graceless maneuver, her legs flailed, and her body slid over the center console into the passenger's bucket seat. The gearshift gave her right hip a painful poke, and Mary's head made contact with the passenger's side door. Her glasses twisted on her nose, and Mary's heart clanged against her breast.

Stunned, she could not speak. The papers she'd been holding flew into the air and now fluttered amidst the incursion into the Buick's front seat.

Just moments before, Mary sat quietly ruminating over the disability payment and two social security checks that she held in her hands. The Buick's front bumper pointed in the direction of a check-cashing store in a nondescript mini-mall near the Santa Monica Freeway.

Now a strange man with a knife trembling in his hand, gunned the engine and put her car into reverse. Dumbfounded, Mary blinked at him as she righted herself in the passenger's bucket seat.

The car made a semi-circle of tread marks out of the parking space. He floored the gas pedal and peeled out of the lot. Mary gripped the armrest for support as the car tore up La Cienega and careened around the corner of Olympic Boulevard.

The man's eyes sought the rearview mirror, and nervously scanned the road behind them.

Mary lifted tentative hands and readjusted her mangled glasses. The seatbelt alarm beeped incessantly. She didn't know whether to fasten the buckle or jump out of the car.

She dared to look at the one who commandeered her Buick. Did he intend to steal it? If so, why hadn't he pulled her out?

The man was younger than Mary, maybe in his late-thirties. He wore a business suit, rumpled, but not cheap. A Rolex timepiece encircled his left wrist. Despite the sweat on his brow, the stranger appeared too dapper to be a common thug.

"I was set up," he said in bewilderment to no one in particular. "Harrison! I can't believe he set me up. Wearing a wire, that son-of-a-bitch."

The Buick spun left onto Highland Avenue, headed north, and Mary momentarily choked on her spit. The roads, still glistening with winter rain, were slippery; too perilous for this type of driving.

Groceries she'd bought only a half-hour earlier tipped over in the Buick's backseat. Mary looked over her shoulder to see her purse and microwaveable cups of macaroni and cheese drop to the floor mats and roll around, joined by a pint of Ben and Jerry's Phish Food Ice Cream and a pound of bagged apples.

"Dammit, Harrison!" the man cried. He gave a hard whack to the steering wheel with his hand, which caused Mary to jump. "I could have paid everything back, and no one would have been the wiser." Wild blue eyes beseeched Mary. "He turned me in. Why did he turn me in? Jesus, the agents were waiting right outside!"

Mary's heartbeat quickened, and she glanced into the side mirror, wondering if the police were following them.

"What am I gonna tell Jeanie?" the man asked wretchedly. "She doesn't know I screwed up. Oh, God! What do I tell my wife?"

Mary turned around in her seat to brave a look through the rear window of the car. Her eyes frantically searched the ribbon of road trailing behind. No police followed. No sirens cut the air around them. Was it possible that no one had seen him assail her in the parking lot?

With the initial shock diminishing, Mary made a closer inspection of her unwanted companion. The weapon he held was an excellent Swiss Army knife. From her limited vantage appoint, it appeared the man's shoes, although freshly scuffed, looked expensive. Mary's eyes traveled up to the stranger's face. High cheekbones, blue eyes, an aquiline nose, and an aristocratic gravity to his lips gave the stranger a near regal comportment. This criminal surely fell into the white-collar category. That factor made Mary less fearful of him.

The Buick raced past Wilshire Boulevard where the nearby Tar Pits beckoned. Mansions that marked the edge of Hancock Park fell like dominos as the car sped by, their Spanish Revival façades blurring into a running strip of wrought iron, stucco, and arched windows. The wet road amplified the sound of screeching tires.

"I can't believe Harrison didn't give me a chance to make it right," the man said. "Instead, he fed me to the wolves! Fed me to the Feds!" He suddenly giggled—the skittish sound of the accursed. His desperate laughter filled the Buick as Mary recovered the breath she lost at the last red light he'd blown through.

They received horn blasts and shouts from the indignant drivers they left in their wake, but the man ignored their execrations. His eyes darted from side to side. Like trapped pinballs, they rolled over the landscape of his red-rimmed eyes.

*He's been crying*, Mary realized.

Maybe she could reason with him before he got them both killed. She opened her mouth to speak, but another horn blasted to her right and cut off her words. Her knuckles ached and turned white as she dug her fingers into the armrest to keep from being thrown around.

"I'm not a bad man," he said in a voice lacerated with sorrow. "I just..." His refined features compressed and he began to sob.

Watching him, Mary managed to say, "I'm sure you can work things out."

The young man used his sleeve to wipe tears and perspiration from his face. He shook his head violently and pressed the gas pedal once more.

The tires gave an abrupt screech as the Buick veered around a Volvo. The Volvo driver leaned out of his vehicle, shook his fist, and yelled. His angry curses got lost under the roar of the Buick's engine.

"Goodness sake, where are we going?" Mary cried out, despite her efforts to keep calm.

The man glanced at her. The hopelessness in his eyes told her that he didn't know.

The traffic, like a thick and lumbering trail of ants, caused them to slow. His outraged hands shook the wheel. His eyes frantically combed the street ahead, searching for an open escape route.

"What happened?" Mary asked him, once again regaining her composure. If she could prompt the young man into conversation, he would most likely calm down. Mary was good at getting people to talk about themselves.

The stranger's face scrunched up again, and he made a short mewling sound, but no tears came. The sweat of his despondency, tinged with the memory of an expensive men's cologne, filled the car with a strange, but not unpleasant, scent.

"To every problem," Mary said in a kind voice. "There is a solution. Nothing is hopeless."

The stranger took a quaking breath and said, "I've been skimming cash out of our business, and my partner found out about it." The man exhaled, and his breath came out in shards, slicing the air and bleeding his anxiety all over the Buick's interior. "I begged him not to press charges. I promised to pay it back. The shareholders wouldn't be the wiser. But Harrison—he'd already been working with the SEC."

Mary swallowed. This stranger was no petty embezzler. The crime had to be significant if the Security and Exchange Commission had become involved.

The Buick continued along Highland and wove in and out of traffic.

"Harrison is your partner?" Mary asked as she clutched the armrest. She tried to keep her voice steady.

The man nodded.

"And you've been embezzling from your company?"

The man winced at her words, but he nodded. He looked like he might cry again.

"It's not the most horrific of crimes," Mary said, her tone purposely halcyon and soothing. She relaxed her grip on the armrest slightly. "It's not like you killed someone."

He manipulated the Buick onto the Hollywood Freeway and headed north, zigging around the cars.

Mary regarded the highway nervously. Where was he taking them? Did he have a plan?

Being a recent transplant, Mary didn't know this part of the city. She felt a small spasm in her back, residue from her collision with the gearshift. Her back protested again, and a tiny moan escaped her. The man turned to her.

"I'm sorry. I—I would never do this to someone. I got caught up, that's all." He looked back at the road and picked up speed, as if pressing the gas pedal would keep his dilemma at bay. "I won't hurt you."

His voice betrayed the frailty of a lie. Mary suspected that the man had no idea whether or not he'd need to hurt her. He was a loose cannon; a man on the edge. In his state, he could kill them both. Mary had seen many kinds of people in her sixty-five years. She'd seen them happy and sad, fearful and brave. She recognized desperation when she saw it.

Desperation sat in the seat next to her.

"Jeanie is your wife?" Mary asked.

Wrong question. The man stifled a sob, and his shoulders shook at his folly.

Mary regretted she had gone to cash the checks when she did. If she'd gone yesterday or even this afternoon, this stranger would not be sitting in her car. If she'd only parked on the opposite side of the parking lot, maybe this despairing white-collar criminal, this *man*, would not be holding her hostage.

"What were you doing in that parking lot?" Mary asked.

"I didn't know where I was," the man replied. "I ran from our offices. I ran, I used Uber, I ran again. I needed to get away before the agents came."

"Before the agents from the SEC came?"

He nodded.

The talk seemed to mollify the stranger. His overall demeanor relaxed and his hands grew steadier on the wheel.

They whizzed past Universal Studios. Mary had always heard about the theme park. She enjoyed theme parks. They were the ultimate arenas in which to get duped and beguiled, and then beg for more. She let her eyes roam over the park before it disappeared from view.

She turned to the stranger driving her car. "How did you know they were coming for you?"

"My partner Harrison freaked out and started screaming at me. He said, 'I know what you've been doing!' He pointed a finger in my face and called me a scumbag. He told me the federal agents knew all about it and any minute they would be coming for me. That's when I bolted for the door."

"What do you plan to do?"

He slammed his hand against the steering wheel again and cried, "I don't know. I can't tell Jeanie that our lives have been built on a lie. The house we own, our cars, the private school for our kids—my God!"

"Weren't you making enough money at your work?" Mary was greatly interested in what people earned.

"I was," the man whined emphatically. He looked like he might cry again. "I don't know what got into me. I saw that I could do it, and I did it. I can't explain why."

*I can*, Mary thought. *You got greedy.* She sighed. *Happens to the best of us.* Aloud she said, "I'm sure your wife will stick by you."

"I've failed her. I've failed my kids."

"You made a mistake, that's all." Mary peered out the window in concern. "Where are we going?"

He shrugged manically and shook his head.

He picked up speed, passed the 405 interchange, and continued through the San Fernando Valley. Mary needed to ready herself for any opportunity to escape. In the meantime, she would keep the stranger talking.

"'To err is human,'" she offered as they whipped past cars. "Not everyone is an angel."

He made no response to that.

"Look," she said in another attempt to keep him engaged. "People make mistakes."

He swerved off the freeway onto Malibu Canyon. He ignored the red light and made a left toward the beach. A volley of honking horns trailed them as they drove in the direction of the Pacific Ocean.

Mary held on for dear life to the dashboard before her. That last reckless turn had caused a crick in her neck.

Where in the world was he going? She thought ridiculously of the Ben and Jerry's pint and how the ice cream was most likely melting all over the Buick's carpeted floor mat. What a waste.

"Do you know where you're going?" she asked him.

He plowed on, ignoring her. The man hunched forward in the seat, both hands still tight on the wheel with the blade of the pocketknife wedged under his fingers. "I don't have a plan. I—I need to keep driving."

"Do you have a name?" Mary asked. "What can I call you?"

"The Angel of Death," he answered curtly. "What does it matter?"

Traffic was sparse on the mountain road, and the man picked up speed. As the car rounded the curves of the winding canyon, Mary felt a wave of nausea roll through her middle.

"You matter," she said, swallowing the sickly sensation. "Could you please slow down? I think I'm going to throw up."

To her surprise, the man decreased the speed of the car. Encouraged, Mary kept talking.

"You have a wife," she reminded him. "You have kids. Think about them."

"I've failed them. All of them."

"You're young. You'll recover." Her eyes made a trek over his face, his polished-looking hands, and his tailored suit. "You look wealthy enough."

"That's just it. I've blown the money." He shook his head. "On what? Cars, a boat, our vacations—all first-class! God knows Jeannie and I didn't need a second home in Hawaii, but it's like an addiction. I keep telling myself to quit the lifestyle and put the money back. But I can't. I didn't. Who will ever understand that?"

"I understand that," Mary told him.

"I don't know how long Harrison knew about the discrep-

24

ancies in the books." His voice suddenly became fierce. "I only know the bastard turned me in. We've known each other since we were kids, and he turned me in!"

"But it's not like killing someone," Mary said for the second time. She reflected on that for a moment and then said, "You'll go to a Club Fed type jail if you go to jail at all. You can afford a lawyer, can't you?"

The man sighed heavily.

"See? You'll probably get off," Mary said.

"What about you?" He swiveled his head toward her. "What's your name, anyhow?"

"Mary. Mary Fitzpatrick." She let her eyes roam the mountains bordering the canyon road.

"Well, Mary Fitzpatrick. It looks like you were in the wrong place at the wrong time. You have a husband?"

The car fishtailed as it hit the bumps in the center.

"Please slow down!" Mary cried.

He evened out and decreased the speed.

"No, I don't have a husband," she said, eyeing the road ahead of them with worry. The turns were tight, and they were traveling too fast. The car hugged the hills to their right. On the opposite side, the road bordered a sheer, steep drop to the canyon stream below.

Mary could swear that the last person they'd passed whipped out a cell phone and photographed the Buick as it sped by them. Surely, someone would have called the police by now.

"You have kids?" the man asked her.

"No." Mary barely heard the question. "I live alone." She tried to calculate how long it would take for the police to arrive.

"Los Angeles can be a cold and lonely place for a nice old lady."

She cocked an eyebrow over her spectacles at him. She smiled despite her predicament. With her gray hair, glasses, and dowdy clothing, Mary knew most people considered her much older than her years. That was okay with her. She wanted them to think that.

"I'm new here," she admitted. "I've only been in L.A. for a few weeks. And to be honest, I'm fine living alone. I've had company aplenty in my past. I ran a boardinghouse for a while near Sacramento."

"A boardinghouse," the man repeated flatly as he drove.

"That's right. Before that, I ran a boardinghouse in Arizona. And before that, in Kansas. In fact, I've run boardinghouses for years. I started on the east coast and kept moving west."

"Ending in L.A.," he stated.

"Ending in L.A.," Mary confirmed.

"People always end up here." He threw his head back and laughed. "The end of the road."

"Oh, I don't know about that," Mary said. "I look at it as a place to start over. To redefine myself."

"To get out of the boardinghouse business?" His tone was sarcastic.

"Don't get me wrong," Mary said. "I'd still do it if I could. My tenants were the elderly and infirm. Society's lost souls. The people who are easy to forget about."

"So what you are saying is that you're one of the good ones." The man gave her a smarmy look. "You wear a little halo over your head? Is that right, Mary?"

Mary offered him a sweet smile. Then she hoisted herself rather painfully from the passenger seat and reached into the back to lift her purse from the floor.

"Hey!" He warned her, repositioning the knife in his hand. "What are you doing?"

"I'm getting my insulin. I never took my shot after lunch." She looked at him and said in a wheedling voice, "Please let me take my medicine."

She pulled out a small vial and a syringe. As she filled the syringe, she said, "If I don't take insulin, I could go into a diabetic coma. Don't worry. I'll hurry."

The man regarded her in concern. Now that his face was relaxed, Mary could see he was a fine-looking young man.

"I'm sorry," he told her. "I'm sorry I involved you in this."

"Then, young man, why don't you let me out?"

The stranger appeared to contemplate that. Finally, he pulled over to the narrow shoulder and put the car into park.

"Go," he told her.

As the man viewed the road ahead, perhaps considering the aftermath of his decisions, Mary jammed the needle of the syringe into his neck. He uttered a small cry and struggled with her. The stranger's pretty-boy hands gripped her shoulders, but they lost strength in a matter of seconds. He fell back hard against the driver's seat with a dazed and amazed expression in his red-rimmed eyes.

Mary retracted the syringe and dropped it in her purse.

"Flurazepam," she said. "It's a sedative. Perfect for your current state of mind, I might add. You've been overdosed."

Mary retrieved the social security checks scattered on the front seat. She turned the man and raised his eyelid with her thumb. He might have passed out. If not, he was on his way.

"I guess I owe you an explanation," Mary said as she primly placed the checks in her purse. "These don't belong to me. One of the checks belongs to an elderly tenant of mine, who, in his senility, granted me the power of attorney. He was buried in my backyard up until a week ago—until a bitchy neighbor complained to the authorities about the stench. I tried to say the smell was from fresh fertilizer, but you know how nosy neighbors are. The bitch didn't let it rest."

Mary began to search for the disability payment. "On top of that," she continued. "A big mouth social worker who worked with one of my more mentally challenged tenants, began asking where her charge had gone. Apparently, she didn't believe my story that a distant relative took him away."

Mary reached down and swiped the rectangle of paper from where it lay near the man's pricey loafers. "Can you believe that? I've been cashing the disability checks for over a year, and now the social worker decides to grow a conscience and check on the imbecile's whereabouts."

Mary did a quick scan about the car, determining what to take and what she should sacrifice to the bottom of the canyon. Her eyes fell upon the man's wristwatch. She unclasped his Rolex and said, "They were digging up the bodies when I said I needed to use the bathroom. Who can deny a nice old lady a restroom visit, right? So, I grabbed what I needed from the house and crawled out the bathroom window."

Mary deposited the Rolex into her purse and then searched the man's pockets. She extricated the cash from his wallet, and then replaced the billfold where she'd found it.

"Then I went to my friend Jeb's house down the block," she said. "I took his car and some cash. For all I know, Jeb is still sitting in that easy chair where I left him, most likely making his own brand of stink."

Mary scanned the interior one more time and then sighed. "I did like this car. Drives like a dream. Got me to a place where I knew I could disappear. I was debating whether or not to cash the last of the checks when you came along. Maybe it was a good thing you did. By now the police have probably identified the bodies in the backyard, and are most likely keeping alert for the checks. Still, it's an awfully tough habit to break. It's an addiction, like you said."

Mary put her face close to the young man's. "Now, I'm sure you can understand that I can't have you get arrested anywhere near me. And I certainly cannot report the car as being stolen. So, thanks a lot, dickhead, because now I have to lose the Buick. I'm thinking, though. This might work to my advantage. Maybe they'll assume you lost your marbles and stole from an old man in Sacramento, like you stole from your partner in L.A." Mary reflected on that for a moment, and then shook her head at the absurdity of her logic. "Then again, maybe not. At any rate, sonny boy, I've got to go." She dropped her purse on the side of the road, and came around to the driver's side. "And so do you."

Mary waited for a car to pass, and then she opened the door and pulled the steering wheel to the left. She reached over the paralyzed man and put the car into drive. The car ambled forward, and Mary jumped back to stay clear. She watched the car move in a slow wide arc, then jogged behind it and gave the back bumper a solid push. The wheels turned faster. Mary took shelter under a nearby outcropping of boulders.

She watched the Buick cross the opposite lane and drop off the cliff.

Dumbass, she thought resentfully of the younger man. There went her Buick Regal. The nicest car she'd ever driven, and one she had intended on keeping. Mary had even changed the license plates.

A loud crashing sound reverberated between the mountains. A minute later, the whoosh of an object catching fire met her ears.

There went her ice cream, too.

What else could she do? The car had to go. If the man talked about a particular Buick in which he'd taken his drive of desperation, Mary would spend her retirement in a penitentiary.

She sighed and looked beyond the rocks to the hiking trails crisscrossing the Santa Monica Mountains. Her old lady shoes would have to do for an evening hike. She certainly couldn't stick around here, not with the fire department and the police on their way. All those years of running from one state to the other, keeping one step ahead of the law. So exhausting! L.A. would be her last stop.

Remnants of storm clouds broke apart over the ocean.

Mary climbed a hill to take in the vista of blue water.

She could fade easily into the crowds of a big metropolis. If, in the event no legitimate means of making an income came her way, she had another recourse. Opening a boarding-house. Sure, why not? A fine cross-section of people existed in Los Angeles. Lost and lonely people with nowhere else to go, searching for a warm outpost in a cold city. Elderly folks with pensions. Disabled outcasts, shunned by their relatives. Mary did not discriminate, not as long as the prospective tenant came with a monthly income check. After all, who wouldn't feel at home with a kind, capable, and caring woman?

Mary hefted the purse over her shoulder and began to walk toward the Pacific.

# Method Actor
## G.B. Pool

He said I had it in me, that killer instinct. But he couldn't have known about Gloria. That happened when I was sixteen. Water under the bridge, like they say...and Gloria, too. The producer said I was what he was looking for. Somebody who could kill his wife with a smile on his face. He offered me a part in his latest movie if I could come to California and didn't lose that sharp edge. He told me that twice.

The producer saw me in an off-off-Broadway play in New York City. One of those improv places on Canal Street near the river that would never make it to the Palace. Another guy told me he was thinking about doing a theatrical version of *Taxi Driver* and took my name. Said he wanted me to play the lead. But I never heard from him again. That was months ago, and nobody ever saw the guy after that. I remember he kept winking at his girlfriend. He was conning me. That's the way a con man operates. I know the signs. I saw it in a movie.

I told my roommate, Jason, about the deal to go to Hollywood, at least about the big part in a movie. He said he got the same offer from the guy and was thinking about taking him up on it. I didn't believe him. Jason always had a better story than anybody else did. He also thought he was a better actor than I was. He was wrong on that one, too.

I told everybody I was heading to California to be in the movies. Jason said he was going to do that himself. He asked me how I was gonna get there since I didn't have a car. He had one. He said I could go with him if I paid for half the gas. I could do that…sort of. I spent a lot of my money on clothes so I could dress the part of an actor. I had an image to maintain. The same one the producer saw when he offered me that job if I'd do that extra bit of business for him. The clothes paid off.

Jason bored everybody about his Hollywood contract. I knew he wasn't offered the same deal I was given. Jason never played a tough guy on stage. He was the sensitive type. James Dean to my Brando.

Now here I was sitting in a cheap motel in Los Angeles, waiting for my call to the producer to go through. I was looking at the guy's fancy business card and listening to canned music.

What pissed me off was I didn't get a card from the movie guy. Jason did. But the guy asked *me* to come out here and kill his wife and get a part in his movie. Not Jason.

I asked Jason how he got the business card while we were on the road. He laughed. He was always laughing. He had his teeth whitened and flashed that phony smile of his. He said the producer saw something in him—probably his own reflection in those teeth. Jason said the producer saw an inner something in him that would light up the screen. The producer said it was something the camera would love. Something that would grab the audience and leave them wanting more—I thought I was going to barf. The producer told me I had an edge. That was all, except the part about getting rid of his wife with a smile on my face. The producer had a grin on his mug when he said it. I knew what that meant.

Jason said I didn't have any acting range. All I could play was a tough guy, and that wouldn't get me very far. It got me to California. Jason only got as far as Arizona. I told him I could put lots of emotion on the screen. I'd just think about something that made me mad, like him laughing at me for not having a fancy set of wheels or any money or having to sleep in the car while he spent the night in a motel. That made me mad. But what really griped me was him having the producer's business card. It should have been mine.

The son-of-a-bitch laughed at me when I told him I thought we had a flat tire, but he pulled the car off the parkway anyway. I can still remember the sound of the bones snapping when I broke his neck with my bare hands. I'll call up that emotion when the cameras rolled. I would just think of Jason saying it was him the producer wanted and not me.

So there I was standing behind his car in some remote hellhole in the desert. Just sand and no people. Except for that highway patrol officer who drove up right as I was pushing Jason into the trunk. The officer didn't see Jason. Just me. I told him I stopped to answer nature's call. He got a laugh out of that. I got back in the car and drove off.

I left Jason in a ditch right at the state border. You could see the WELCOME TO CALIFORNIA sign from there. At least Jason got to see California…sort of.

There was a detour on the parkway that led to what I thought was a restaurant. It looked like the Taco Bell in the Bronx except there was a palm tree next to it. It turned out to be an agricultural checking station. I thought maybe California had toll roads, but they just wanted to make sure I wasn't bringing any fruit or nuts into the state. "Just me," I told the guard. I even said I had a movie deal. He gave me one of those looks like he didn't believe me. It was the raised eyebrow stare. I was good at that expression, too. I'd practiced it until I could raise just one brow and hold it.

He waved me through, and I headed for Los Angeles. There's nothing in that part of California except sand. I started thinking maybe the cities dried up and blew away. After about a million miles, I found a batch of fast food places. No pastrami. No cheesecake. No delicatessen. There was a pizza place. I'd settle for that. But it wasn't like Luigi's. Not even close.

But that wasn't my only problem. When I looked in my wallet, I saw that I had spent most of my money on gas. And then I realized I hadn't taken Jason's wallet before I dumped him in that culvert. I couldn't go back looking for him. I'd run into that highway patrolman for sure.

I had enough money left for one more tank of unleaded and a hotel room, but I might not be eating for a while. That's when I saw a girl in a pair of short jeans and a tank top standing along the side of the road. She had a cardboard sign she was holding up. It said: *Hollywood or Bust.*

I pulled over.

"You going to Los Angeles?" I asked.

"If that's near Hollywood, I am. I'm an actress." She sort of posed there like one of those centerfold girls. I'd seen tons of pretty girls in the theater district in New York. They were a dime a dozen. This girl was worth a little less.

"You got any money for gas?" I asked her.

"Yeah. I got some money. You goin' to Los Angeles, too?"

"Yeah. We share the cost, or you're back on the pavement. Got it?"

She checked over my car, then me. Then she tossed her suitcase in the backseat and climbed in. She said her name was Addison. I told her my name was Leonardo, and that I was an actor, too.

"You don't look like a Leonardo."

"What does that mean?"

"It means your name's gotta fit the person you want to be. I feel like an Addison or maybe a Stephanie today. I wanted to be Delilah, but sometimes I forget how to spell it, so I figured I better pick something easier. So what's your real name?"

"Jason," I said, trying that one on for size. "Do I look like a Jason?"

She cocked her head. "No. Your car looks like it belongs to a Jason. It's kinda fancy. I like guys with fancy cars. You look more like a guy who would drive an old Chevy—or steal one."

"What name should I have?"

"You could be a Nick. Or how about Rad? I went to school with a boy named Rad. He's in prison now. Or maybe you could be Shade. Now there's a name. It would go with your black T-shirt and jeans. Just pick a name you can spell." She laughed. "Where you from?"

"New York."

"Were you ever on Broadway?"

"Just finished a play. I was the lead. A producer saw me and—"

"Yeah, yeah, yeah. He asked you to be in his movie. I hear that from 'producers'—" she made quote signs with her fingers, "all the time. All they want is me in their bed for the night. Never gets any farther than that. What do you have to do for him to get in his movie?"

For a dumb blonde, she was asking an awful lot of questions. I kept driving.

"So what did this big producer guy say to you?" she asked again since I hadn't answered.

"He said I had an inner something that would light up the screen. He said I had a face the camera would love. Something about me would grab the audience and leave them wanting more."

"He said all that? Wow. I just get propositioned and a few bucks for my time. I bet some of them weren't even in the movie business. But they paid for it. Big time. So this guy thought you were that good, huh? What movie are you gonna be in? Why didn't he fly you out here? Would there be a part for me in that movie?"

She yakked for another hundred miles until I saw the gas gauge was low. I pulled into a filling station and filled up. She paid. I told her I paid the time before and now we were even.

When I started the car, it coughed and wheezed until the engine turned over.

"That doesn't sound good," she said as I pulled onto the road. "The car's probably overheating. Did you check the water in the radiator? If there's a leak, you could be dry. I had a boyfriend who had that happen to his car. Nearly ruined that piece of crap. Had to get a new radiator 'cause the old one cracked or exploded or whatever they do. I don't know much about cars, but I know when one sounds like it isn't gonna make it. Yours sure sounds like that. Maybe you need an oil change. I'm not gonna split the cost of that with you. I don't even think this is your car. What did you do, steal it? Maybe I should look for another ride. I have—"

I gripped the wheel with my left hand and hit her in the side of the head with my right. I heard her head hit the glass and crack. Her head, not the glass. She crumpled in the seat while blood oozed out of the back of her head. I pushed her down to the floor just in case anybody could see in the car while I was driving.

I kept watching her, but she didn't move. When I got close to Los Angeles I touched her and she was getting stiff.

There was a small road off that section of parkway and I took it. I drove a little ways and then pulled in behind a few straggly trees. Boy, nothin' grows in this desert without water. There wasn't anybody around, so I dragged her out of the car and dumped her behind a prickly bush covered with bright pink flowers.

I found a few dollars in the tiny pocket of her short jeans and then got back in the car. I went through her suitcase and found even more money. She must have been good in bed because she had a lot of dough. And she had a gun.

A few of the guys in the neighborhood back home had one. Never fired a gun myself except on stage. Always liked doing that role. I'd stick the thing in my belt and strut around, and look like I wanted to shoot everybody. You just have to call up some old memory and live it there on stage and squint a lot to let everybody know you meant business. I'd think about my old man when he used to beat up my mother. Not that she didn't deserve it 'cause she used to beat up me and my sister.

The stupid engine took even longer to turn over this time, but I managed to drive a few more miles before the car started banging and clanking. I was on the outskirts of Los Angeles when I saw an exit sign, so I got off just as smoke began pouring out from under the hood. I pulled into the weeds and stopped.

This was another *Tobacco Road* garden spot. I got out and walked into the center of a town that was three blocks long. Three *short* blocks. I saw a used car dealership and had a thought.

I jogged back to the car, wiped most of Addison's blood off the seat with an old sock, and changed into my nicer pair of slacks. I put on a black sports coat over my black T-shirt, slicked back my hair, and tucked her gun in my waistband. Then I strolled into the dealership's office like I owned the world and asked the guy behind the counter if he could give me a few bucks on my car. Said I wanted to get rid of it since we already had two cars and I was going to buy the wife something nice. He looked me over, and said he'd check it out. He was the owner of the place. I told him I had parked up the street. I said I ran out of gas.

He got the kid who worked on the lot to tow the car into the work bay while I filled out some papers.

"We'll check her over to see what we can give you on it. You live around here?"

"No. From out of town. Here on business. Decided to surprise the wife with a diamond bracelet. I'll fly home."

He looked at me again. I could tell he was thinking about something.

"You got the pink slip on this here car of yours?'

"A what?"

37

He took a step back. There was something in his eyes that said I screwed up my lines. I moved toward him. His helper was still in the lot. I saw him through the front window. The owner stepped back some more.

"Get out now, and I won't call the cops," he said.

I yanked the gun out of my waistband and pulled the trigger. Once, twice, three times. Nothing. The damn thing wasn't loaded.

The guy grinned at me like *I* was the idiot. I stepped toward him and hit him with the butt end of the gun. He stopped laughing and fell to his knees. I had dropped the gun by then, but the guy didn't scream because I had grabbed his throat before he could open his big mouth. He was a short guy. Short and fat. His neck was thick. It took both hands. I didn't hear any bones break, but his face turned red before his eyes bulged and he went limp.

I snatched a handful of keys on the rack behind the counter. They were to the vehicles on the lot. One had a big #19 on it. The kid who towed my car was still busying himself around the area. I walked out the door, went over to Jason's car, grabbed my suitcase, and then went looking for car number nineteen. The parking spots weren't marked. I pressed the button on the key, and the car next to me chirped. I jumped a foot.

I eased around to the other side and pretended to be admiring the silky lines of the slick, silver car. I opened the driver-side door and dropped into the front seat. With the key in my hand, I stared down at the dashboard. The stupid car didn't have an ignition.

"How the hell do you start this thing?"

The kid wiping down the vehicles in the lot looked over the top of the car he was polishing and smiled. I smiled back and got out of the silver car.

The next key I looked at was #5. The key didn't have a button to push, so I wandered around the front of the lot trying to get a clue where it was parked.

"What number do you want?" called the kid.

"Five."

He pointed toward the first row of cars, and then glanced back at the office. I walked over to the row he indicated, but still didn't know which car.

"The fifth one," he called out.

As I walked down the row of vehicles, I kept looking back at the kid. I spotted number five, and looked at him again. This time he stopped wiping down the red Corvette he was shining, and started to walk to the office. I got into the driver's seat of the older model car, shut the door, and turned over the engine. At least this four-wheel chariot started like a normal car.

By then the kid was mounting the steps to the office. I gunned the engine and got out of there. But the old buggy was nearly out of gas. I'm sure lucky I took Addison's money. I filled up and headed into the big city.

That was just a few days ago. I dumped the old car after I found a place to stay.

And here I sat in a crummy motel in Hollywood, waiting for the producer to come on the line. I told his secretary I had his card and that he had seen me in a play in New York and that he had asked me to call him when I got into town. She asked my name again and I told her. I gave her the name of the play and that her boss said he had a special part for me in an upcoming movie.

She put me on hold again.

While I waited, I noticed the television in the motel room went to the local news. They were running the story about the car dealership guy getting strangled, and about the car towed into the lot. The cops noticed the blood in the front passenger seat and evidence of another body in the trunk. They were looking for a young, good-looking man in a black shirt. Good-looking. I liked that.

They were also hunting for a guy named Mike Corlon. That was the name I had written on the dealership form.

The news reporter kind of smirked and said, "Do you think he meant Michael Corleone? You know, like the gangster in *The Godfather*." The news guy also said that maybe the killer was trying to be funny. Or maybe he didn't know how to spell the name.

That made me think of Addison…Delilah…whatever her name was. We both had trouble with spelling our aliases. But, hey, I'm an actor. We don't have to know how to spell.

Anyway, it turned out her name was Daisy. Somebody found her body. And here I thought California was so big nobody would find her. It's easier hiding a body in the East River near Astoria. And ol' Daisy had a rap sheet. Seems she would pick up guys along the highway, pull a gun, and steal their money. Got to hand it to her. She sure had the Hollywood actress act down pretty good. She might have made it big in the movies.

The producer's secretary finally came back on the line.

"Mr. Woodruff can see you tomorrow at ten. Do you know how to get to the office?"

"Yeah. No problem. Ten."

I spent the rest of the day trying to figure out where the hell his office was and how to get there by bus. Then somebody told me it would be easier to take the subway. I thought the guy was being a smart ass since he knew I was from New York, but they really have a subway in Los Angeles. I could walk to the subway entrance on Western, and go north to the Universal City stop. Piece of cake.

I wore a black shirt with the black T-shirt underneath. I used a laundromat to wash my jeans and I cleaned up my shoes. None of the stuff I got from Jason fit, so I dumped it in a Goodwill bin. I sure wish I had taken his wallet.

I got to the meeting on time. The subways run every ten to twelve minutes. Just like home. I could get used to this.

Woodruff's secretary pointed to his office and I walked in.

Woodruff was a big man. I guess he ate regularly. His head was shaved, but I don't think it was a fashion statement. Guys his age, fifty-ish, were "follicly" challenged. He was kinda sizing me up like he didn't remember me.

"Where are you from again?"

"New York." I said it with attitude. This bum didn't know me from Adam.

"Long way from the Big Apple. How'd you get out here?"

"Flew. Don't have a car. Nobody I know has one in New York."

"That's New York for ya. I saw some really good plays when I was there. You...you were in that artsy one on Canal Street. Right? Just the 'killer' I was looking for. Didn't know if you would take me up on my offer. Glad you did. Really glad you did."

He *did* remember me. I knew I had presence on the stage. And Jason said I was totally forgettable. What did he know?

"Well, I'm glad you came to see me. I don't give my card to everybody I meet. Sometimes fate just lets things happen."

He smiled. I knew what he meant.

This guy was so cool. He remembered me, but he wanted to keep this strictly professional. No need to advertise the deed I was to perform. And I could improvise, too. Did it a million times in acting class. Give me a scene to play, and I'll deliver.

"I've played a lot of bad boys on stage. I can do the same thing for you."

He gave me a knowing nod. "I'll have you meet my wife and get that over with. Then we can schedule rehearsals. My location scout has a few places lined up. I'll have my secretary get you a script. Familiarize yourself with the part. Are you busy tonight?"

"Tonight?"

"Yeah. If I can get this thing with my wife taken care of

first, the more time I can devote to the main scenes in the film. Did we talk about this in New York?"

"Not much, just the part about your wife."

"Oh. I was pulling what hair I have left out over that one. Read the script, then come by tonight and we can take care of the old ball and chain." He laughed at that. "And thanks for doing this. It means a great deal to me."

"Sure."

"My secretary will arrange for a car to pick you up." He stopped and looked at me. "I'll make it worth your while." He gave a small nod and went back to the work he had on his desk.

Woodruff's secretary was waiting for me. She had me sign a contract and then handed me a script.

"This one's marked up already, but there will be rewrites before they even get you in front of the camera. You know how it goes." She looked me up and down. "You'll be great in the part. He does know how to pick 'em."

I took the script.

"Where are you staying?" she asked.

I didn't want to give her the name of the fleabag joint that I could afford, but I had seen a better hotel a few blocks away that would work.

"The Hollywood Star Hotel."

She did one of those slow turns with her head that said I had made a joke. Only thing was—I didn't know the punch line, but I knew how to ad lib.

"Any place to hang my hat," I said.

"At least it's on the main drag and not one of those cheesy Hollywood day spas that charge by the hour. Dumps like the Nomad Inn or The Last Retreat, for God's sake, are strictly for wannabe actors when they first come to Tinseltown and end up selling themselves on the street."

The last motel she named was mine. No wonder the manager was surprised I wanted to rent a room for the week.

"The Hollywood Star was the only place I could find," I said, and shrugged. "I'm moving into an apartment the first of the month."

She gave me one of those looks that said she half believed me. Then she said, "Have you ever seen his wife in a movie?"

I was surprised she asked about the wife, but then I took a closer look at this babe. She could have been in the movies herself. She filled out her sweater like a Victoria's Secret model. Oh. I get it. I was getting rid of the "ball and chain" so this tootsie could move into the main house. Happens all the time.

I shook my head in answer to her question.

She pointed to a picture on the wall. In fact, there were several pictures of the same famous face. Jeez. Woodruff's old lady was Lydia Marshall. She had a great career. She had to be a good ten years older than Woodruff. Maybe they couldn't do another facelift on her or maybe she was getting too temperamental, and he didn't want to put up with her anymore.

I get it. This was *Sorry, Wrong Number* meets *Double Indemnity*. Instead of the husband being blackmailed, he wants the wife dead to collect the insurance. Sure. He needed the money. I looked around his office. Everything looked old, except for the hot secretary. She had a lot of good miles left on her.

"What do you think of her?" I asked.

She hesitated and looked away. Boy was that a sign of guilt. She knew what her boss wanted me to do. "She has a mind of her own. I guess that's what you get when you've made so many Oscar-winning movies. You take care of her, and Don—Mr. Woodruff—will do what he can for your career."

So it's "Don" to Little Miss Cute Tush Secretary. I bet she uses his first name whenever nobody's around.

"The car will be at your...*hotel* at seven. Casual dress."

She was hiding something. I could see it in her face. It was one of those looks that said she knew our secret. I raised a conspiratorial eyebrow, and she gave me a slight nod.

I tucked the script under my arm and left. I rode the subway back to the Western Avenue station and scoped out the Hollywood Star Hotel. On second look, it was a little seedy, too. The couple heading to an upstairs room at that hour kind of told me the place wasn't exactly a Christian Science Reading Room.

I walked back to my motel. I ironed my wrinkled slacks and shirt. I had to borrow the iron from the scrub lady who was cleaning out the room across the hall. The place needed to be fumigated before they let anybody else occupy it. I knew the maid expected a tip, but I'm sure she knew she wouldn't get one from me. She gave me that ten-second stare and her hand went out to me, palm up, but I ran my own hand through my hair like a 1950's rock star, ignoring her, and went into my room and closed the door.

The rest of the day was spent reading the script. I got the leading man's part. The character's name was circled and all his lines were highlighted with a yellow marker. I guess Woodruff wanted me to find my part easily.

The storyline was dark. My character was moody and tough. There was a part for an older woman who has a nasty boyfriend who roughs her up and gets his head blown off in the first scene. As I kept reading, the woman's role ate up half the script. If this was Lydia Marshall's part, Woodruff must want her out of the way fast, so he could put another actress into the role before too much film was in the can. I wondered who they had in the wings. Old Lydia Marshall would be perfect for this role.

But my part, the male lead, was awesome. This guy was cool and quoted Shakespeare. I'd have to brush up on the bard before cameras rolled. I'm glad I didn't get stuck with the part of the guy who gets killed. He was one tough s.o.b., but kind of stupid, if you know what I mean.

Woodruff saw something in me that spoke to him, he wanted me in the lead, and I wasn't about to disappoint him. And all it would cost is me getting rid of his wife...with a smile.

I was on the sidewalk outside the other hotel at seven. A limo pulled to the curb, and at first I thought it was a hearse, it was so long. I got in. Man, this was great. We drove up into the hills to a high-class neighborhood like you see in the movies. But this time *I* was starring in the picture.

The limo dropped me at the front door, and a man was waiting there to let me in. He was dressed better than I was, but come to find out, he was the butler. I thought they were only in the movies. He showed me into a room the size of the lobby at the Plaza. He even offered me a drink. I said I'd take a beer, and his eyebrow went up. Everybody must be able to do that in Hollywood. Then the idiot poured the beer in a glass. Both my eyebrows went up on that one.

A few minutes later Woodruff came in. He was wearing a different suit than what he had on in the office this morning. It looked pretty sharp considering the size of the guy's gut.

"Did you read your part?"

"Yeah. Thanks for marking the scenes. I've been practicing all afternoon."

He gave me an odd look like maybe I was kidding him, but I wanted to thank him for highlighting my lines. I had almost as many as the leading lady.

"I want you to take care of this thing with my wife now. She's been nagging me for a month, and when I saw you in that play I thought you could take care of her for me. I couldn't find anybody here in L.A. who had that killer look. I guess Californians have gotten too soft."

We both laughed.

"Where is she?"

"In the library." He pointed to a pair of big wooden doors.

"I take it the guy who showed me in here will handle things when I'm finished."

"Whatever you need. Do you want another beer?"

I shook my head.

"Thanks again for flying out here to do this. But it will make the movie shoot a lot easier once my wife's taken care of. You married?"

I shook my head again. I was getting into the part and had to concentrate.

"Marriage can make you do things you never thought you'd do. Maybe I should have tried this with my first wife. She was an actress. It would have been a lot easier—and cheaper."

He gave a short laugh. I wondered if he got rid of that "ball and chain," too.

I walked into the room. I'd never seen so many books except when I had to do detention in my high school library. Lydia Marshall was sitting in a big chair reading a script. I wanted to tell her she didn't have to bother. Her old man was replacing her in the part. She looked up, and I saw that famous face. It looked kinda rough now. Just like she was supposed to look in that first scene when the young tough beats her up before he gets his head shot off. Special effects will do a great job with that.

She was wearing a chunky necklace that looked like it was made of broken beer bottles. It covered most of her neck, but even from where I stood I could see the sagging wrinkles.

"Are you the boy Don picked? He said you had something."

I didn't like the "boy" part.

"Do you know your lines? I suggested a couple of changes and the studio will send around the rewrites by Thursday. I'll tell you what I want you to do when the time comes. Come a little closer." She looked me over. "At least you're tall enough. A lot of the guys I've worked with are shorter than I am, and I have to wear flats. I hate wearing flats. My legs are still my biggest asset and the camera loves them. My personal trainer makes sure they stay that way."

She dropped her script and stood up. She got closer and studied me.

"Yeah. You do have that look. Hate to mess up that face, but the part will be memorable."

I smiled at her and stepped closer. Something about the move made her nervous. She put her hand out like she was going to push me away.

There was fear in her eyes.

"Do you want to do the first scene when I come into your bedroom?" I asked. I knew that scene got me very close to her.

"Bedroom? Your scene is in the living room. Just follow the script. You only have three lines. I do most of the dialogue."

She kept talking, but I had tuned her out. What she was saying didn't make any sense anyway. That was probably all the new stuff she wanted the director to add. What she didn't know was the rewrite her husband had in mind. I knew that part.

I smiled at her again. Her eyebrows went up as she tried to back away.

My hands were around her throat by then. She managed a few screams. One really loud one. I pushed her down on the couch so I could pin her under my knee as I squeezed, but the old gal's legs were in great shape.

That's when I heard yelling behind me. I turned my head and saw Woodruff. He was screaming at me. The old fart who had opened the front door was there, too, with a baseball bat in his hand.

Woodruff kept yelling. I kept smiling just like he wanted me to while I was trying to kill his wife.

Then I heard a gunshot. It echoed in the room. I didn't

know where it came from, but the noise hurt my ears and my chest seemed to be on fire. I rolled sideways and Lydia slipped out of my reach. The room started to swim in front of me, but I could still see Lydia as she slid off the couch and onto the floor. She was shaking her head.

I turned around and caught a glimpse of Woodruff with a gun in his hand. He had knelt down next to his wife. He was playing his role really well. You know, the distraught husband part. Boy, he sure had the angst down. I could almost swear he didn't want me to kill his—

# The Best LAid Plans
## Anne David

L.A., exciting glamour capitol of the world, polar opposite of the day-in and day-out tedium of the farm, a life left behind. Irene had dreamed and planned and saved for her escape for as long as she could remember. Now she was here, living on the doorstep of Hollywood, so close to fame and fortune. But not the fame and fortune of stardom, not as the actress who garnered accolades from a worshiping public, but as the woman to see if you wanted a good tomato, or fantastic potting soil if you wanted to grow your own.

Irene planted tomatoes when necessity forced her to establish the first garden. It needed plants, and tomatoes were the largest plants available at the garden store ready to go into the ground. They were already several feet tall and they covered a lot of space. That first year the crop was average, nothing spectacular, enough for her and a few for her neighbor. It was in the second year that there was a startling difference, in not only the size of the fruit but also in the abundance, and they were delicious. It was her neighbor's suggestion that she rent a stall at the local farmer's market to get rid of the surplus produce that propelled her into a business that was definitely not what she had planned.

The tomatoes were such a success that word spread there was a new tomato lady at the Silver Lake Farmer's Market. There were farmer's markets in every part of the Los Angeles basin, a salute to the fecundity of the California climate. You could find one on any given day of the week, and news of new offerings spread through them like wildfire among the habitués of those food bazaars. The stall at the Beverly Hills Farmer's Market that had tender salad greens, unavailable at any supermarket; the filet beans, haricots verts to the chefs shopping for their restaurants, arriving from the Central Valley in bushel baskets on the backs of pick-up trucks and unloading at the Santa Monica market.

A source of good tomatoes always made the market news and Silver Lake became a foodie destination. Lines formed at Irene's stall before the market opened and she would sell out in the first hour, so it made sense to expand her garden. She could certainly use the tomato money to supplement what little she earned waitressing at a bistro on Sunset Boulevard.

During the winter she built another planting bed like the first, a raised bed filled with potting soil from the same nursery, and planted the same tomato plants in both beds in the spring. Again the results were startling, but in a different way. The original planting bed produced robust plants with an abundant, tasty crop, as usual. It was the second bed that was odd. It was normal. The tomatoes were okay, but nothing like the others. Of course, the original bed hadn't begun producing the super crop until the second year. That must be it, that and the fact that she always covered the first bed with a tarp at night. She did that to make sure that the raccoons and coyotes that roamed the hills of Silver Lake didn't get into the garden and dig. But maybe that contributed to the success of the tomatoes. She had read somewhere that tomatoes needed warm nights to develop their flavor. Maybe the covering fulfilled that need, and so she built a tarp frame for the second bed. But the fruit from the second year was no better than the first. What was the difference? Both beds had the same soil, the same plants, the same amount of sunlight, and the same covering at night. Her bafflement led her to delve into tomato horticulture and the science of the soil composition that tomatoes needed.

Her research into the soil requirements for tomatoes led to the potting soil recipe, which she began to bag up and sell alongside her tomatoes at her market stall. She found that there had to be a delicate balance in the pH quality of the soil and an adequate supply of nitrogen, phosphorus, and potassium in just the right amounts for nightshade plants to flourish. But, as it turned out, you didn't just buy a bag of nitrogen or phosphorus. There were products that provided those nutrients: lime to correct the pH factor, blood meal to supply nitrogen, bone meal for phosphorus, and wood ash for the potassium. She was puzzled at first by the fact that she hadn't added any of those things to the potting soil she used in the original garden bed. She just bought as many bags of commercial dirt as she needed to fill up the frame that she had erected from a prefab package purchased at a large garden supply warehouse. When she realized that she actually had amended the soil as suggested, she quit eating the tomatoes from that bed.

Irene had arrived in Los Angeles at the Greyhound bus station shortly after her twenty-first birthday. She shed the name Elvira Klotzman in favor of Irene Ross on the long road trip from the farm in Minnesota. A substantial stash of movie magazines in her travel bag, the source of her information on breaking into the movies, reported on the many stars who had changed their names. No shame in doing that. Better John than Marion, or Marilyn than Norma Jean. Irene seemed glamorous, but dignified, and there didn't seem to be any Irenes on the movie scene right now. Irene Dunne was the last one she knew of, so there wouldn't be any confusion with someone else.

The seedy people wandering around outside of the Los

Angeles bus station and the general dinginess of the street dismayed Irene, and she realized that she had no idea where to go. She had some money saved from her waitressing job at the Prairie Café to get her started, and her mother had pressed a twenty-dollar bill into her hand as she boarded the bus.

"Be careful." Her mother was a woman of few words. "You can come home anytime."

Her father just stood with his hands in his overall pockets, chewing on a toothpick. "Take it easy, girl."

None of them were demonstrative, so no hugs or kisses. She did have a slight lump in her throat though, because as far as she was concerned she wasn't coming home again. She would never return to the backbreaking work of a farm, with the endless chores and the smell of the place on your clothes and in your hair, and the dirt always under your fingernails. The long hours aged a person beyond their time. Look at her mother.

"I'll write." And then she was on her way.

She stood on the sidewalk outside of the bus station with no idea what to do. There were a few taxis lined up at the curb, but she had no destination to give them. She retreated back into the building and found an information desk, unattended, but littered with pamphlets and flyers promoting nearby restaurants and hotels. The one advertising the YWCA caught her eye because she had heard of it. Irene carried the brochure back out to the first taxi in the line, climbed in, and gave the address.

The room at the Y was cheap and clean, and her inclination to crawl into the bed and pull the covers up over her head was strong, but instead she went out to find something to eat. She bought a newspaper along the way, opened it to the apartment rental section, and was overwhelmed. The sheer numbers defeated her at the start, and she fought down the urge to pack her bag and go home. But maybe the woman at the desk could help.

"You mean you've come out here to L.A. with no job?" The woman peered at her over her glasses, obviously skeptical of that plan.

"No, not yet, but I intend to get one right away." Irene figured she had enough money to tide her over for three months, if she was careful. "I need an apartment first, I think."

"Do you have a car?"

"No, not yet," she said again.

"Well, you're a brave one, I'll say that for you." The woman was spreading the rental section out on the desk and beginning to go down the columns. "No car in L.A. Hmmm… so that means you need to find a place on a bus line."

She gave her several leads, which Irene followed up immediately. Two were actual apartments, one furnished, one not. Both smelled. The third lead was a little distance away from the downtown area but on a bus line, and she took it the minute she saw it. It was an actual house in an area called Silver Lake, a small house, a little rickety. The owner called it a cottage, built in the '20s. It was perched on top of one of many hills in the area, an incredibly steep hill that had left Irene breathless halfway up. Only one bedroom, but that's all she needed, a small wood-burning fireplace, and a large backyard facing south, with full sun all day long. From one vantage point she could see the tips of the downtown office buildings in the distance. The woman told her that Judy Garland had lived down the street at one time.

The pine trees and palm trees, towering eucalyptus and brilliant bougainvillea running rampant through the hills, were another world away from Minnesota. She paid the rent for the first and last month, which took a large chunk out of her money but was worth it. This was where she belonged, and she would do whatever it took to stay here.

The furnishings were minimal but sufficient. She only needed to buy bedding and food at first. She had brought a towel from the Y. After three days of canvassing the neighborhood, she found a job at a coffee shop that lasted for a month. But the money she earned barely covered her groceries for that month, and the rent was still due. Her savings were dwindling fast, so when a waitressing job opened up at the bistro next door Irene leaped at the chance. Besides a salary there were tips, and that would keep her going until she found something in acting.

She wasn't the only one working at the restaurant interested in show business. The bartender had a speaking part in one of the daytime soap operas, which he said was a big break for him. It gave him a lot of face time with producers and directors, and you had to have face time to get anywhere. Cindy, another waitress, was interested in modeling and commercial work. She brought her professional portfolio in to show Irene. It referenced jobs that she had already had, with a page devoted to her past training and future aspirations. And she had Zed cards.

"You're not getting in the door without a Zed card. It's your business card, sort of." She could see the confusion on Irene's face. "Don't worry, I'll help you. Everybody wants to see how you photograph, if you've got camera personality. You just need some glamour shots, and I know a guy who's cheap."

The photo shoot was an eye opener. Of course Irene had used makeup, after all she had been the star in several high school productions and was an old hand at stage makeup, and an avid reader of style magazines, too. She followed their tips for enhancing your natural beauty with a myriad of recommended products. But she hardly recognized herself after the makeup artist worked her wiles on her face and hair. She really did look glamorous.

The shoot and the cards were more of a drain on her budget than she admitted to Cindy, but worth the expense now that her acting portfolio was beginning to come together.

Along with her new Zed cards, she developed a resume sheet that sounded quite professional, at least she though so: lead role in *Our Town* at the Barnum Theater, the name of the auditorium at her high school back home; studied drama with Patricia Keller, her high school drama teacher. Naturally, she omitted the references to high school. Several roles in the drama department productions at the local junior college where she had spent a year and a half showed up on the resume as well. She was ready to knock on doors, but discovered another stumbling block.

"You can't just walk into an audition cold," Cindy explained. "You have to have an agent. This is a tough business to break into, and nobody's getting discovered walking along Sunset Boulevard anymore. The agent is your foot in the door."

"So, how do I get an agent?" Another hurdle, but she wouldn't let it stop her.

"Well, you can start with mine. It's a small agency and they are *usually* looking for new faces." She pulled a card out of her purse and handed it to Irene. "I'd ask Jason who he's working with, too." She nodded toward the bar.

The bartender gave her the name of his agency, but wasn't very encouraging about the outcome for her. "They handle some pretty big stars. They don't normally take on newcomers, but it can't hurt to try."

Irene tried both of those agencies, and a dozen more, but was turned away at each of them. "We're not accepting new talent at the moment. Check back in a few months." She left copies of her portfolio with each one in the hopes that they might call her, but they didn't.

"You need to get out and meet people," Cindy advised. "I know some places where agents hang out and maybe you can do yourself some good."

\* \* \*

They drove out to Burbank in the San Fernando Valley, home to a number of studios, and hunting grounds for would-be starlets hoping to snag an agent. The restaurants catered to the Happy Hour crowd of the lesser-known hopefuls, both talent and agents. An agent's reputation could be made overnight by discovering the next big star, so they were looking, too.

Irene wore her newest dress, a green paisley jersey that hugged her body. She had picked it up at small boutique just off Sunset Boulevard that sold "gently used" clothing. She did her best to repeat the hairstyle and makeup look that appeared on her Zed card. She felt pretty. Cindy loaned her a neckace made of imitation jade that was a different shade of green than her dress, but said no one would notice because the lighting would be dim.

It was dim when they entered the restaurant, dim and glamorous. The heavy wood of the bar and the red leather of the booths gave Irene a sense of sophistication that she had never experienced back home. This felt like the big time. It was seven o'clock on Monday evening, and the bar was crowded with singles. Cindy, at ease in the mix, nudged her way through the crush toward the bar. Irene followed. When they were close enough to place an order, Cindy asked her what she wanted.

"I'm not sure. I don't usually drink." Back home the drink of choice was beer.

"I'll get you a gin fizz. They're pretty harmless." She raised her voice to the bartender in order to be heard, and when the drinks were pushed across the bar to her, she paid. "This first one is on me. After that you're on your own."

"Thanks." Irene felt sure that this would be the only drink she would need. She could nurse it.

The crowd pushed in on them and Irene was caught up in a vortex of small talk, mostly unintelligible in the under roar of the crowded room. She felt out of place. It was obvious that the men and women, some young, some older, knew how this game was played. Cindy was in the thick of it. She had monopolized three actor-looking sorts, at least Irene assumed they were actors from the bits of conversation that she could hear, and had left Irene to her own devices, of which she had few. She wasn't talking to anybody, and the embarrassingly belittling feeling of being the wallflower at a senior prom washed over her. She wanted to leave, but obviously Cindy didn't. Irene escaped into the calm of the ladies' restroom, which was short-lived when the door opened abruptly and two laughing women burst in.

"Oh! My! God! Did you see the guy I'm talking to?"

"Yeah, he's hot. Is it anyone we should know?"

They each headed into a stall but the conversation continued.

"I think he's got a part on some daytime show."

Irene thought of Jason, their bartender. Maybe he was here. She hoped so because she knew she could talk to him.

"They all say stuff like that. You shouldn't believe it."

The toilets flushed and both women reappeared, splashing water in the sinks, combing their hair, leaning in to the mirror to reapply their makeup.

"Well...he's hot!"

Then they were gone and it was as if Irene didn't exist. She was ready to go home. She made her way back to the spot where she had last seen Cindy, but there was no sign of her. Irene scanned the crowd anxiously, to no avail. What was she going to do? How would she get home? She couldn't afford a cab. A bus—but she wasn't even sure where home was from here.

"You look like you just lost your last friend." The man had thinning sandy hair, and slightly rounded shoulders, and was taller than Irene, but just. His jacket was open, his tie loosened, and a drink in one hand, probably not his first from the looks of him.

"My friend. She's disappeared." Again she scanned the bar, but no sign of Cindy.

"Well, that's not much of a friend."

"I'm sure she'll be right back. I'll just stand here."

"Great. I'll just stand here with you. What are you drinking?"

"A gin fizz." Irene relaxed just a little. At least she was talking to someone.

"I'll be right back." He moved away from her towards the bar and she could see that he was older than she had first thought. She looked around again but still no Cindy, or Jason, so she was relieved to see that the man was coming back.

"Here, try this." He handed her a drink that looked like a pink martini. "Nobody drinks a fizz after noon."

"It's beautiful, what is it?" Irene hoped that didn't seem too unsophisticated. She should probably know what this was.

"It's a cosmo. A cosmopolitan." He took a sip from his own drink, which had been replenished. "It's gin. You'll like it."

She did like it. It was delicious. She discovered that the alcohol was helping her open up and she found herself telling this man, Roy, all about her ambitions to become an actress. He seemed interested.

"You got an agent?" He stubbed out another cigarette and shook the melting ice cubes in his empty glass. "You've got to have an agent to get anyplace out here." He signaled to the bartender to make another round for both of them.

"That's what I found out. I've been looking, but so far I haven't found one."

"I can help you out. I know some agents." He was lighting up again.

"Really?" Cindy was right. Maybe she was going to do herself some good.

The drinks arrived and he pulled his billfold out of his

inside breast pocket, fanned some bills, selected one and paid the tab.

"So it doesn't look like your friend is showing up. Is she you're roommate?"

"No, I live alone. We work together." Irene took a sip from this second drink. "The problem is, she drove and I don't have a way home if I can't find her."

He shrugged. "No problem. I'll give you a lift. Where to?"

"Silver Lake."

"No problem," he repeated. "But look, I haven't had dinner and I'm hungry. How about dinner, and then I'll take you home."

The dinner was the best that Irene had ever had. The dining room seemed elegant with its white tablecloths and gleaming silverware. Roy ordered a bottle of red wine and insisted she have a glass with her steak. He seemed to know a lot about wine, and many more topics as well, which he elaborated upon as the evening grew late. Finally, they were out on the sidewalk and getting into his car, a low-slung car, a Porsche he said, with only room for the two of them. Irene was feeling magnificent, on top of the world.


When Irene awoke at five in the morning with a pounding headache, the world had turned. The room was spinning and she rolled over to the edge of the bed and sat up. The spinning stopped but the headache intensified. She needed to make it to the bathroom before she threw up. She leaned against the wall then pushed away and moved slowly toward the dim light of dawn that came through the bathroom window.

She tripped over something in the hallway and fell to her hands and knees. Her hand brushed across the bare back of a shadowed form on the floor. She recoiled in revulsion. A man's body. Her head was spinning and she could feel the bile rising in her throat. She pushed herself up and lunged into the bathroom, falling against the toilet bowl, retching. It seemed an endless time until her body quit heaving and she could press her forehead against the cool porcelain of the commode.

Something terrible had happened, she couldn't remember what, but she knew it was awful. When she could steady herself to stand, she leaned into the sink and splashed her face with cold water, drinking spasmodically from her cupped hand. She buried her face in a towel and held it there, pressing hard, for what seemed a long time. Finally, she looked back into the darkened hallway. The body was still there.

The man was sprawled face down on the hall floor, half undressed, no shirt but wearing trousers and socks, the back of his head matted in blood. She looked down at herself. No dress, but still wearing her underwear, blood spattered down the front of her slip. Then she saw the log next to the body. It was a piece of split firewood that had been part of the small pile next to the fireplace. The wedge side of it was bloody. Irene turned back to the sink and looked into the mirror. Her hair was wild, matted with hairspray and dried blood, and blood was caked on her face and on her chest. She knelt down by the toilet and was sick again.

When she could, she leaned back against the bathroom wall and tried to remember. Dinner. She remembered that. She remembered the gleam of the candle in the middle of the table and the sound of the wine pouring into her glass. She had never had red wine before, or any wine for that matter, and she liked it. She remembered him parking the car. But she couldn't remember the drive to her house, only the parking, and the only place open nearby was down the hill, and she remembered the man complaining about the uphill climb.

Then it swept over her, the derisive laughter: hayseed; all alike; go home; fool; dinner's not free...dinner's not free... dinner's not free. The feeling of rage swept over her again! Again! Again! She had a life here. Not back there. This would not keep her from this life. Her new life. She felt herself slipping down the wall and onto the bathroom floor. The tile was cool on her face. She closed her eyes, the horror that was becoming her life obscured in an alcoholic fog.

After a time, she stood up, turned on the shower and pulled off her clothes. She let the water run from hot to warm over her body until it began to cool down, then poured shampoo onto her head and frantically scrubbed it in, allowing the suds to wash over her, the rusty water swirling around the drain. The water turned icy but she stood there for a long time, and, when she finally turned it off, she knew what she had to do. She pulled her jeans and sweatshirt from the back of the door, put them on, and squeezed the water out of her hair with a towel, watching herself in the mirror as she combed the wet strands, running through the plan in her mind.

The body first. She unclipped the plastic shower curtain from the hooks that ran across the rod, wiping it down with the towel as she went. She threw the towel over his head and then spread the plastic over the body, tucking it under on one side and then the other, shoving against the right side and rolling him over onto the curtain. She could feel the rigidity in his arms and knew enough about dead bodies from growing up on a farm to know he would soon be frozen into place. Purple mottling from the blood pooling in his bare chest showed through the translucent plastic. She yanked on the curtain until she had him securely wrapped.

The log was next. She picked it up and stared at the blood and the hair caught in the small shards of wood that made up the raw face of the log, took it into the living room, knelt down by the fireplace, and began building a fire. She struck a match and held it to the wadded up newspaper that was stuffed under the kindling and the logs and watched until she was sure it was going, and then turned to the disarray in the room. Her dress, his jacket, their shoes were strewn on the floor and one of her portfolios was splayed across the small coffee table. She remembered that now. She offered it and he laughed.

"This is crap!" he snorted. "Don't show this to anyone in the business. They'll laugh you out of town."

"I thought you could help me." She remembered the feeling of the blood rushing to her face and humiliation sweeping over her, the shaming realization of the truth in what he said.

He laughed again, more of a sneer. "No, I'm not helping *you*. I'm helping myself. Just collecting on your debt. Dinner wasn't free, you know." He took a long pull at a flask that he had brought in from the car. "Go home, blondie, there are hundreds of girls out here—probably thousands—with the same idea. You're all going to make it big in the movies, and you're all pathetic." He stood up, and said, more to himself than to her, "I must be really drunk to end up here...another hayseed...another loser in a cast of thousands." He steadied himself against the wall. "Where's the bathroom?" He picked up his shirt, which had been discarded in his thwarted attempt at sex, and headed into the hallway.

She remembered the rage again. It was all consuming, and she grabbed up the log and swung it up and over her head and down onto his with all the force she could muster. There was a dull thud, and then he pitched forward onto the floor. She hit him again and again. He wasn't getting up and she wasn't going home.

She picked up the clothing from the floor, pushed her dress into the laundry bag, and then went through his jacket. She found his wallet in an inside pocket and his car keys in an outside one. She put the keys on the table, removed the money from the wallet, which she shoved down into the trash bag along with the whiskey flask, his bloodstained shirt, and her slip, and took it out to the garbage bin sitting at the curb. Today was trash day and the trucks were rumbling in the distance. She folded his jacket and tie and put them into a brown paper grocery bag, and his shoes into another one.

She was calm now that she had a plan. She had to get rid of the body, and soon, and the only way she could see to do it was to bury it. She couldn't use his car to take it somewhere else for several reasons, the main one being the condition of the body. It would be too stiff to shove into the car by tonight, and someone would surely see her. While the street was dimly lit, the one streetlamp on their block was outside her house. Besides, she didn't know how to drive his car. Burial in the backyard would have to do.

There was a small shed built against the side of the house, and she had noticed the garden tools when she stored her suitcase in there. She found a shovel, a rake, and a wicked-looking hoe, all rusted, along with an old hose and a partially used, dried out bag of potting soil. There was a bottle of liquid fertilizer, the lid screwed on crookedly and cemented to the bottle by the brown spillage that had dried with age, a few more partially used bags of plant food, and soil amendments. One of them was lime.

Irene took the tools into the backyard and began clearing the dead grass from the hard baked earth. The yard was secluded from the prying eyes of neighbors, with a tall wooden fence on one side overhung with orange bougain-villea, and a chain link fence covered in ivy and bordered with a tall stand of bamboo on the other side. There were no neighbors behind the houses on her block because they backed up to a steep ravine. Her only protection from a slide down the hill was an extension of the chain link fence from her neighbor's yard.

She chipped away at the weeds and crusted dirt, and began to think this idea wasn't going to work. She even looked over the fence and thought about pushing the body down the steep hill, but that wouldn't work either. There were houses on the street below, and a body in their backyard would obviously have come from up above. She turned back to the shovel and the hoe and eventually broke through to softer earth and began to make some headway. By noon she had a shallow trench carved out, approximately seven feet by three. She needed a rest.

As she leaned over the kitchen sink, splashing her face and then drinking a tall glass of water, she could see from the window that her trash had been picked up and the plastic bin was halfway out in the street. She went out the back door, in order to avoid the hall, along the narrow path between her house and the neighbors, and unlatched the front gate. As she was rolling the empty can out of the street her neighbor came outside.

"What are you doing over there?" Linda was always curious, but usually in a friendly way. "I've been listening to you digging and scratching all morning."

"You have?"

"Are you putting in a garden?"

"I thought I'd give it a try." Irene appreciated an explanation having been given for what she was doing.

"Well, if you're thinking of just planting straight in the ground you're going to be disappointed." She was tugging her trashcan up over the curb. "The soil is too poor. It doesn't even make a decent graveyard, and I should know," Linda didn't seem to notice the stricken look that appeared in Irene's eyes. "I tried to bury my cat last year when she passed. She had feline leukemia."

"Oh...I'm sorry." Irene's mouth had gone dry.

"That's okay, she didn't suffer. I had her put to sleep at the vet's." She paused and Irene started to turn away. "I should have had her cremated, I guess, but they wanted a hundred dollars and that was too much for me."

"Yes, that seems expensive." Irene was tired of the conversation but didn't want to seem rude, so she stood there.

"That's when I found out it was a lousy place to bury something. You can't dig a hole deep enough to keep the raccoons from digging it up. I buried the cat twice and then I just wrapped her in a sheet and put her in the trash."

"Oh, sorry about that."

"So, the reason I'm telling you this is that I tried to plant some flowers in the hole I dug for the cat, but they wouldn't grow. I even gave them a lot of plant food and kept them watered."

Irene just shook her head, but she was beginning to worry about her own situation.

"You need to plant in pots or a raised bed. That's what I did. Now I've got lots of flowers for the house and the yard looks nice."

"I wouldn't know how to do that." Irene was getting nervous that her plan was too stupid. Why did she think she could just bury a body and not be found out?

"Oh, it's easy." Linda looked pleased. "I just went to this lumber yard and they had a do-it-yourself planter box kit. They had all sizes, but I got the small one. It's all I need. Anyway, they have plants, too, and dirt, and they delivered it all up here. For a fee, of course."

"Oh sure, I guess there's always a fee."

"Have you dug up a lot?"

"Well, yes, some."

"That's probably not a bad idea. Put your raised bed right over where you've been digging. That way your roots won't run into the rock hard dirt we have around here."

"Yes, that's a good idea." Irene was beginning to see a plan.

"You won't have wasted all that effort this morning." Linda had turned back to her house. "I'll get you the name of the place I went. I won't be a minute."

She returned with a slip of paper with the address of the garden supply store and the assembly instruction booklet for the prefab bed. "Here you go. This is what I got. It's really easy."

"Thanks." Irene took the papers and started for the gate,

then turned back. "I think I'll do some more digging this afternoon. Just to loosen up the ground, like you said."

"Good idea! Good luck."

By three o'clock Irene had widened and deepened the trench enough so that she felt sure the body would fit, and then showered, dressed for work and left a little early in order to make three stops. The first one was at the man's car. She dropped the car keys in the street next to the driver's door, a gift, perhaps, to one of the many scavengers who rifled through the trashcans in the neighborhood. The Goodwill bin was next. She shoved the sack with the jacket and tie down the chute, and then walked on a few blocks where she set the bag with the shoes in a doorway next to a sleeping derelict.

The burial wasn't too difficult. She had started as soon as she got home from her evening shift at the restaurant, around ten-thirty, and was finished well before Linda came home from her job at County General Hospital at midnight. She was able to manage the body by dragging the shower curtain down the hall and out of the back door to the trench. She had already scooped the ashes from the fireplace, the only connection to the murder weapon, into a bag and had poured them into the hole. She peeled back the plastic, gagged at the smell, but rolled and shook the makeshift shroud until the body settled into the grave, fitting nicely. She remembered the bag of lime in the shed, got it and sprinkled all of it over the bare chest of the man, then shoveled the dirt on top, packing it down with the back of the shovel. She folded the plastic into a compact square and shoved it into the empty ash bag. It would go in the trash bin tomorrow. She thought about offering up some sort of prayer, but wasn't sure whom she was praying for. She showered and tried to rid herself of the noxious smell.

* * *

The raised garden bed had been a brilliant idea all of those years ago, the vital ingredient that made her plan work, and she often wished she could thank Linda for suggesting it. The actual grave was not as deep as she wanted because she had hit rock and had to give up. But the added soil made it closer to four feet deep, maybe more. She had ordered tomato plants delivered along with the kit and the soil, and paid for all of it with the cash from the billfold. Because the raccoons and coyotes digging in the soft earth were always a worry, she rigged a covering for the plants using painters' drop cloths and plastic tubing. Each night she covered the bed, and each morning she uncovered it. It had been good for her peace of mind and, as it turned out, good for the tomatoes.

Now her peace of mind was shattered. She had realized long ago the flaw in her plan, a rather major one when you thought about it. Over the years she had seen old houses in the neighborhood sold for a lot of money, torn down, and new houses or condos erected on the spot. The construction always included excavation.

The letter in her hand today told her that her house was next. The owner had sold the house to a builder and expected the demolition to begin within the next several months. The woman reminded Irene that her last month's rent was paid and hoped she was giving her plenty of notice. She had been a good tenant.

Irene needed another plan. Her first thought was to dig up the grave, but she gagged at the thought of what she would find, besides what would she do with the remains. She had to leave. She ruled out going back home, not that she wanted to do that, when she remembered that she had listed her Minnesota driver's license on the rental agreement. She could be tracked there. Mexico wouldn't work. What would she do? Waitressing was her only skill and she didn't speak Spanish.

In the end Irene's plan was simple. She changed her name, packed her clothes, withdrew her meager savings, and boarded the Number 4 bus for Downtown L.A. and the anonymity of the sprawling city.

# Lead Us Not Into Temptation
## L.H. Dillman

*Which is more important to a person's character: nature or nurture? Can humans be born evil? Or are some of us made evil by circumstance?*

Carolina Roundtree pondered these questions on a warm Monday morning while mopping the terrazzo tile in the kitchen of a Bel Air mansion. She always had to be thinking about something besides whatever her hands were up to at the moment. A lifetime of sweeping, washing, and wiping might cripple the mind of a weak individual, but a strong person does not let her brain go fallow no matter how tedious the job—the same way a person of integrity does not dive in to the temptation to behave badly, no matter how strong the lure. She had made this very point to her great-nephew, who had come to live with her at the start of the summer.

"You understand me, Dante?" she had asked when he'd first arrived, backpack over his shoulder. They were standing in the baggage claim area of Terminal 7 at LAX.

"Whateva," he'd replied with the smug indifference of a punk from the south side of Chicago. The Englewood district, where Dante had spent his first fourteen years, was one of the meanest neighborhoods in America.

"'*Whateva?*'" she demanded, loud enough for others to hear. He was lucky to have a sixty-something great-aunt willing to step in when everyone else had given up. She figured he owed her some respect. "I think you meant to say, 'Yes, Aunty Cee'."

Embarrassed, he mumbled, "Yes, Aunty Cee."

They waited in silence for his luggage, Carolina stealing glances at the boy beside her. Not really a boy any more, she realized. Since she'd last seen him, he'd grown six inches, broadened across the shoulders, lost the plump in his cheeks, and gained a shadow over his upper lip. His voice had dropped too. For better or worse, he could pass for eighteen.

"Los Angeles is going to present you with a number of opportunities, both good and bad," she told him. "Of course, you'll avail yourself of only the good ones."

He screwed up his face. "Run that back for me?"

She heaved a sigh, her tremendous bosom rising and falling under her blue dress like a thundering wave. Then she rephrased: "You best stay out of trouble while you're here. Walk a straight line and show respect twenty-four-seven. Also, tell the truth. You abide by my rules, Dante, we'll get along fine…"

The unspoken "or else" was that she'd put him on the next return flight to the Windy City, where he'd soon enough fall back in with the hoodlums and hussies of Englewood. Only this time, as a repeat offender, he'd be charged as an adult.

"Aight." He snatched his suitcase as it tumbled from the chute. "Why'n't you say so?"

"Wrong answer."

They headed out of the terminal, Dante shuffling along beside her. She frowned at the sight of the ragged hems of his low-slung pants sweeping the blacktop. He probably needed a whole new wardrobe, and she'd probably have to pay for it. *Well, fine. Family is family.* She was standing in for her dear-departed sister, Georgia, who'd been the boy's grandma and surely would have done whatever it took to correct his course before it was too late.

"What do you mean, 'wrong answer'?" he asked as they

entered the cavernous parking structure.

"I mean, if a person wants to advance in this world, they've got to have a decent vocabulary. They can't sound ghetto."

He snorted. "Drake and Kendrick and Snoop and them make bank. Be doin' way better'n you, Aunty Cee. No offense."

She grabbed him by the arm. "You don't have the slightest idea about me." Standing in the middle of the garage, forcing cars to detour around them, she delivered a primer on the lack of prospects for a penniless black female when she was his age in the early 1960s. She told him that, notwithstanding her lack of formal schooling, she'd strived to become an educated woman, devoting countless hours over the years to reading the classics of literature and philosophy, the fundamentals of science and history, and much more. Maybe someday he'd understand the value of such intangibles. "As for material assets, I've done quite well, thank you—well enough to rescue your black behind." He tried to pull away but she held on. "And don't get me started on those rappers. For every one of them, there's a hundred men dead or in prison for following the messages in those terrible lyrics."

"If you say so."

She loosened her grip. "I do."

Once inside her old white Corolla, she confiscated his iPhone and headphones before he could disappear into a haze of hip-hop. "You mind your p's and q's, Dante, and we'll see about you getting your music back."

He sulked all the way to Leimert Park.

The following day she enrolled him in summer school. For five weeks, he spent his mornings studying English, Algebra 2, and Religion at St. Ignatius. In the afternoons, he helped Carolina's husband, Alfred, at the vacuum repair shop on

Venice Boulevard, or, if business was slow, as it often was, they'd go fishing off the Santa Monica pier. Nighttimes, they stayed home and watched Discovery Channel or, if the men had their way, sports or Showtime. No way was Carolina going to let the boy roam free after dark.

Dante's mid-summer grades at St. Ignatius were a pleasant surprise (two Bs and an A-) so she gave him back his music and allowed him to hang out with friends after school. In return, he helped her pick out a new iPhone and showed her some of its more advanced functions. Impressed with his improved attitude and manners, Alfred said it was too bad they couldn't afford to keep him and send him to St. Ignatius year-round. Carolina was not yet convinced. People can change, but not that fast.

When summer school ended and Alfred traveled to San Diego for a reunion of medic-corps veterans of the *USS Kitty Hawk*, Carolina had no choice but to bring Dante with her to work. Monday morning, they set out for Bel Air, where she had a twice-a-week job. In response to his ogling the mansions they passed, she quoted from Matthew 19:24: "'Tis easier for a camel to pass through the eye of a needle than for a rich—"

"Look at that." He cut her off to point out a Bentley Flying Spur speeding their way.

*Oh dear.* She would need to add "irony" to the list of topics for discussion with Dante, a list she was keeping on the Voice Memo app of her new iPhone. They had arrived at the entry to 510 Bedford Terrace.

"Who owns this place?" Dante asked.

"Ming and Wei-Lin Laing." She typed the code into the keypad at the gatepost.

"Are they, like, famous?"

The boy was far too keen on celebrity. "Don't say 'like'. Makes you sound dumb."

"Well, are they?"

"Not in this country." Carolina had never met the Laings, who lived in China. All her dealings were with Jackson Wu, their U.S. business manager, who lived in San Francisco.

"How much they pay you, Aunty Cee?"

"*Do* they pay. Enough."

More than enough, really. Five hundred dollars a day, one thousand dollars a week, direct-deposited into her account by Jackson Wu on behalf of the Laings. She'd had to pinch herself when she got the job two months ago. The money couldn't have come at a better time, what with the balloon payment on the house due at year's end, and Alfred hardly working.

The wrought iron gate swung open, and the old Corolla wheezed its way up the cobblestone drive. When the residence came into view, Dante let out a whistle. The Mediterranean-style mansion presided over its own hilltop. Flanked by towering palms and tropical plants, the house resembled an exotic movie set. And no wonder: the Laings had bought it from an ex-Hollywood-Big-Wig whose last three features had bombed.

"Holy—How many rooms does it got?"

"Does it *have*." She parked the Toyota. "Twenty-three, not counting the tennis pavilion. Most of them aren't used, thank the Lord, or else I couldn't get through them in two days."

"How come most of 'em aren't used?" Dante asked as they walked to the entry.

"Because only one person lives here." Carolina explained that while Mr. and Mrs. Laing owned the place and paid the bills, only their daughter, Amy—whom she referred to privately as Little Miss—occupied the home.

"How old is she?" Dante asked.

"Eighteen. She'll be a freshman in the business school at USC in the fall."

"Doesn't she get lonely?"

"She entertains a lot." Carolina fished in her purse for the house key. "Listen, Dante. When you're employed by this caliber of people, you learn to be discrete, to overlook transgressions, to keep confidences."

"Huh?"

"I mean, I don't get all up in their business, and I don't go flapping my mouth about their peculiar ways or the things I've seen under this roof." She unlocked the door and waved him in. In the foyer, they removed their shoes in observance of Chinese custom. "Now, I know I don't have to worry about your having sticky fingers," she whispered.

"'Course not."

She just about believed him. All the same, she'd find a way to pat down his pockets before the day was done.

Rather than Asian-influenced, the décor was Spanish Colonial. According to Jackson Wu, the estate had come fully furnished. The Laings had merely sent over a selection of their jade and ivory, a few silk rugs, and some paintings. Carolina handed her great-nephew a vacuum and told him to get started on the first floor. Next, he was to pick up all the empty bottles, dump the ashtrays, and dispose of it all out back.

"You got that, Dante?"

"Sure, Aunty Cee."

An hour later, she looked up from mopping the kitchen floor and spotted him walking across the rear lawn. *What a handsome young man,* she thought, *and how respectable-looking, with his upright posture and preppy polo shirt.* You'd never guess he held a prominent position on the Chicago P.D.'s Street Gang Watch List. *If crime is a product of circumstance, can it be prevented in the right environment, with the right influences?*

"They sure enough go through a ton of booze," Dante said from the doorway. "Didn't know Chinese people drink so much."

"Little Miss is more Canadian than Chinese." Carolina relayed what she'd learned from Jackson Wu: Amy Laing had attended boarding school in Vancouver. Her folks moved her down here after she got into some kind of trouble up there. That last part was gossip, so Carolina didn't repeat it.

"Do her parents know she parties this much?" Dante asked, stepping into the kitchen.

"Don't you dare dirty-up this nice clean floor. Go stand over there." She backed out of the room in advance of her mop, her bulbous rump pushing her great-nephew into the butler's pantry. "Do they know? I doubt it."

"You aren't going to tell them?"

"It's not my place. Anyway, I don't have their number."

Once, early in her employment, she did phone the Laings' business manager. "Is anyone looking after Amy?" Carolina had inquired. "I know teenagers like to have fun, but you should know she's having a *lot* of fun." Jackson Wu then explained, in a tone that left no room for debate, that although Mr. and Mrs. Laing were very busy people, they did try to visit their daughter once a year; that Amy had been living apart from them since age eight; and that supervision was outside both his and Carolina's job descriptions.

"Suggestion number one is, drop it," Wu had said. "Suggestion number two is, focus on cleaning."

"So you really think she's okay?"

"You'll have to trust me."

"Sure, Mr. Wu. I understand."

But Carolina hadn't understood, so she'd done a little reading. Amy was part of the "parachute kids" phenomenon. Wealthy Chinese citizens buy their children F-1 visas, drop them into California, and house them in upscale suburban neighborhoods with minimal oversight—all in pursuit of a U.S. education. Well, Amy was getting an education all right, just not the one her folks intended.

"Let me guess," Dante said, leaning on the counter.

"That's her red Tesla in the garage?"

"Yep. New last month."

He shook his head, no doubt marveling at the freedom and good fortune bestowed on a girl only four years older than he. To Carolina's way of thinking, Amy Laing wasn't lucky at all: her parents had set her adrift on a raft made of cash. When, inevitably, she started to sink, they would foot the bill for a rescue. The folly was not all that different from the errors that had led to Dante's three appearances in Cook County juvenile court.

"Where is she?" Dante asked.

"Sleeping it off, most likely." With whom, was the only question. Carolina had seen enough upon opening Little Miss's bedroom door to cause her to put off cleaning upstairs until after noon. "I don't approve," Carolina added, hanging the mop on a hook in the pantry. "And I don't want you consorting—"

From the next room came the whooshing sound of a Sub-Zero refrigerator door opening. Little Miss was awake. Had she heard them? Carolina straightened her back and walked into the kitchen, motioning for Dante to follow.

"Good morning, Amy. How are you?"

Dark eyes looked out from behind a curtain of tousled black hair. Soft lips hung open. Bare bowlegs stood at the end of a trail of dirty footprints across the damp tile.

"Hey," she said.

The sight of a college-bound woman still in her Jurassic 5 pajamas at eleven a.m. on a Monday irritated Carolina. *Business school, my derriere*, Carolina thought. This gal's going for a bachelor's degree in Dom Pérignon and a masters in ménage à trois.

"This is my nephew, Dante, from Chicago. He's helping me out with some of my clients."

Dante jerked his chin. "Hey."

"'Sup."

"Hope we didn't wake you with our clatter," Carolina continued cheerfully.

"No prob." Amy kept her eyes on Dante as she took a seat at the counter. "I'm gonna need some coffee, Carolina."

"I'll be happy to get that." She bustled over to the Keurig machine.

"Nice ride," Dante said. "The garage door was open. New model, huh? Sweet."

"I'm still learning how to drive it."

He smiled. "I could school you."

"Dante doesn't have a license," Carolina said. "He's only fourteen."

"Damn, you look at least seventeen," Amy said, crossing and uncrossing her bare legs.

Something in Little Miss's voice raised the hair on Carolina's neck.

"I bet you hear that a lot," Amy added.

"Yeah," he said, folding his arms across his chest and sliding each hand under a bicep to push the muscle out. Carolina recognized the trick from her early days with Alfred, when he'd acted like one of the chest-puffing frigate birds on *Wild Kingdom.*

"You visiting, or you moving here?" Amy asked Dante.

"We'll see how it goes," Carolina answered.

"I like L.A. so far," he said. "It's chill."

Amy grinned slyly. "You have no idea."

"Yeah?"

"Come to one of my kick-backs and see."

"Dante's too young for that." Carolina set a cup of coffee on the counter in front of Little Miss. "I forgot. Do you take milk or sugar?"

"I like mine black."

The room fell silent.

\* \* \*

At noon, as Carolina and Dante were unwrapping their baloney sandwiches, Amy appeared in the doorway. This time, she wore booty shorts and a white crop-top so thin that her little nipples showed like copper pennies under a hanky. Carolina scowled. All the designer clothes hanging in that girls' closet, and she had to dress like a thrift-store waif?

"Hey, Dante," Amy said. "I need help reaching something up high. Can you come upstairs?"

He sprang to his feet. "No prob."

Carolina followed a minute later. Alone-time with Little Miss was not in Dante's best interests, no matter what his gonads told him. She climbed the grand staircase, tiptoed down the hallway—though the floor creaked anyway under her great weight—and stopped outside Amy's open door. The king-sized platform bed was empty. The teens weren't in the bedroom at all. Their voices were coming from the walk-in closet.

"The big blue one on the left." That was Little Miss talking.

Dante grunted. "Got it."

"Thanks. Can you set it on the dresser?"

So, the girl really *had* needed help reaching something on a high shelf. Carolina figured her instincts were just off that day.

After lunch, aiming to keep the two teens apart, Carolina asked Dante to clean the pool cabana. Amy chose that afternoon to work on her tan. From the window, Carolina watched her strut around in her white thong bikini, swaying her hips to the beat of Beyoncé, and finally settling on a chaise lounge. Naturally, Dante had to take a break and talk to her, and naturally, after five minutes in the baking sun, he had to remove his shirt. He had a well-muscled chest and arms, and his skin gleamed like rich chocolate. Carolina heard Little

Miss ask, ever so sweetly, if he worked out.

"Dante!" Carolina called. "I need you in here for a minute."

Amy spun around. "Don't you have work to do?"

The insolence took Carolina's breath away. Feeling disrespected and powerless, she thought about quitting right then and there. But she had no other job lined up, much less one that paid five hundred dollars a day. So she held her tongue and stewed, angry with Little Miss and angry at herself for yielding to the girl.

Amy lifted her hair and asked Dante to take off her necklace so she could apply sunscreen to her shoulders. Naturally, he obliged, examining the gold locket before handing it back. At least Little Miss slathered on the suntan lotion herself. Carolina couldn't wait for the day to end.

"See you Friday," she said to Little Miss when the clock struck five.

The girl ignored her. "'Bye, Dante."


"I'm sorry I took you up there," Carolina said on the way home. "I shouldn't have put you in that situation."

"I was having a good time," Dante replied from the passenger seat.

"You two were getting awfully cozy."

"Chill. Nothing happened. Besides, she's eighteen, Aunty Cee."

So the girl was old enough to consent. Still, that didn't make the liaison wise or good. "Remember what we talked about at the beginning of the summer? How we need to do what's right even if temptation's pulling us in the other direction?"

"Oh my God."

Carolina felt entirely disconnected. Was it impossible to bridge the five-decade gap between them? She sighed, thrusting her bosom so far into the steering wheel that she honked the horn. He laughed.

"Listen, Dante, I may be old, but I've got good eyes. Amy Laing's a dangerous—"

"She's being friendly 'cause we're both new to town. We're in the same boat."

"Hers is a yacht. Yours is a rubber dingy."

"So?"

"So she doesn't like *you*. She likes the *attention*."

He shifted to face his great-aunt. "If she's so bad, why do you work there?"

They came to a red light. The ancient Toyota idled noisily.

"I need the income."

"Then you're giving in to temptation, too."

Carolina stifled a gasp. "It's not the same."

"You let her treat you like shit."

"Watch your language."

"Just sayin'."

Carolina opened her mouth but no words came out. The light turned green. She slammed her foot onto the accelerator. They didn't talk the rest of the way home.


"The boy deserves some fun with people his own age," Alfred said the next night. He'd just returned from the reunion and was relaxing on the couch with a beer. "Not Amy Laing, no. But young people. He's been stuck with two old coots all summer."

"Who's the second old coot?" Carolina asked with a harrumph.

"I'm serious. He's worked hard, hasn't caused us any trouble." Alfred took a swig from the longneck. "You can't keep him under wraps forever, Carolina. He'll blow his lid."

Alfred had a point, she had to admit. So, on Thursday, when Dante announced he was going to a movie with a friend from St. Ignatius, she did not object.

"Are you meeting at the theater?" she asked. "I can give you a ride."

"Jeff's picking me up," Dante said, checking his wallet.

"Okay, then. Be back by eleven."

"Eleven-thirty."

She chewed the inside of her lip. "All right."

At seven-thirty, a black Nissan Altima with dark windows pulled up in front of the house. It was only Alfred's hand on her arm that kept her from going outside to meet this Jeff.

"You be careful now," she called after Dante.

"'Course, Aunty Cee." He waved, then got into the back seat.

The Nissan sped off. She turned around with a frown.

"What's the matter?" Alfred asked.

"Why'd he get into the back seat?"

"Coulda been another friend from St. Ignatius sitting up front."

"Maybe." Either that or it was one of those Uber cars.

At ten p.m. Alfred went to bed. Carolina stayed in the living room with a hot toddy and a Walter Mosley novel. She didn't get much reading done. Eleven-thirty came and went. Dante didn't answer his cell phone, and he hadn't given her Jeff's number. She cursed herself for not getting the name of the theater or even the name of the movie—which a more experienced guardian would have thought to do—and cursed Dante for breaching her trust. By twelve-thirty, she was imagining the worst: a car accident, a goofball prank gone wrong, an encounter with the LAPD—or a tryst with a certain Asian seductress.

She grabbed her purse and headed out into the night, knowing that Alfred would have called her crazy. He would have pointed out that Dante could be anywhere in this vast metropolis. Not exactly *anywhere*, Carolina would have countered.

Twenty-five minutes later, she punched the code into the security panel on the Laings' gatepost. She expected to see cars lining the private drive, but there were none. The house was unlit, save for a yellow glow bleeding through an upstairs window. She parked and got out, leaving her purse but bringing her new iPhone, which she checked for messages one last time. She listened for sounds of hijinks, but all was quiet. Had the party ended early? Or was she being crazy? She unlocked the front door. The house was silent. Was anyone even home?

Then she heard a tiny mew—like a kitten—coming from the second floor. Little Miss had no pets. *Oh dear.*

At the top of the staircase, Carolina heard another sound. This one sounded more human than feline, and more like a moan than a mew. She considered the possibility that it wasn't her great-nephew but some other supplicant ensnared between Amy Laing's loins—in which case she'd get fired for nothing. It was a risk she had to take. The floorboards creaked as she made her way toward the bedroom. Ten feet from the door, she thought she recognized her great-nephew's voice. An image of Dante in a state of carnal ecstasy flashed across her mental screen—a sight no aunty should ever have to see. *Damn that boy for being so selfish.* All manner of complications and catastrophes flooded her mind. What if Little Miss gave him a disease? What if she was making a sex tape? What if she got pregnant? What if she regretted the liaison and claimed rape? Of all the dire scenarios, that last one scared Carolina the most. *Damn that boy for being so dumb.* She activated her cell phone's Voice Memo app and whispered, "Remember to have 'The Other Talk'."

"Dante!" She flung the door open.

The room appeared empty. No limbs entwined on the mattress, no clothes strewn across the floor. Were they in the closet? Carolina took two steps in. Then she heard a grunt behind her.

She spun around. Up against the wall, Dante was sitting in a chair, fully clothed, his hands tied behind his back, his ankles bound, his mouth covered with duct tape. A few feet away, Amy Laing sat in a matching chair, dressed in silk, and free of ropes. She had a gun.

*What in God's name?* Carolina's pulse pounded in her ears.

"I've been waiting for you," Little Miss said, pointing the weapon at Carolina. "Didn't think it'd take you this long."

"Waiting for me?" *Hold it together.*

"I knew you'd come after him."

Carolina searched Dante's face for an explanation. Muted by the tape, all he could do was shake his head. "Let him go," she said. "He's too young for your kinky games."

"Damn, you're dumb. You're totally missing the point."

"I suppose I am." If not for that gun, Carolina would have slapped the smirk off the girl's face.

"Lemme break it down for you." Amy stood. "You've been stealing from me for two months, practically since the day you started. My family's jade, my dad's ivory Buddhas, two paintings, a rug. You swiped it all."

"I've no idea what you're talking about."

Actually, Carolina had noticed the jade collection shrinking. She'd left a message for Jackson Wu last week to cover herself, though she hadn't mentioned this to Little Miss. As for the paintings, rug, and Buddhas, they must have disappeared before Carolina was hired.

"You sold it all for cash," Amy said, stepping forward. "I'm guessing you took it to your neighborhood fence in South Central."

*The ignorance.* "I'm not from South Central."

"Whatever. Then you bring this home-skittle to work with you. Supposedly, he was gonna help clean our house, but really he came to help you clean us out. That's right, you work as a team. While you distracted me in the kitchen, he went looking for my jewelry. Oh yeah, you're real good—'cept I caught you."

"You have an epic imagination."

"I've got proof," Amy said, taking another two steps. Dante was now slightly behind and to the right of her. "Your nephew's fingerprints are all over my blue jewelry box. Everything's gone. He stole the diamond earrings Daddy gave me, and an emerald ring, and a Cartier watch I got for my birthday, and a bunch of other stuff. At least a hundred thousand dollars' worth."

Now Carolina understood why Little Miss had lured Dante upstairs. The "something up high" had been the jewelry box. She'd tricked him into supplying his fingerprints in order to frame him. There was a lesson for him in this. Carolina only hoped he wouldn't have to learn it in prison. She saw him tugging at his wrist-ropes and rubbing his ankles together.

"And you, you were the brains of the operation," Amy continued, waving the gun in Carolina's direction as though to intimidate her. "You have the house keys and the code to our security system."

"That doesn't prove anything."

"Wrong. Check the trunk of that ugly old car of yours. You'll find my gold necklace, the one with the locket? Actually, the police will find it. You must've left it by accident when you hocked the loot."

So that's why Little Miss had asked Dante to remove her necklace out by the pool. After collecting his fingerprints, she'd planted the locket in the Toyota while Carolina was busy cleaning. Devious. But why?

One possibility came to mind.

"Your parents are coming for a visit, aren't they?" Carolina asked.

"You're smarter than I thought."

Carolina was accustomed to being underestimated. "You

sold the art and jewelry," she told the girl, "and now you need an explanation for why it's gone missing because your parents will surely notice."

"They notice everything." Amy rolled her eyes. Behind her, Dante wriggled out of his leg ties.

"So you're going to blame us."

"Duh. I'll tell them you were counting on me staying out partying, but I came home early and caught you guys red-handed."

It was a clever scheme, though Carolina wouldn't give Little Miss the satisfaction of hearing her say so. The Laings would believe their daughter's story, as would a lot of other people—possibly including the LAPD. All they'd need to know was that Carolina was a black housekeeper with a less-than-stable job history, a curious turn as a witness to a Malibu homicide last year, and a pile of debts; and Dante was a black juvenile with a rap sheet that included grand theft and breaking and entering. Of course, if they bothered to dig below the surface, they'd uncover plenty of holes in Amy's story. Wouldn't they? At the moment, Carolina could think of only one.

"But you invited him up here tonight, and I came later out of fear—"

"Who says?" Amy shrugged. "Not me. Not the security cameras outside—I switched them off. Not some Uber driver who'll never be found. I'm telling the cops you came together."

It now dawned on Carolina that Little Miss had no intention of turning them in because that would allow them to tell the police what really happened. No, the girl planned to kill them, then call the police and claim she'd done it in self-defense. She was smart enough to stage the scene and plant the necessary evidence. Amy Laing had the heart and soul of a killer.

*Stay calm. Think.*

Carolina took a long look at the gun. It was light enough for Little Miss to hold in one hand. With a small caliber firearm, accuracy mattered. Depending on the girl's skill, Carolina was probably within lethal range. Dante was a goner for sure—unless he could escape. He had one hand free and was frantically picking at the other knot.

"I don't understand why, though," she said to keep the girl talking. Dante needed one more minute, maybe two. "You couldn't need the money."

"L.A.'s so fucking expensive. Everything's about how rich you are. My friends, they all know the difference between a genuine Chanel bag and a knock-off, and you know how much the real ones cost? No, you wouldn't. They start at three thousand, okay? And my personal trainer charges, like, two-fifty a visit."

*Talk about the banality of evil.* Carolina had the urge to whump the brat upside the head, gun be damned, but instead she said, "Can't you ask Mr. Wu for more allowance?"

"He's a tight-ass. He says it's up to my parents, but they're totally clueless about L.A."

Carolina feigned sympathy. "They've never lived here."

"I'm supposed to settle down and go to college, right?" Little Miss spat the words. "Okay, but they need to be realistic. Like—" Glancing behind her, she spotted Dante tugging at the last rope. In one smooth motion, she went to him and brought the pistol to his left temple. "Don't even think about it."

Carolina's heart sank. There went his chance to escape—unless she could distract Little Miss long enough for him to get free. To her surprise, Amy ordered her to untie him.

"No tricks," Amy said. "Then we take a walk."

A walk? Of course. To make their murders appear to be justifiable homicide. Little Miss couldn't shoot them against the wall. What the girl had failed to take into account was the mark that the duct tape was going to leave around Dante's mouth. A clue for the coroner. Great.

"Move," Amy commanded.

Keeping her eyes on the gun, Carolina knelt at Dante's side. When she'd untied him, she removed the tape. His first words were: "I'm sorry."

She wiped a tear from his cheek. "Isn't your fault."

"Shut up." Pointing the pistol first at one, then the other, Amy said, "Now, both of you stand up and move to the middle of the room. Starting with you, Carolina."

*This is it.* If Dante was to survive, Carolina had to draw the girl's fire. She had no reservations; she'd lived a full life. First, somehow, she needed to alert Dante to get ready to run.

"Hurry up." Amy clicked the safety off.

Slowly, knees popping, Carolina rose. As she prepared to lunge, the idea for a signal came to her. "Greater love has no one than—"

Dante leaped in front of her. Little Miss pulled the trigger. He crumpled to the floor.

Fueled by fury, Carolina heaved herself at Little Miss. Her momentum knocked the girl over and dislodged the pistol from her hand. Amy started to rise, but Carolina immediately shoved her down and sat on her chest. Then she balled up her fist and delivered the wallop the girl had coming. Amy's dark eyes fluttered closed.

Carolina saw that Dante was alive, thank God, but bleeding from the left upper arm. He had saved her life—he, a fourteen-year-old boy whom she had recently labeled stupid and selfish, untrustworthy and dense.

"How badly are you hurt?"

"I think just scratched." Wincing, he crawled five feet to where an unconscious Amy Laing lay pinned under his great-aunt's substantial body. He lifted the gun with his right hand and raised it to Amy's head.

"No!"

"She deserves to be punished."

"You pull that trigger, you're the one who'll be punished, and I don't mean by me."

"She was going to kill us," he said, his voice cracking with emotion.

"But she didn't, Dante."

"So we're going to let her get away with it?"

"That's not what I said." Carolina pulled the iPhone from her pocket, checked the settings, and allowed herself a tiny smile. "Justice may be blind, but she can hear A-okay."


At precisely nine o'clock the next morning, Carolina picked up the telephone in her living room and keyed in the number for the Laings' business manager. Waiting for Jackson Wu to answer, she watched the procedure underway on the couch. Dante lay on a sheet in his underwear while Alfred checked the wound and changed the dressing. Her husband's training as a Navy medic came in handy when a trip to the hospital was impractical due to the questions those ER docs were required to ask of gunshot victims.

"Steady now." Alfred squirted hydrogen peroxide onto the gash.

Dante bolted. "Motherfucker!"

"Watch the language," his great-aunt scolded.

"Oh, give him a break," Alfred said.

"Yes, Mr. Wu? This is Carolina Roundtree. There's something we need to discuss. Remember when I called you about the missing jade? Well, it turns out..." She described the terrible trauma she and her great-nephew had endured at the hands of Amy Laing, how they'd almost lost their lives, and how Dante had, in fact, been shot. A photo of his injury was on its way via email. "All because Amy wanted more spending money," Carolina said. "It sounds preposterous, I know—"

"Unfortunately, it doesn't." Jackson Wu released a long,

tired sigh. "She's had…issues. I had hoped L.A. would be a fresh start."

"Apparently not. In fact, I'd say Los Angeles brings out the worst in her. Can't she go live with her parents?"

"Not an option. It's complicated. She's got to stay in America."

"Well, don't her folks have property in another, um, U.S. jurisdiction?"

Jackson Wu allowed as how the Laings owned an oil field in North Dakota, and he wondered aloud whether there might be an opening for the fall term at the state university in Fargo. The thought of Little Miss lugging her Louis Vuitton through the frozen tundra brought a smile to Carolina's mouth.

"But I don't think Amy will agree to that," Jackson Wu said.

"I don't think she has a choice."

"What do you mean?"

"It's a good thing I had my smartphone with me last night—not that I expected to record Amy's confession, of course, but I did. Start to finish."

"You recorded it?"

She pressed the "play" arrow on the little screen and held the device to the receiver. Six minutes and eight seconds later, the recording ended.

"Oh my God," he said.

"I'm debating whether or not to give it to the local authorities."

"Please don't—"

"I'm leaning toward yes."

"North Dakota is doable, definitely. I'll make it happen."

"I'd get on it ASAP, if I were you, Mr. Wu. That's suggestion number one."

He groaned. "Is there a number two?"

"Why, yes there is." She caught her great-nephew's eye.

"Poor Dante, he's going to carry the scars, literally and figuratively, for years. He'll need a lot of care and attention."

"Christ…How much?"

She named a price in the mid-six figures, enough for Dante to spend four years at St. Ignatius and four years at a college of his choice. "You can direct deposit the money as per usual, Mr. Wu, and I'll make sure Dante puts it to good use."

"Okay, but, now, what're you going to do with the recording?"

"As long as Amy doesn't set foot in this state or cause any more trouble, nothing."

"How do I know you'll keep your word?"

"You'll have to trust me."

When she'd hung up, Dante scrambled to his feet to embrace her with his good arm.

Uncharacteristically at a loss for words, she simply nodded.

*Nature or nurture? Most likely both.*

# Highland Park Hit
## Gay Degani

A three-hour layover in Atlanta turned my six-and-a-half-hour flight into ten. I don't get why anybody leaving Louisiana should have to fly all the way to Georgia just to get to L.A. That kind of logic makes my nose itch.

I'm waiting out front of an LAX terminal in a good amount of California sunshine. Cousin Clovis, bless him, is more than an hour late. I call him for the umpteenth time, getting a busy signal or voice mail. Between flying east to go west and standing on hard cement, my fifty-year-old body feels like mules are marching all over my feet and parading around *ma tête*.

But I can't be angry at Clovis. His daddy was my mama's youngest brother, who fell off a damn oil rig out on the Gulf and drowned. A lovely man, him, just lovely, but his wife, Clovis's mama, ran with a fast crowd. We come from a long line of Cajuns, and though we don't speak much French anymore, we always take care of our own, so Clovis spent most of his time at our house. I've got five brothers—six counting him—along with four sisters. Fanchon Landry, that's me, called Fig since I can't remember. I'm the oldest. I still love those sweet purple July treats.

My moving to the West Coast is Clovis's idea. He sees me as a role model for his teenage daughter. Glancing down at my fingernails, unpainted and ragged, I think, *really*? Not so sure I'd be my own first choice, but starting fresh, I need that.

After getting laid off, my life devolved from high school art teacher to clerking at the Walmart and binge watching *Dateline* and *Law & Order* reruns.

One of my nieces—Charles's Bernadette—insisted I'd need a way to get around L.A., so she installed that Uber app on my phone. Good for her. Good for me. When I finally decide Clovis isn't coming, I summon up my own ride. We role models know how to take matters into our own hands.

My Uber driver crams me and my two big suitcases, carry-on tote, and oversized purse into her tiny Toyota Corolla and takes off. We charge up an on-ramp and immediately slam into a genuine L.A. traffic jam, automobiles stretching for miles. Inching through this sprawling megalopolis is blowing my mind with its palm trees, tangle of freeways, and dusty mountains rising up behind all these mirrored skyscrapers. Beautiful, yes, but isn't this supposed to be earthquake country? But I don't judge. I'm from the swamp. We deal in hurricanes and saltwater incursion.

My fantasy of ritzy Highland Park—based on how much money Clovis told me he spent on a house—implodes as we peel off the Pasadena Freeway. Its crowded main drag, older stores, scraggly bushes, and music thumping out car windows, remind me of Beauport, except this place is surrounded by rolling hills instead of delta flatness. I think about the wet lush growth of home, whiff the Intracoastal Canal, see my cute little shotgun house on a tract of land my grandpa's grandpa homesteaded, selling off bits and pieces through the years to make a town. I bite down a homesick pang. Clovis needs me. His daughter Taylor needs me. Since they moved out here—he got a job teaching petroleum engineering at a bigger small college—his daughter is in full-bore-rebellious-teen mode, and his wife has left him for the man who sold them their "lovingly updated" California ranch.

The Uber driver turns onto a street crowded with parked cars. She finds a spot in front of a gray, one-story house straight out of HGTV. The yard is dark mulch, dotted with the occasional spiky cactus and a few clumps of flowers, the kind of minimalist planting Tarek and Christina would spring for on *Flip or Flop*.

I rub my nose. This doesn't make sense. How can this tiny home possibly contain four bedrooms? The way Clovis bragged about vessel sinks and overhead rain showers in the bathrooms, I expected a Kardashian-like mini-mansion, but it's Clovis's house all right. That's his old Mitsubishi van sagging in the driveway.

I loop my carry-on through the handle of my biggest suitcase, drape my heavy purse over my shoulder, and trudge up the cement path. The front door's ajar. Bumping it open with my shoulder, I trip my way inside, my toe catching on the loose weather stripping along the threshold.

Late afternoon sun streams through the house, so bright I'm temporarily blinded, but I find myself quickly wrapped in my cousin's bony arms. He's trembling, and I can't be sure but I think he's crying.

His nose is running like it did when he was a kid, running to tell me how the bully down the block sat on his head or the cousins teased him for being such a crybaby. I smooth back his hair and say, "Talk to me, *cher*. What's wrong?"

"She's gone."

"Who's gone? Deborah?" He can't be this upset about that now. She left him six months ago. He must mean his daughter. "Taylor?"

"They took her."

"Who took her?"

His wet gray eyes are frantic. "Whoever shot *him*."

I twist around, eyes following his pointing finger, noting the house's open concept space: living room, dining room, kitchen, even the backyard through the sun-lit sliders, all on view in a single glance. Then I swallow hard at what I see next. At the foot of the quartz island, on the dark wood floor, lays a man's crumpled body.

Adrenaline surges through me. I suck in breath and turn to guide a shaky Clovis onto the sofa.

"Stay here," I say, and, offering up a prayer to Detective Lennie Briscoe from *Law & Order*, I creep into the kitchen and stoop to take this poor man's pulse, but there's a hole through his neck, round and deep. A bullet hole—I know this from TV—the skin around it shredded, blood trickling onto the floor. His flat dead eyes seem to ask me why this happened to him. I don't know. I throw up. Twice.

Glancing around for a gun, I glimpse the laminate flooring buckling in corners, the dishwasher missing its door, a blackened electrical outlet, and Clovis watching me. I wipe my mouth, and say, "Did you call the police? Are they on their way?"

"Yes, yes, of course I—"

"Shhh!" I hear the soft clack of a wooden gate shutting, the latch catching, and I turn toward Clovis. "Is that Taylor?"

"Taylor?" He struggles up from the sofa.

An engine barks awake outside.

I hiss, "Stay here," and head for the door, which I left ajar. I think, *Fingerprints!* and use my sweatshirt sleeve along the door's edge to pull it open and rush through. Down the path, I pivot left, then right. Spot the black back fender of a car turning the corner, some kind of sticker in the middle of rear window. A blurry orange and black? I pick up speed, but by the time I round the curve, it's gone. I picture it in my head and mumble, "Sedan, mid-size, not an SUV or a crossover, sticker in the window."

Back in the house, Clovis, still on the sofa, asks, "It wasn't her, was it?"

"Would she be in a black sedan?"

He puts his head in his hands and murmurs "No."

My whole body buzzing, I don't know what to do with

myself. I haven't watched twenty years of *L&O* reruns without learning you don't mess with a crime scene, and I don't want any of *my* hairs and fibers mixed up with the perp's hairs and fibers, especially since I've already barfed DNA all over the victim.

I sit on my suitcase. It slides around beneath me on its four wheels, just as unsteady as my own two legs. I ask Clovis, "Who is it—that man?"

He rakes his fingers through his thin blond hair. Looks at me. "Trey Hamilton—". He stops, a catch in his throat. "Deborah's new husband."

"Oh my God."

"I know how it looks, Fig, but I couldn't *kill* him."

"Then you'd better tell me exactly what happened."

"Okay. Okay." He slumps against the back of the sofa. "Trey was bringing Taylor over after school so she'd be here when I got back from picking you up at the airport. But I forgot my phone, and when I got here he was—in there—not alive, and Taylor wasn't here either. I mean, where would she go? All I can think is that they must've taken her. Whoever did *that* to Trey."

Clovis points toward the dead man in front of the kitchen island. Damn this whole open-concept trend anyway. Right now I'd give a toe for a nice thick wall between that dead man and me.

"Okay," I say, trying to shift my focus from murder to possible kidnapping. "Maybe she wasn't with him. Did you call her cell?"

"I've done nothing *but* call her cell, and Deborah's cell, and the school. Trey's a con artist. He conned me, he conned a lot of people. He fixes up houses so they look good, but it's just smoke and mirrors. Everything falls apart, and he sold one to the wrong person. An Eastern European gangster bought one for his mother to live in, but it burned down because Trey skimped on the wiring. She survived it, but Trey said the guy put out a hit on him."

"A hit?" I feel a nervous thrill at this, TV crime show junkie that I am. "But why would Trey get shot here in your house?"

"I guess they were following him. I don't know. Maybe they wanted to make it look like I did it." He sobs, mumbles, "All I care about is that Taylor's safe."

Sirens sound in the distance, coming closer, and we sit still, listening, until cop cars stop out front, doors slam, officers yell they're coming in. I half expect to see Lennie Briscoe burst through door. I hope and pray he'll have Taylor with him.

Most law enforcement buildings on TV are dingy and crowded, but this one is ultra-modern, its glass and steel façade jutting out into the air like the beak of a giant bird. As an art teacher, I admire its smooth clean lines. The blue-and-white lobby mimics a hip hotel with its open staircase set against a bank of windows, and a long reception desk suggesting five-hundred-thread-count sheets and chocolates on pillows somewhere above. Still, not a hotel I ever want to check into.

Now I'm sitting on a bench here in the lobby, next to a kid's table and chairs complete with crayons in a pencil holder and a couple of torn coloring books reminding me that criminals have families too.

They dragged me into an interview room as soon as we got here, but Detective Pena figured out pretty fast that I'm a hundred percent clueless. Clovis, however, has been cooped up with them for hours.

I don't know what they're doing to find Taylor. I don't know how to get in touch with Clovis's ex-wife. Did they send someone up into the Hollywood Hills where she lives with this Trey Hamilton to tell her what's happened to her daughter? To her new husband?

Detective Pena—not quite as good-looking as Rey Curtis on *L&O*, but not bad—promised me a cup of coffee when he settled me here. I have yet to see it. I yawn and blink. The adrenaline buzz is wearing off. Twenty-four hours without sleep has, as my grandma used to say, filled my eyes with pea gravel.

I have no place else to go, so I play with my cell phone, scrolling through until I find Bobby's number—Bobby who I've been with for most of my adult life. We met in junior college, and when he joined the Army and wanted to get married before boot camp, I said no, thinking he'd knock me up, and I wasn't ready to raise my own kid since I was just getting free of my sibs. Then he stayed in the service for years, and when he finally came back having lost a foot to an IED, he didn't want to strap me with a gimp. I didn't care. I was ready, but he let the years pass. When I finally decided to move to California, he guessed we could get married if I stayed, but I'd made up my mind. Timing is everything.

Like if my flight hadn't been delayed, I might have been at Clovis's house when the shooting happened. The shooter or shooters—not sure how many—might have killed us all. I shiver. Massage the palms of my hands.

Glancing up, I notice two women—one of them young and slender—talking to the sergeant behind the counter. Something about them makes me stare at their backs, then when the girl looks around, face red from crying, I leap up, heart hammering, recognizing Taylor. Relief floods through me. I hope someone's told Clovis that Taylor's okay. With him squirreled away in some interrogation room, he must be frantic over what might have happened to her. I want to run over and hug the girl, but I hold myself back. There's no place for me in this, not yet.

Then a uniformed officer buzzes open a door, and I watch

as Taylor, all dark spiky hair, and her mother, transformed from drab mouse into tan California blond, disappear into the police department's inner sanctum.

I wait.

Finally, Taylor and Deborah reappear in the lobby.

I jump to my feet. "Deborah! Taylor!"

They hurry past me, not hearing or not wanting to hear, and push out the glass door. I follow behind. The air is hot and smells of exhaust.

The police station is on a corner. Cars are parked bumper-to-bumper along the narrow cross street while those traveling east and west on the main road are barely moving, bumper-to-bumper too.

"Wait!" I call. "It's me, Fig."

It's the girl who turns around. Shades her eyes with her hand to look at me. Her mother grabs her arm and drags her close as she pushes the crosswalk signal.

"You're okay." I try to give Taylor a hug, but she backs away. "Your dad thought—well, he was worried about you. And, Deborah, I'm so, so, sorry about your—friend."

Taylor starts to say something, but Deborah interrupts, "Go home, Fig. There's nothing you can do. You can see that, can't you?"

The light changes and they hurry across. I trail behind, feeling like a little kid looking for someone to play with. I ask, "What did the police say about Clovis? Do you want me to wait for him?"

Kitty-corner to the police station, in a Staples parking lot, a white Mercedes chirps, and they head for it.

"Please," I say. "I want to help."

The girl turns on me. "Can you bring my dad over to my mom's when he's done?"

Deborah climbs into the car. "They can go back to Highland Park."

"Actually, we can't," I say. "It's a crime scene. Off limits until they release it. I don't even know when I can get my luggage."

"So come over then and bring my dad," says Taylor. "If he was worried about me, he'll need to see me, and I want to see him."

"Okay. Give me your number and I'll call you when he gets out of the interview."

Deborah's voice is sharp and low, "Taylor, I mean it. We need to go."

The girl does that young-person-thumb-thing with my phone, then hands it back, waving as she heads around to the passenger side of the car.

Back inside the police station, I ask the uniform behind the counter if he knows anything about Clovis. He says no, so I retake my seat, and think about my confrontation with Deborah. I'm not surprised. We've never gotten along, her looking down on us, finding excuses not to come to family dinners, graduations, even weddings. She's not Cajun, coming from Georgia, meeting Clovis when he started teaching at a small college in Atlanta.

I'm falling asleep on my bench by the stairs when Detective Pena, the one who interviewed me, sits down.

"How're you doing?" he asks.

"Fine. How's Clovis? Does he know that Taylor's okay?"

"He does."

"Can we leave now?"

"*You* can leave, but we need to hold onto Mr. Carney for a while."

"You're holding onto him, but you're working the clues, right? The fingerprints on the side gate? What about the black car I saw leaving the scene of the crime? The sticker in the window narrows it down, the orange and black one? Clovis explained his theory about that Russian threatening to kill Trey? He's got to be the perp."

Laughing, Pena holds up his hand. "We say suspect, not perp. You watch a lot of TV, don't you? Look, I understand you want to help. We know about Yakiv Rudenko's threat to Trey Hamilton, and he's Ukrainian, not Russian. We're taking everything into consideration—"

"So Clovis didn't do it."

"Please, Ms. Landry, everyone blames the Russians or the Ukrainians or the Mexicans. Just let us do our job. Here's my card if you need to talk to me. Your suitcases are at the crime scene?"

Suddenly exhausted, I sigh. "Yes."

"Call me tomorrow, and I'll let you know when you can claim them. Now, do you need a ride somewhere, to a hotel, a friend's?"

"Actually, that would be great."

"Okay. Wait here, and a uniform will take you where you want to go."

"Thank you."

He pulls himself off the bench and hands me his card.

"Thanks."

With a wave, he starts to walk away.

"Detective?"

He turns toward me, his "Yes?" sounding reluctant.

"You didn't arrest Clovis, did you?"

"Yes, we did."

"But why?"

His brown eyes meet mine reluctantly. "Because he confessed." He nods and heads behind the long white counter, disappearing through a door.

I call Taylor and tell her I'm on my way, I have a ride, and hang up before she asks about her dad. This is something I want to handle in person.

\* \* \*

Trey Hamilton's house is up in the Hollywood Hills, a large two-story Mediterranean, tile roof, large arched entry, a thick wooden door with wrought iron trim, eight-paned windows. A house they might give away in HGTV's annual Dream Home Sweepstakes. I ring the doorbell as the cop car pulls away.

I try again, but no one answers. I glance around, and except for a gray SUV parked in front of the house next door, there's no sign of anyone being around. Weaving through some bird of paradise plants, I go up on tiptoe to peek in the window. I can see a light in what could be a family room toward the back. Taylor must be watching TV or listening to music.

I turn around and my heart jolts, legs wobble. The sun has disappeared behind a hill, but there's no mistaking the huge man standing in front of me with a gun in his hand. He shakes it at me, and points toward the open front door. Only now do I dare look away from the gun. Did he just come *out* of the house?

He's square-faced with tats on his neck and hands and probably everywhere else, a pair of Ray-Ban sunglasses perched on top of his shaved head.

I whisper, "The Russian."

"Ukrainian," he says, with an accent. "Now move it."

When we get into the great room—another open-floor plan, one giant space including kitchen, dining, and family room everyone lusts for on *House Hunters*—Taylor leaps from the couch. "Fig!"

"Hey." The man whips the gun toward her. Taylor pales, plops down.

He gives me a shove and I stumble onto the couch next to her.

"This is good," he says. "Now we find out what's going on."

I look at Taylor and she looks at me.

"Don't do that," he says. "Don't look at each other. Look at me. I'm the one with gun."

I stiffen. Taylor stiffens. Our eyes must be as big as dinner plates.

He paces a little, looks around the open space, and then wheels toward us. "Don't move. You move, I shoot."

He ambles over to the island, says, "This is fine place. Marble countertops. Sub-Zero refrigerator. I see only best will do for Mr. Trey Hambleton. You think he watch *Property Brothers.*"

I say, "*You* watch *Property Brothers?*"

"Favorite show. Boss's too. Ah, this why we so upset with Mr. Hambleton's work, but we not kill him."

"His name is Hamilton," I say.

"Like the musical?" he asks, eyes wide.

"Yes, like the musical. Now what do you want from us?" I ask.

"What you think I want, girlie?" More gun waving, extremely close to my nose.

His eyebrows are puny for a man of his size. I wonder if he has them waxed. Somehow noticing this puts spunk in my voice. "You wanted Trey Hamilton dead."

He leans in close enough for me to smell his sour breath. "Not what we want."

"Someone killed him," I say.

"You are right. Someone kilt him, but not me. My boss did not tell me to kill nobody today. Did you see me kill him?" He taps the gun on Taylor's nose.

"Leave her alone," I say.

He taps me on the nose. "Did *you* see me?"

"No, but Clovis figured it out and told the police."

"Covers tracks, of course." The big man's smile is smug. "But we have alibi."

Taylor starts to say something, but I cut her off. She must be having her first inkling that her father just might have done the shooting, something I've struggled to keep out of my own thoughts. He had reasons. Trey conned him into a house that's falling apart, *and* he stole his wife. People have killed for less. I see all this in a flash, then turn to the tattooed man. "If you didn't shoot him, why bother coming here?"

"Because my boss not want his name told to cops. Your friend—how he named?"

"Clovis?" I ask.

"Ah, what kind name is this? Hmmm. Boss not want cops in business, um, his business, right now. I make deal. Your friend, your Clovis, confess crime, I not kill you."

I blurt, "Then you can leave because he already confessed."

Taylor, "What?"

If I'd told her this over the phone, she wouldn't be looking at me with such blazing eyes. I say, "I'm sorry. I didn't mean to tell you like that, but this Big Ox—"

"No need to call bad name," says the Big Ox.

"But Dad couldn't have done it, Fig. You know him better than anyone. He couldn't kill a fly."

I've seen Clovis swat a stream of red ants off his legs with no sympathy for the critters at all, but I don't say this.

I turn back to the Ukrainian. "If you don't want to be called a Big Ox, what's your name?"

"I don't give a shit about him, Fig. What did my dad say? Why did he confess?"

"Taylor." I grit my teeth. "I would like this Big Ox—"

"Orek."

I roll my eyes. "Okay, *Orek*—I want *Orek* to stop waving his gun in our faces and leave. His boss is waiting to hear he's off the hook."

I will her to shut up. She tightens her lips together, lets out a long breath.

"Orek," I say in my most reasonable voice. "Since my cousin has confessed to the murder of Trey Hamil..."

But he's moved to the patio door, back turned, flicking the outside lights on and off, on and off. It's full dark, and with the party lanterns strung across the pool, reflecting in the water, it would be magical if the Big Ox wasn't the one playing with them.

Leaving them on, he turns and says, "This Trey Hambleton flip house?"

"Hamilton." Taylor corrects him. "He didn't flip it. He moved *into* it."

"Boss would like house. I bet electricity here first class. No way house burn down."

Hearing something in his voice, an edge, I glance at Taylor, then say, "Orek, don't you need to tell your boss—"

He lifts his gun and swings around, points it at me, points it at Taylor—I stop breathing mid-breath—then he shoots out the TV, a big seventy-two-inch Panasonic. The sound is deafening. Taylor and I clap our hands over our ears and scream.

"I not bossed by women." He raises his scrawny eyebrows.

I may have just peed my pants, and my brain goes on speed-dial. "What I meant to say, Orek, is you don't have much time because the cops are dropping off my suitcases, and I don't think you want to be here when they come."

"I not afraid of cops."

"But think of the mess you'll be in if they find you here. You'll look guilty. There might be gunplay."

"I like gunplay."

"It will make your *boss* look guilty."

He frowns. "How I know you not lie about confession?"

"We can call the police and have them tell you."

"I don't talk to cops."

"Taylor can call and ask for Detective Pena. She can put it

on speaker. You just need to listen."

Orek looks at his watch, a huge expensive one, more of a clock, then he huffs, "Okay."

So that's what we do. I dig out Pena's card. Taylor calls and asks the detective to confirm that Clovis has confessed, and he does, and she starts to cry, and I swear Orek looks upset for her. After she hangs up, he says, "I will tell boss. It be okay. He will buy house."

I make a key-to-the-mouth motion to keep Taylor from saying anything more, and stand to walk Orek out. We start toward the front of the house, but he suddenly stops in the kitchen. I think, *what now?* The big Sub-Zero has caught his eye. He steps over to it and opens the freezer door, rummages through, and takes out a large package of Kobe steaks. Grunts. I force a smile and follow him through the hall and entryway to the outside.

He strolls down the driveway to the street and climbs into the gray SUV parked in front of the neighbor's. I don't breathe until the motor flares and his headlights disappear.


Back in the house, Taylor is still on the couch, arms folded across her chest, staring into her lap.

Wearily, I flop beside her and say, "I don't think he'll be back."

"My dad didn't kill Trey," she says.

"So we should call Detective Pena again and let him know what just happened. Orek showing up here tells me the Russians probably had something to do with this."

"Ukrainians."

"Whatever. Anyway, I'll call him and then I'd like to take a shower. By the way, where's your mother?"

"At Leslie Witter's."

"The actress?"

"Mom's gone Hollywood."

"How'd she meet Leslie Witter?"

"Spinning."

"Making yarn?"

Finally, a smile from Taylor. "No, it's indoor bicycling."

She leads me down a hall off the family room into a small bedroom. "It has its own bathroom. Where's your suitcase?"

"Back at your dad's."

"Oh right. Well, go ahead and shower, and I'll bring you some clothes." Finally she says, "Maybe Trey's sweatpants will fit. And one of his T-shirts."

I don't like this on so many levels, but I have to clean up, my clothes sticking to me like swamp grass after so many hours, so I shrug. "Okay."

I'm dressed in Trey's clothes and eating a ham sandwich in the kitchen. Although the shower's revived me, I want very much to climb into bed and dream about home. Dream about Bobby. Taylor's still upstairs, I assume taking a shower of her own. I also want to talk to her, find out where she was if she wasn't at the house in Highland Park when Trey was shot.

I always thought I would make a good detective—I managed to get Big Ox Orek out of the house—but that's not really detecting. More like outwitting? On *Law & Order*, it seemed Lennie Briscoe and whoever his current partner was— Mike or Rey or Ed—would ask a question or two and that would instantly lead them down a path littered with clues. I need to start detecting, but where to start? In real life it's hard to even find a path, let alone come across anything helpful along the way.

I finish my sandwich and push the plate away, turn on the breakfast stool to look at the lights strung across the pool. The Big Ox left them twinkling.

A door opens behind me, and a banshee scream splits the room. Hands over my ears again, I twist around to see

Deborah leaning against the garage door, face drained of color. Our eyes meet.

"Are you trying to give me a heart attack? What the hell are you doing here in my husband's clothes? What are you doing in this house? Who let you in? Taylor? I'm going to kill that girl."

"I didn't mean to scare you."

"Oh shut up," she says as she stomps toward the stairs, then halts. "What happened to my TV? What is going on around here? Taylor! Where are you?" Back to me, "She has no right to bring you here. I've had enough today, do you hear me, *enough*. Taylor!!"

"Stop yelling!" The girl traipses into the room. "My father's in jail and who knows what you've been doing."

Deborah's mouth puckers and she dissolves into tears. I rush over as she falls against me—smelling of booze—mumbling, "What am I supposed to do now?"

I whisper, "It's going to be all right. Today's the hardest day. Taylor, could you help me get her to bed?"

The girl is on the brink of refusing, but she gives in and we manhandle her mom up the stairs and into her bedroom. I start to help Deborah remove her clothes and she bats furiously at me. "Get off me. Get off!" She spins away and lands halfway on the mattress, half off. We try to push her onto the bed, and she kicks me hard in the thigh. I step back from her, both hands up. She's calling me names I wouldn't think she'd use in front of her daughter—witch, bitch, whore, asshole—but Taylor is stone-faced.

"We're going to leave you, Deborah," I say, my voice shaky. "Will you be okay?"

"Like you care."

"She always does this," says Taylor. "She'll be fine."

"Get the hell out of here."

"I'll be downstairs if you need me."

"*Get out!*"

At the top of the stairs, I ask Taylor, "You think she'll be okay?"

"She's always okay. She's drama."

"She lost her husband today."

"And I lost my dad."

"Let's go downstairs and talk."

"I can't," she says. "Really. It's been too much."

"Can't I ask one question, though? Wasn't Trey supposed to bring you to your dad's house today?"

She looks at me with damp, sad eyes. "What difference does that make now?"

"I'm just trying to see it all in my head. See what might have happened."

"I don't want to think about it anymore."

"Okay. We can talk it over in the morning. Maybe we can go see him."

"What we should be doing is finding him a good lawyer since for some reason, he's gone and confessed."

"And why do you think he'd do that?"

"I don't know. The cops must have tricked him. I'm going to bed."

She pivots away down the hall to her room.

I ask, "Where would he have gotten a gun?"

She stops, but doesn't turn around. "He didn't have one and he didn't do it. It was Trey's—" She stops herself.

I take a step toward her. "Trey's what?"

"What?"

"You started to say Trey's—something."

"No I didn't. Can't we talk about this tomorrow?"

I take another step closer to her. "What were you going to say?"

"Can't you leave me alone?" And she hurries into her room and shuts the door.

* * *

As tired as I am, I don't go to bed, but lie down instead in the family room, stare at the ceiling, my brain roiling. The house is quiet around me as I mull over what Taylor started to say. "It was Trey's—*what*? His gun? No way Trey committed suicide and he certainly wouldn't give his gun to Clovis? It was Trey's—fault? Because the houses he flipped and sold were crappy? For driving Clovis to murder? For Trey ripping him off, both house *and* wife? Is Clovis a killer? Maybe I should've been suspicious after finding him with a dead body in his house, but it's still hard to accept. Yet we never really know what anyone is capable of.

Poor Taylor. Did she witness the murder? See her dad pull the trigger? That would account for her behavior. I'm amazed she's held it together this long, considering everything, her dad, Orek, her mother.

And Deborah. L.A. has messed with her mind for her to up and desert her marriage, her family after so many years. Midlife crisis? How much did her departure affect Clovis? Enough that he would kill Trey?

I flip over and face the shattered TV. As much as I want to blame Trey's murder on the Russians—Ukrainians—it doesn't feel right. Taylor didn't seem to know Orek, and if she'd watched him kill Trey, she couldn't have been as calm as she was. Something is just plain screwy.

I try and relax. Drift off. But the black car is there, playing on my eyelids like a movie, swinging around the corner in Highland Park. I sit up. If Taylor had been there, she might have been the one driving that black sedan.

Pulling myself up from the couch, stumbling a bit, I race to the door to the garage. Open it. Flip on the light.

There are three cars, a slick hunter-green Jaguar, the white Mercedes I'd seen before in the Staples parking lot, and in the last bay, a black sedan. My heart thumps. I step down into the garage.

I'm in a trance, edging my way toward this last car, the

one that must've been driven by Trey to deliver Taylor to Highland Park, so she could be there in Clovis's house when her cousin Fig arrived from Louisiana.

In the middle of the rear window of the black sedan is an orange and black sticker.


I go upstairs and tap lightly on Taylor's door.

Her dead-tired "Come in" is immediate.

The lamp glows on the bedside table. She's on the floor, leaning against the side of her bed. I close the door behind me and join her on the floor. Hold out the dishtowel-wrapped object I've brought with me. She takes it, feels its weight.

"I found this in the black car in the garage. Will you tell me what happened? I can guess, but you should tell me."

She unfolds one side of the cloth, then another, revealing the 9mm gun. She doesn't look up. I wait patiently until she stops sniffling and wipes her nose. "Trey—he was always messing with me, you know?"

"Tell me."

"He had these hands, all manicured and soft, and when he'd talk to me—even when my mom was in the room—he'd touch my hair, my neck. That's why I cut my hair so short. But he was always on me. One time..." She sucks in a stutter of breaths, eyes on her hands still holding the gun.

I stay quiet.

"One time, more than one time, he'd press me against a wall and—touch me. My mom? I tried to tell her, but she wouldn't listen. She said I was just trying to get back at her for leaving Dad."

I wait.

"So, this time, when he dropped me off, he came in with me. Said he wanted to check out all the complaints my dad had about the house. I didn't want to let him in, but what could I do? The house is falling apart."

She stops, the tears on her cheeks shining in the lamplight.

"Go ahead, Taylor. I'm listening."

She nods. "As soon as we got inside, he grabbed me. Shoved me on the sofa. Pulled off my tank top. He was so heavy."

She clinches her teeth, rubs her palm over her temple and says, "I—I don't know how I got free. I think I kneed him, but he rolled off and I ran into the kitchen where Dad keeps his gun—"

I can't help myself. "This is Clovis's gun?" My cousin's the last person I thought would ever have a gun.

"He bought one when we moved to Highland Park."

I want to ask why, but can't distract her from her story. "Okay. Go on."

"So," she says, gasping a little. "So when Trey came after me—he was so angry—I was so scared, I shot him."

She begins to cry, and we sit there, me patting her shoulder until she looks up, swallows hard, and says, "I called Dad. He was on his way to pick you up at the airport, but he turned around and came back."

"And he said he'd take the blame for you? He didn't want your life to be ruined, did he?"

She nods her head, swallows hard. "How did you know?"

"I know Clovis and I know what he'd do for someone he loves."

"I told him no, and he came up with the story about—Orek's boss."

"So when that story didn't convince the police, he confessed."

"I feel so bad for him. I should have told that detective the truth. I wanted to but I was so afraid of what would happen to me—I mean Mom blames me for everything—and I thought Dad's story might work, but it didn't."

"Taylor, none of this is your fault. None of it. Are you clear on that?"

She nods her head, then buries it in my shoulder. I let her cry a bit, then say, "We'll go first thing in the morning to see Detective Pena, take the gun, and get your father out of jail, okay?"

We stay this way for a while, then she asks, "How did you figure it out?"

"Just couldn't believe your dad would kill anyone unless he was protecting someone he loves. And the timing felt off to me from the beginning. It seemed—I don't know—forced somehow, just off. It seemed your dad shouldn't have been there at the house when he was. He should've been at the airport when it happened."

"We saw you unloading your luggage out front and that's when he called the cops. I snuck out the back."

"That makes sense. And where did Clovis, of all people, get a gun?"

She huffs an almost laugh. "Trey got it for him. Highland Park is up-and-coming, not *there* yet."

My body lets go of its buzz. I smile a little, thinking of Detective Lennie Briscoe. What kind of wisecrack would he come up with for this one? I gnaw on my cuticle. I may be an unemployed art teacher with minor retail experience, but damn, I might make detective after all.

# Independence Day
## Avril Adams

The 4th of July. The country's Independence Day. It was Ava's, too, although, she was still unsure of what it meant to be free. She set the lipstick, "Crimson Dynamo," and the Colt automatic on the vanity. Ava hadn't handled either of these for the five years she'd been jailed at Tehachapi State Prison, but she hadn't lost her touch with the only things a girl like her really needed.

The sun was setting but it was still hotter than a flat iron on the Sunset Strip. So while the rest of the celebrants waved Old Glory and exploded fireworks on the grassy mall across the street, Ava slipped down to the bar of the Hotel Vieux Carre for a Manhattan or two.

The bar was all dimmed lights and dark mahogany, unquestionably masculine with colorful liquor bottles backlit by glowing gold mirrors. When Ava walked through the door, the temperature felt as if it had dropped by twenty degrees. She paused for a moment, adjusting her eyes to the darkness. Men in business suits sat quietly at a couple of tables, drinking their dinner. A group of tourists ate hors d'oeuvres in front of the television. She surreptitiously searched the shadows for the solitary man who might not be noticed, the single guy who could easily blend with the woodwork, the lone wolf.

The wolf sat at the bar in a bulk warehouse suit, hairy cheek propped on his palm, slowly stirring a martini with its olive. Ava recalled the face in the photograph Frank had given her. It was the same, a little heavier, but easily recognizable. She strolled casually between the empty tables, to a place two stools to his right. Smoothing her tight skirt and stretching her long shapely legs, she took her seat and placed her Gucci shoulder bag on the counter. He sized her up as she knew he would, then turned. He stared at her in the mirror for a while, a Who's Who of covert expressions taking turns with his face. After a decent interval he turned her way again. "From around here?" he said, his flat Midwestern accent darkly steeped in possibilities, like Oolong tea in boiling water.

She deducted style points for the *cliché* line, and lifted a bare, nonchalant shoulder. "Not exactly."

"Nobody is, in this town, I guess. What I mean is—" he said. "I didn't mean to intrude."

"It's okay," she said. "I don't mind. I'm from Palm Springs."

"I know it well, used to golf there in the winter," he said. "Whereabouts?"

"Just outside the city limits," she generalized, since she'd never set foot in the place, only seen pictures of its iron red hills and cactus fields. "Near the foothills. In a new development."

"That town is growing like a mushroom cloud, if you know what I mean. Mostly canes and walkers though. The broken-hip migration," he said. "Where's the fun in that?" A wink.

"Where, indeed?" she agreeably replied. She began to enjoy tossing logs on his fire and watching them crackle.

"Dry heat and the golden years. Like an El Dorado within the City of Hope," he said.

Ava added a few style points for a sense of humor. Maybe he'd laugh all the way to the cemetery. He said, "I'm from Nevada, Reno. Back in the Old Indian Territory, it was nothing like L.A. It was a city with a past, full of gamblers, mean outlaws and even meaner hookers."

"Sounds like everywhere I've ever been," Ava said. "And not just in the past." She laughed.

He seemed to relax. Good. The ice was broken.

"You're a real charmer," he said, rubbing the graying stubble on his chin. He gave her that watery look with his eyes, the one where his pupils enlarged to the size of a kid in a Keane painting, big enough for her to fall into if she were so inclined. "Buy you a drink? Name's Harry. Harry Engels." He offered his hand.

Ava took it. *I know who you are, Conrad Oliver.* "Danni," she said. No last names necessary. She thought "Harry" gave her a puzzled look and was still scratching that itch when a cherry bomb shattered the quiet and exploded so close it must have been detonated on the sidewalk in front of the enormous picture window. She flinched. Her nerves were showing. The ones she wasn't supposed to have. "I thought those things were illegal," she said.

He grinned, cheeks folding back into long, deep dimples. When he placed his hand reassuringly on the bare flesh of her shoulder, his palm was cold and dry. This time she controlled her urge to flinch. "Better get used to it," he said. "For the next twelve hours, there'll be no rest for the wicked."

Harry wasn't *that* bad looking, she thought, just yawningly ordinary. Boilerplate. He was a decent height with good shoulders. Thirty-five or so. Dark hair. Blue eyes. A fresher haircut might propel him a hair's breadth north of average.

Killers could look like anything, she granted, same as meat in the case at the butcher's. But whether the homicidal types seemed like ground round or prime rib, they all came from the same crazy steer. This meatball had a neglected, divorced look about him, so cartoonishly hang-dog it made her want to laugh. She wondered how he'd appear in the casket after the formaldehyde filled up the slack under his baby-bloodhound eyes.

"If you're still offering," she said, "I'll take a manhattan. Dry. Make it a double." She smiled. It was so easy to make men happy.

While the bartender mixed the drink, Ava reached into her bag and fished out the compact and lipstick tucked beneath the thick wad of Benjamins. The bundle would get a lot thicker when the job was done. Enough for a fresh start. Enough to change her face and her address. Maybe get married, settle down. She could smell the money, bills so fresh she'd held them up to the light to check for counterfeits. Straight off the presses, they still had the whiff of dirty socks, filthy lucre, buried in her bag. She felt reassured when her fingertips grazed the cold steel of the loaded Colt.

She pushed up the lipstick's sprocket until an inch of the deep red wax tube peeked out. She believed men secretly enjoyed watching women transform themselves from boring hausfraus into armor-plated goddesses with the application of a bit of face paint. Gazing into the mirror, she carefully traced the outline of her sensuous lips, coloring them in with "Dynamo" while Harry pretended not to notice.

When the drink arrived, it was frothy instead of still. She didn't much care for it that way but, under the circumstances, the preparation of a cocktail seemed unworthy of making a fuss.

She patted the seat beside her and said he could join her if he wanted. He seemed nervous. As he moved closer to the stool, he offered her a cigarette from a silver case, which she declined. "I quit those coffin sticks five years ago." She told him she'd gone cold turkey but not that she'd done it the hard way, behind bars, sharing a steel toilet with a psycho drug trafficker. He lit one for himself and fumbled with small talk. She let him twist in the noose until his legs stopped kicking.

"So what brings you here?" she said. "Business or pleasure?" The corners of her lips turned slightly upward when she said "pleasure." *Easy does it, Ava. Take your foot off the gas.*

"Neither." He glanced, discreetly she thought, for a wedding ring. She folded her left hand, hiding the crooked middle finger broken during the escape. Frank had sent his own man from the mortuary to push her into a false-bottom coffin for the getaway.

"Art, you might say. I'm a writer. Freelance."

"What are you freelancing?" *As if she didn't know.*

"I'm covering the Coburn murder trial for *People's Gazette Magazine.*"

"The Coburn murder trial? That gangland murder up in the hills a few years ago?"

"That's the one," he said with emphasis, circling a thick finger around the crest of his glass. Ava shivered, her well-shaped breasts contributing their part to the performance.

She set her drink on the bar and poked at the ice cubes with a swizzle stick while she thought of something to say that would imply she had some sympathy for the victims. "So they finally got the killers," she said. "I remember seeing the coverage and thinking what they did was so cold-blooded." She held her fingers like a pistol. "Each one of them, two to the head, pop, pop, execution-style. Weren't there four people in that house? Four college students?"

"I believe so," he said, thoughtfully, after a pause. "Yes, four. You have a good memory, Danni."

*One of them was Frank's niece, you Dumbo. You could have just taken the cocaine, but you're a killer at heart. So you're gonna be number five, Conrad Oliver.*

"Some of the gossip rags say those guys on trial are innocent," said Ava.

Harry's eyes examined the bottom of his glass. The corners of his mouth turned down, laden with cynicism and doubt. "Innocent?"

Ava gave Harry a hard stare, insulted by his condescension. Did he take her for a nitwit? "Of course, they're not innocent," she said. "Those types never are. I'm sure they're guilty of plenty, even if it's not those murders."

Harry avoided her eyes again. "Guilty. Innocent. Just words. Who knows? Sometimes it's all a matter of degree. And that, in a word, is why I'm here—to follow the drama of those questions up until the final verdict."

They both fell silent for a moment. Ava knew Harry had been on the road for years, changing addresses, occupations, trying to cover his scent with Frank's bloodhounds after him. Apparently he was getting sloppy, wanted a real life, and thought the pursuit had ended. He'd gone back to his old profession, maybe because he wanted to insert himself into the investigation the way a lot of psychopaths did. That's where he was naive. Frank was old school. Frank would pursue him to the ends of the earth and to the end of time. Harry's ego had let the bloodhound slip its nose right under his pant leg.

Ava sipped her drink. It was unusually strong. The bitterness tasted good. The whiskey corkscrewed languidly through her chest like a living thing, like kundalini fire.

"The *Gazette's* putting me up at this palace. I couldn't afford it otherwise," said Harry, eyes roving in a one-eighty around the room. He was sheepish, as if he were confessing to being on the dole. "It could be a while. Sometimes these murder trials can go on for—"

"Weeks. Months. I know. You should enjoy being here, while you can."

Harry seemed to deflate. "Well, enough about me," he said. "What about you?"

"Me?" she said, toying with the small silver cross at her throat. "I'm not at all interesting, Harry. Not like you. I'm on my way to San Francisco to visit friends." He seemed satisfied with her answer. By his expression she could tell that he was finally about to ask what she had been expecting him to ask for the last tortuous hour.

"Danni...you know...I really like your name..." He dropped his head shyly. "If you'd like another drink and have nothing better to do tonight, I'm in room twelve-twenty-four."

She paused just long enough, a handful of beats, to make him wonder. Then she smiled. "I just might take you up on that, Harry. It's my birthday, you know."

A bottle of brut champagne on ice cooled on a small stainless steel table along with two wine glasses and another plastic bucket of ice, filled from the dispenser in the hall. His room was identical to hers right down to the taupe color scheme and the framed abstract prints on the wall.

Harry had taken off his dark brown suit coat and hastily removed his black-framed glasses with the muttered explanation, "reading," and placed them on his bedside nightstand. Ava saw his white T-shirt through the lightweight, summer fabric of his long-sleeve shirt. He gave off the awkward, corn-fed vibe of Clark Kent, novice reporter for the *Daily Planet*, not the bleeding edge of a big city crime blotter.

"Sit anywhere you like," he said, his tone cheerily ironic, pointing at the only two available chairs shoved under the table. Her other choice, she decided, was the queen-size bed which he was apparently too much of a gentleman to suggest. "Take off your coat."

"Too much air conditioning. I'm a little chilled," said Ava, shivering.

Outside the picture window, night was falling. The fizzled sun had trailed off into a delicate band of orange and pink which became the new horizon. Fireworks began to burst, at first in single volleys. She could hear them whistle and sizzle as they roared into the sky. The crowd applauded as each missile burst and rained down cascades of shimmering reds, blues, and golds. These single firings were soon followed by an off-beat rocket cannonade, a twenty-one gun salute to two hundred years of the republic.

"Happy birthday, Danni," he said as he poured the champagne. "How many is it? How many years today?" She didn't answer. He replaced the bottle in the bucket and touched his glass to hers. "Ballpark, hon." He made a gesture of zipping his lips.

"A gentleman never asks a lady her age," said Ava.

"Maybe I'm no gentleman," he said without smiling.

Ava thought for a moment. What harm could it do to tell him her age? She started to admit to twenty-five, her actual years if she subtracted the five she'd spent caged for her bank robbery. But the habit of secrecy kept her mouth shut. *Isn't it always the small things, the little details, that get you killed?*

The lines in her face had lengthened and deepened with prison, but she'd managed to keep her figure and the pretense of youthful buoyancy while she'd felt about as perky as any other mackerel sealed in a tin can. She looked up at him through her mascara, sipping the champagne. "Too many to remember. Too few to forget."

"Very mysterious. Sounds almost ominous," Harry said, "like a scene out of an old movie, words Susan Hayward might have spoken as they were rolling the credits on her walk to the gas chamber."

"I don't know anything about Susan Hayward. It sounds like I should."

Harry rolled the bowl of the glass in his big hands. "A fantastic broad. She played Barbara Graham in *I Want to Live*, a party girl the decent people on the jury didn't like. So they gave her the pellets for joyriding with thrill-killers." He paused for a moment, taking Ava in. "You have her hair, you know."

She didn't know; didn't care. She was nothing like that

woman. She would never take that walk. *What am I waiting for? I should finish him off right here.* She put her hand in her coat pocket and felt for the gun.

Harry excused himself, said he was heading for the bathroom. Ava downed her glass and the cold champagne, following the hot whiskey at the bar, loosened something inside her. She didn't feel quite right. Drinking this expensive booze was like sliding into a pair of fine silk pajamas and discovering they were really fine silk snares. When Harry got back, quicker than expected, she said, "Let's go out on the balcony. Bring the bottle."

They stood on the balcony finishing their glasses, Ava's right hand in her coat pocket, gripping the .22. It barely made a bulge in the loose fabric. Across the street the main event of the night was under way. A recording of a cannon boomed.

As the climax of the *1812 Overture* reached a fever pitch she heard Harry say, in a whisper, as if he were conversing with someone in another room, "Who sent you, Danni?" In Harry's hand, Ava saw the big black eye of a .38 revolver staring her down.

She heard herself say, "Frank."

"Frank Kovitsky?"

"Yes."

"Why?"

"You know why."

"I think you've got it all wrong. Frank's got it all wrong."

"Maybe," she said, "but does it really matter? Your epitaph is written, Conrad. You killed the wrong people."

"Well, may they all rest in peace," he said, coolly.

"Not good enough for Frank. No loose ends."

"I heard Frank might send a woman. I even got some identifying details, but I thought that was crap."

"He knows how much you like women, Conrad."

"I don't like women who want to kill me."

"I don't want to kill you, Harr—Conrad. I have to."

"You won't get that chance."

"If not me, then someone else. At the carwash, the diner, coming out of the dentist's office. You'll be lucky if you don't see it coming."

Conrad bared his teeth, pissed off and defiant as a coyote backed into a gully. He lowered the gun's muzzle over its target, her heart, dead center.

"How did you know, Conrad?"

"You knew too much. And that finger."

Ava didn't need to aim. The Colt did the thinking for her, making that tiny round hole in Conrad's chest when she pointed it upward. And it was just at the moment when he slumped over and she fired two more, *pop, pop,* into his head, that the recorded bells began to ring, hundreds of them, thousands even for the finale, and the victorious cannon began to sound—like musical thunder, singing high and low. And Ava knew how it must have felt to scrawl her name on that bloody declaration of L.A. freedom and to fire the first shot for her Independence Day.

# Mimo
## Lynne Bronstein

Back in the seventies, if you were walking in Venice at night, you might have seen her standing in a doorway, singing softly to herself. You would have had to look straight ahead or even down because she was tiny, not more than five-foot-one, and she herself joked that her bones were like noodles. You would have known her by her hair. It was always some color not found in nature, blue-green or vivid red or purple with silver streaks. She didn't have it done in a salon, she never could have afforded that, so she got the dyes from somewhere and did it herself in public restrooms or friends' homes. She spiked it and put some sort of grease on it, and it stuck up from her head like alien plant life.

She came wrapped in old kimonos, worn camouflage jackets, denim vests and jeans, velvet robes, falling-apart lace gowns. Her nose was a bit beaky and there was a scraped area on one side of her face. She'd survived a motorcycle crash years before.

She called herself Mimo. People thought she was mispronouncing Memo. She pronounced it with a short "i." Was her name Mimosa? Miriam?

Few people knew her real name. Welfare knew what it was. Mimo used friends' addresses, and at one time or another had a post office box. She lived nowhere and everywhere. She slept on peoples' couches, in shelters, or on the street. Sometimes people told her she ought to get a permanent place to live, and she shook her head and said, "I don't want to live anywhere."

"Why, Mimo?" they would ask her.

And she always answered: "I'm free this way."

That sounds like a good beginning. That's how I wanted to frame the story when I made notes for a "human interest" article I never wrote.

Me? My name is Roger. I'm a journalist when they pay me, which doesn't happen much these days. Back then, I had a few gigs for small local papers and I lived in Venice, too. I thought of myself as a friend to the down-and-out. Who was I kidding?

I recognized that I was one of the fortunate people in Venice—the housed. I had a very small and very messy apartment, and I lived on canned goods and wore the same two or three shirts over and over. But I was a wealthy member of the genteel class compared to many of the people I saw on Ocean Front in those days. The old white-haired man I thought of as "the old prospector" who muttered stuff to himself and waved a cane at the passers-by, shouting "Get out of town by sundown! I'm the law around here!" The sword-swallowing dude who was finally taken away because he owed the IRS. The man in the band uniform who sang obscene lyrics in an operatic voice.

And Mimo.

I saw her most often on Ocean Front Walk or when I walked along a Venice street and saw her emerging from an alley, probably after sleeping there.

I became Mimo's confidant by accident. One day I just started walking along with her and she opened up to me, and after that I heard dozens, hundreds, of stories about Mimo and from Mimo herself.

She told people many tales about her background. The

names often changed, although, most often, her place of origin was Chicago.

"I lived in Chicago once," she would say. "In a high-rise apartment house. I had a washer-dryer. I was a happy house-wife married to George. But then I became unhappy with it all."

Once she confessed that she'd actually grown up in a small town farther south, in Kansas or Nebraska. She said she remembered working in a cornfield.

One day she was walking down Ocean Front with me and she suddenly stopped and whispered, "We have to turn around! Walk the other way."

I had no idea why, but I followed Mimo's instruction and we walked north instead of south. Mimo seemed to breathe heavily for a while and then her zany smile returned.

"Why, Mimo?"

"I think I saw my ex-husband, George."

"Are you sure?"

"Well…" Mimo shrugged. "He looked like George anyway."

"But wouldn't he be back in Chicago?"

"Oh," Mimo said. "Chicago. That's right."


When she shut her eyes and drifted away from human communication, people said she was schizo or autistic or something-or-other that made her crazy that way so she couldn't be reached.

Doctors prescribed this or that medication, and she would give the pills away or sometimes sell them, but selling was not even her thing; she despised "commercialism" even if it left her hungry and without a roof on a rainy night.

When she shut her eyes she was often thinking of *him*, remembering when she rode with him across the U.S. back in the 1960s, from Chicago to Venice, on the back of his motorcycle and they wore no helmets. Remembering the two of them in a bare-bones motel room, laughing at a stock painting of a mountain and a sunset above their starchy-smelling bed. Remembering them having breakfast in a coffee shop in Arizona, digging into one plate of huevos rancheros together, drinking coffee for hours until the shop owner kicked them out for not paying.

Remembering the two of them hugging and kissing and hugging some more, and pulling each other's long hair while standing in the surf near the rocks on the South Beach. Remembering him gently biting her cheek and saying, "Be good, baby girl, and I will be waiting for you."

"So he is in Chicago, right?" I asked her. I sensed that she heard my voice coming from far away as she came back to this earth.

"I think he's in stir," she replied. "Yes, I think he is definitely in the hoosegow. He oughta be, anyway."

She loved to use those hokey words for effect. I wanted to roll my eyes but I kept a straight face and said, "But you said you were a happy housewife, married to him."

"Who?"

"Your former husband. That's who we're talking about, right?"

"Henry?"

"No, didn't you say his name was George?"

Mimo shut her eyes.

"Nooooo…"

Then, "Henry was my *husband*. George was my *lover*. There is a difference. Husbands like Henry have no souls."


She had a record. Several of her arrests were for defrauding an innkeeper, that is, not paying for meals in restaurants. Her usual M.O. was to come in, be seated, order food, eat, and then try to slip out unnoticed. Of course someone with her outré hair and clothing had trouble not being noticed.

At the Lafayette Café, the people who ran the place were more compassionate than elsewhere. They told her if she showed up near closing time (they closed after lunch), they could give her some leftovers. She did avail herself of their kindness a few times. But other places were not so nice. She was officially banned from three Venice hangouts for skipping out on her bill.

She also sported an arrest for vagrancy. She had refused to "move on" on one occasion when the cops found her sleeping in a corner of a liquor store parking lot. That bust got ugly. She tried to resist, and the cops (so it was said) got rough with her and she fought back, hitting and biting them. She was gone for a while after that and it was rumored on the street that she was doing hard time.

Then she was back on the street, no worse for wear. She bragged about her arrest and told different versions of a story about the amount of "police brutality" she had endured. In one version, the cops hit her with their truncheons. In another, she said they just verbally insulted her about the color of her hair and then they pulled on her hair. Once she claimed that one of the cops had touched her in an unacceptable way, but when someone suggested she file charges, her face went blank.

After that, whenever Mimo saw a police officer, she did the same thing that she did regarding alleged ex-husband sightings. She turned around and walked in the opposite direction, no matter where she was supposed to be going.


I remember one night when it was raining. It was one of those rains that are neither cold nor warm, just a steady drip, more irritating than anything else. I had only a short walk myself from a friend's house to my apartment, so I ventured out into the damp night with a hat and a newspaper for an umbrella.

I saw Mimo huddling in the doorway of a closed-up store on Pacific Avenue. She was wearing a camouflage jacket and jeans but her feet were encased only in rubber beach sandals. Her hair, at that time dyed purple and silver, was soaking wet.

"Hey, Mimo!"

"Hi, guy," her voice echoed, sounding slightly hoarse.

"You okay? You got anywhere to go?"

"I'm okay. See you."

"No, seriously," I went on. "It's pouring out here. You're wet. Maybe you want to sleep on my sofa tonight?"

"Just tonight?"

"Just tonight. Then you can do whatever you want. I just want you to be dry."

"No," Mimo sighed. "I'm okay. I really am."

"Okay, then."

So I walked on but kept looking back, nervously. The rain came down harder. My newspaper disintegrated and I threw it in the trash. Walking in this rain felt like being dunked in a pool of dirty water, over and over, by a bully.

And when I looked back again, Mimo was gone.


The word on the street one afternoon was that Mimo had been raped. I got a call from a friend who'd heard from another friend. It had happened the night before, another rainy night when Mimo was trying to sleep in a doorway of an abandoned building on Pacific Avenue. She wasn't beaten up, but she was really shaken up and kept saying that the man had been her ex-husband.

A group of women organized a rally that evening at Windward Circle. There were about twenty women and they rattled beads, maracas, small drums, anything that made noise. Someone believed that the perpetrator was a man who was often seen around Venice and that he lived on Windward. The women made noise outside what was assumed to be his apartment.

I went out to look for Mimo and found her on the beach. She was sulking and not very talkative. She had not gone to the police and did not want to go. It took me and the friend who had told me about the rape a couple of hours to persuade her to accompany us to the police station and report it.

"These are the guys who arrested me," she pleaded. "They'll just arrest me again."

The police did not arrest Mimo this time. In fact, they listened to her story and seemed to believe it. That is, except for the ex-husband as the culprit. They did a check and found that he was still in the "hoosegow." The alleged assailant was more probably the man on Windward, but he seemed to have left the neighborhood.

I had made up my mind. The street wasn't safe for her. It was utterly unsafe for a woman, especially such a small woman.

I hated not being able to take her somewhere. She couldn't just be dumped on the street again. I offered her my couch again, temporarily. She wanted to go temporarily to the apartment of a female friend.

I took her to her friend's, but I clamped down.

"Look," I said. "I know you have this thing about being 'free' but we have to get you a place. A permanent place."

Mimo looked more scared than glum.

"Maybe," she said.

Rents were still low in some very old buildings, and Mimo was a special case. I took time off from work to stay with her as she signed forms and talked with welfare people. I accompanied the kind social worker to the apartment that she finally moved into. It was in a green building near the Venice Ocean Front Walk, only one fair-sized room with kitchen fixtures and a bathroom with shower.

Her meds were kind to her, and she seemed to be alert most of the time as she assembled the props for an indoor, secure life: a little table and chair, a bed, dishes and cookware. In the evening of her first day in the apartment, she lit a violet candle.

Neighbors saw her coming and going, carrying a backpack, humming. She talked of getting a cat. Then one day, I found a litter of kittens in an alley. I showed up at Mimo's door with a small black kitten in one hand. Mimo named the kitten Lucky to ward off the old black cat superstitions.

One evening I stopped off at Mimo's new place. It was another rainy evening but now she was in a warm place.

It felt like home. I got to sit in an old leather chair she had found in an alley. I felt a rip on one arm of the chair and I idly pulled a wad of stuffing out. Lucky promptly grabbed the stuffing to play with.

Mimo brought me a plastic cup of lemonade.

"What next," I mused. "You going to get a butler?"

"I've done it," said Mimo. "I have a regular place."

"It's amazing," I said. "A year ago, two years ago, I wouldn't have thought you could do this."

"You helped me."

"But you know that you did a lot of this yourself, don't you?"

"No," Mimo said.

"How do you mean?"

"I'm crazy. You know that."

"I never said you were crazy."

"Then what?"

"You've stabilized. We, a lot of people, welfare and others, got you to where you're stabilized. But you were the one who did it. You should congratulate yourself."

Mimo sat on the floor, cross-legged, and looked up at me. I had the feeling she was going to say one of her outrageous zingers. I ran through a number of things in my head that I could say before she could say anything else.

"I might write something about you." I went on, "A human-interest article."

She opened her mouth. And out it came.

"Do you love me?"

"No, Mimo."

"You're wrong," Mimo said. "You do love me. You know you do."

"I like you as a human being. I'm concerned about you. But if you mean romantic love—no, I don't want to get into that. It's not that kind of feeling—oh, hell. Please don't make me say things I don't want to have to say."

She gave me a look that was surprisingly hostile.

"Don't screw with me, you," she said, almost snarling. "It's not like I'm asking you to sleep with me, nothing like that. But I think you do love me. You're afraid to say it. Because I'm the way I am. Come on, admit it."

I wanted to be anywhere else in the universe at that moment. I had never been the target of her anger before. I forced a smile and said, softly, "It's not the kind of love you mean. I know what kind of love you mean. You've had a hard time. I know. But while I care about you and I'm concerned about you—no, I have to be honest, it's not that kind of love. We're friends. Friends...can be more important than lovers. I..."

And then she was crying. I felt I would never recover, never be forgiven. What could I do? I helped her get stabilized. But it's all I'd been able to do.

I had to hold her in my arms. She cuddled up against my chest and threw her thin arms around me and clung to me. I just let her be for a while. The rain outside came down harder, banging against the windows. Mimo gradually

131

stopped crying. Her body relaxed. When it seemed like she was stabilizing from the reality of the previous moment, I let go and moved toward the door.

"I'll see you soon, Mimo," I said.

When I left Mimo's building that night, I thought I saw someone outside, a man who was waiting. I'm going to have the rest of my life to think about what I thought I had seen. I can spend my life punishing myself for not acting on instinct, but hell, it was Venice and every day, every night, someone thought that there was a crime in progress.

So no one knew what happened on that one particular October night. This much happened that could be agreed upon. There was a scream. Some said they had heard several screams. Some thought they had seen a man running down the stairs.

The police later found Mimo on the floor. She had been stabbed fifteen times with her kitchen knife. There were ten stab wounds on her chest, two on her arms, and three in her abdomen.

There were various scenarios that I played out in my head as I tried to figure out what had happened. When the theories became too depressing and frightening, I shut them off as I would have turned off a bad TV show.

Of course there was also the scenario that would have involved me. I had been the last one to see her alive. Well, I told the cops my story. I must have seemed very distraught. They bought my story. I was not a suspect.

The police hunted the man for weeks. They finally caught up with someone who resembled a man someone swore they had seen entering the building. There was a chase through the alleys of Venice and shots were fired by both sides. The man was dead on arrival. He was identified as George H. (for Henry) Wilton. Either way, she'd been right about the name.

Only Lucky knew what had actually gone down, and anyway, Mimo would have laughed and said, "Nobody can understand Lucky's accent. She speaks feline."

Lucky became my cat. I also took Mimo's leather chair, the one with the rip and the stuffing coming out. I gave away what few possessions she had left to her friends or to charity.

I stood on the beach on yet another drizzly day, listening to speeches by Mimo's friends. A local minister said a prayer for her. Then people scattered Mimo's ashes on the beach and in the ocean.

"That was Mimo," someone said. "She was always scattered."

And to everyone's surprise, including my own, I refused a chance to deliver a eulogy.

"I can't talk about her," was all I could say.

I had a collection of little notes, scribbled on everything from gum wrappers to rent receipts, with thoughts of Mimo. I had intended to write my article about her from these notes. I could have made a speech using these notes.

But instead, I crumpled them in my hand and scattered them the way her ashes were scattered. Then I kicked at the wet sand and left the memorial.

In the evening, I sat in the leather chair, held Lucky and petted her, and thought about Mimo.

I began to write. It was not the human interest article. It read like an editorial or maybe a poem.

"People," I wrote, "come to L.A., to Venice, from points east, from all over. But when they get to L.A. and to Venice, there is no further west they can go unless they take a ship or a swim. The ocean dead ends many of them. For my friend Mimo, the trip ended at the ocean's edge. It was a wall she ran into, head-on.

"She couldn't even see through that wall or over it. Every day for her was simply getting up from wherever she was sleeping, and just walking around within the limits of that dead end zone of streets she called home.

"She would have, if she had realized her plight, called it the hoosegow. Prison."

I read what I had written, scowled, and as usual, tore up the paper.

There was no getting her on paper. I could think about Mimo for the next decade and I knew that no matter what I thought, she would not come back to life, and I could do nothing and there had never been anything that I could do.

And as for her being up against a wall, in prison—what had she told me so long ago?

"I'm free this way."

# Today's the Day
## Mae Woods

Estelle ran a glossy red fingernail down the names at the security gate. The Rossmore Lanai was a glamorous address in its heyday. Now it was dwarfed by high rises and assaulted by the drone of traffic. But a lush garden buffered it from the street and, best of all, it overlooked the Wilshire Country Club golf course. *This looks very promising,* Estelle thought, watching a silver Jaguar glide up to the Club entrance. She located MRS. ELIZABETH BRADDOCK—2B on the roster and pressed the intercom.

Estelle reached into her shoulder bag for a business card. Only one left, and a bit grimy, but it would do: MADAME ESTELLE, PSYCHIC ADVISOR TO THE STARS, ASTROLOGY, TAROT, SPIRIT CHANNELING, PALM READING, RUNE STONES. Luckily, no one ever asked for rune stones. She'd lost two and never bothered to replace them. Today her bag was weighed down with tarot cards, books, crystals, packets of Devil-Be-Gone Sage, and House of Good Fortune Incense. Mrs. Braddock had not flinched at paying a hundred bucks for a half-hour consultation, so Estelle planned to milk out a tarot reading, sell her wares, and be home before Ray left for work.

Estelle buzzed again and the wrought iron gate clicked open. Inside, she paused at a lobby mirror to refresh her lipstick and fluff her henna-red hair. Usually people expected a flamboyant gypsy, and that's exactly how she felt in her flowered wraparound skirt and tight yellow top. She knew it was a bit too youthful for a woman of fifty-five, but a good costume is part of any performance, she reminded herself.

Mrs. Braddock was waiting in the doorway. "Hello, dear. I'm Betty," she said warmly. "Thank you for coming, Madame Estelle. I am most grateful for your help. I realize it might be a bit unorthodox to come to someone's home, but you will see why it was necessary."

"No problem. I'm happy to go wherever I'm needed." Estelle smiled. She looked into the large living room, silently appraising its contents. There was a baby grand piano, photos in ornate silver frames, a crystal chandelier, shelves of leather-bound books, an overstuffed sofa, and armchairs in matching chintz fabric.

Betty led her to a seat at the dining room table.

"I always begin a session with the tarot," Estelle explained, taking the cards from her bag. "It will be our way of getting to know each other." Shuffling the deck gave Estelle a moment to size up her mark. Betty was dressed in a beige silk blouse topped with a blue angora cardigan. Her once-blonde hair had aged into a muted white and was now tightly anchored in a black plastic clip. Estelle imagined that was what Grace Kelly would look like if she'd reached eighty and only weighed ninety pounds. There was a word for that classic style. What was it? Oh right, *money*.

Betty said, "I don't know anything about card reading. Actually, there is a *specific* reason why I called you—"

"All in good time," Estelle interrupted, motioning for Betty to cut the cards. Estelle laid out five cards in a cross and began turning them over. "The King of Cups, the Sun, the Tower."

"Is that good, dear?" Betty asked.

"The Tower represents the chaos that comes before enlightenment. I feel there are good things ahead for you, Betty."

Betty nodded.

Estelle turned up the Ace of Swords, then lingered over the last card. She flipped it over and Betty gasped. *La Morte*. The final card pictured a skeleton with a leering grin.

Estelle smiled reassuringly. "Don't be alarmed."

"But isn't that *death*?"

"It also signifies a new beginning. The old patterns have to die before something fresh and new can be born."

"I don't know what you mean, dear," Betty said.

"You can only start a new lifestyle when you leave your old one. It means you're ready to try something new, and that's exciting and wonderful." Her voice began to swell as she went into lecture mode. "Don't be afraid to—"

Betty cut her off, shakily. "Can we move on, please? I'm not worried about my lifestyle, whatever that is. I called you because I have a *question*—"

"Of course. We all have questions. We all need guidance. That's why we go to the tarot. It can be our roadmap to the future." Estelle gestured to the cards. "Now, your question. I'd like you to think about it as the cards speak to me."

"I *am* thinking about it. What I want to know is—"

"Wait. I'm feeling something." Estelle paused dramatically. "I see money in your future. The Sun represents wealth, and it's right here in the center. Look."

Estelle smiled and waited for her reaction. Betty stared at the cards without enthusiasm.

"Or perhaps you have some financial concerns?" Estelle pried.

"That's not why I called you," Betty said quickly.

"Your question isn't about money?"

"No. You see, I've lost something, something precious to me. That's what I've been trying to tell you. I was hoping you could help me find it."

"What?"

"My wedding ring."

"Oh, how terrible. A diamond? I imagine it's very valuable…"

Betty stared down at her hands.

"How did you lose it?"

Betty paused, and Estelle felt the other woman was deciding whether to tell the truth. Estelle waited, locking eyes with Betty in an expression of respectful sympathy. It worked, as it always did. Betty's shoulders slumped ever so slightly, then she began.

"My husband died ten years ago. We lived in Chicago. I decided I wasn't going to spend another winter in the snow. I moved out here to Hancock Park. I haven't made many friends. I've actually lived in this building for nine years, and I don't know any of my neighbors. Then I met Sergio—"

"Ah, romance. It's never too late."

Betty waved her hand, dismissively. "It wasn't a romance. He's not interested in women, if you know what I mean, dear. We met at a dance studio. My husband and I loved to dance, and I realized how much I missed it. Anyway, I took lessons just so I could go out dancing. And, to be honest, I hoped I would meet somebody. Sergio was one of the instructors. I saw him every week, and we became friends. Sergio was a great believer in psychic predictions, ESP, that sort of thing. Last year he urged me to go on a cruise, insisting that I would meet the man of my dreams."

"Did you?"

"I did meet a man, a handsome businessman. After the cruise, he invited me to visit him in Palm Beach. But marriage was not on his agenda, as it turned out. He asked me to invest in a new company he was putting together. Like a fool, I did. He said we would both be riding high in a month. But then it didn't pan out. When he started to tell me about another 'investment opportunity,' I wised up and called it quits."

Estelle nodded, knowingly.

"But let me back up to Sergio and the cruise. I was packed

and ready to leave the apartment. When he saw I was wearing my diamond ring, he became very agitated. 'No, no! That's very bad luck! A wedding ring will keep you from meeting the right man. It sends a negative vibration. You must take it off.' The ring is worth...well, quite a lot of money."

Estelle leaned closer, listening intently.

"It was nighttime," Betty continued, "so I couldn't put it in my safe deposit box at the bank."

"What did you do?"

"First, I hid it in the pocket of my fur coat. But then Sergio said that was a *terrible* place. If anyone broke in, they would steal the fur and there would go the ring. Well, I didn't much like the notion of someone breaking into my apartment from a man who claimed he could foresee the future. Anyway, I remember looking around. Finally, I found the perfect place. I even remember thinking this is so off the wall, no one will ever find it here. And if they do, well, maybe they deserve to have it."

"Where did you put it?" Estelle prodded.

"I don't remember! I've been home for a month, and I've spent every day looking for it."

"And Sergio? Did he see you hide it?"

"No. He was putting the luggage in the car."

"Have you asked him what he remembers?"

"I wish I could. When I came back, I found a note from him. He said his mother was ill and he was going to Italy to look after her and would be in touch. But I haven't heard from him. I have no idea where he is."

"Do you know any of his friends?"

"No. I asked at the dance studio, and they just said he'd given notice and left town."

"Okay." Estelle took a breath. "Many choices. I must summon a Spirit Guide. This will be a bit more than the hundred we discussed."

"Why? You advertised psychic help and that's all I'm

asking for. Let's just spend the rest of our time looking for my ring. You can follow your spirit vibe or whatever you call it."

Estelle scowled.

"I do intend to pay you more if we find it." Betty walked to her desk and pulled out a ledger-style checkbook. "Here, I have a check made out to cash for one thousand dollars as a finder's fee if you are successful."

Estelle craned her neck to see the check. Betty snapped the book closed.

"Well," Estelle said, "let's get to work. I'm going to ask you some questions to take you back to that night. Let's go to your bedroom so you can show me exactly what you were doing."

Betty led Estelle into a spacious bedroom. The furniture and walls were white, and the plush carpet a soft gray. In contrast, the bedspread of bright pink flowers appeared to glow. Mirrored closets took up the entire length of one wall.

Betty slid open a closet door. Estelle stared at three racks of high-heeled shoes—satin, patent leather, and suede—and noted that today Betty's tiny feet were in soiled, pink terrycloth slippers. Betty began to dutifully recite what she'd done that night. "Okay, I packed three bags, and they were over there by the door." She paused. "No, they were gone, actually. Sergio was carrying them downstairs." She returned to the closet. "My evening wear was already packed," she continued, gesturing to a row of gowns encased in plastic garment bags. "I had decided to leave the mink at home. It might be, you know, dear, a bit too showy."

"Let me see where you first put the ring," Estelle said, stepping forward.

Betty unzipped the largest bag, and a silver mink sleeve popped out. Estelle petted the silky fur as she gently eased the coat off the hanger.

"I put it in the left pocket, I think. Yes, I remember that," Betty said.

"I need to go back to that moment with you." Estelle slipped on the coat and plunged her hands into the pockets. Satin. The touch was immediately soothing. She smiled.

"Are you getting a vibration, dear?" Betty asked, excitedly.

"Yes. Yes, I am."

"Something about the ring?"

"Yes. But I need more. Tell me what other jewelry you have and where you keep it."

"I don't have a safe if that's what you mean. I believe nice things should be used, not tucked away." Betty peeled the tight-fitting coat from Estelle's shoulders and returned it to the closet.

"We should go through your jewelry," Estelle said, moving to an ornate box on the dresser. She picked it up. "Is this where you keep everything?"

"Not everything," Betty said, grabbing the box, impatiently. "I know I didn't put the ring in there. That would be too obvious, don't you think?"

Estelle switched gears. She would try to find a way to come back to examine the jewelry box without Betty breathing down her neck. "Do you remember leaving the bedroom with the ring?"

"Not really. But I'm rather sure I did."

"Okay, back to the garment bag in the closet. I want you to put your hand in the coat pocket and pretend to remove the ring. What did you do next? Did you put it on your finger, or what?"

"No, I carried it like this." Betty pinched the imaginary ring between thumb and forefinger in front of her like a divining rod.

"So, what now?"

"I don't know," Betty said glumly, closing her hand.

"What about in the bathroom?" Estelle charged into the adjoining room, flinging open a medicine chest cramped with lotions and vials of pills.

"Don't waste your time in there," Betty shouted. "I've checked every bottle. Wait. Now, I remember! I went into the *kitchen*." She pivoted, and Estelle quickly followed after her.

Betty's galley-style kitchen was designed for bachelor efficiency. But she had crammed it with food containers, dishware and old appliances. A bulky Mixmaster covered in a discolored plastic shroud was lodged between a juicer and a Mr. Coffee, half full of this morning's brew. A microwave took up most of the space on a small Formica table.

Estelle sighed. "Lots of hiding places. And what about in here?" she asked, entering the pantry. There was a stacked washer-dryer unit, a wall of storage cupboards, and a huge chest freezer. Folded sheets and towels smelling of fragrant detergent were neatly stacked on top of it. *This search could take all day*, Estelle thought. Good thing I'll be charging by the minute.

"I distinctly remember the kitchen. I don't think I went into the pantry."

"Okay," Estelle said, "back up. I want you to hold up your ring like you did before and walk in here again. What do you do next?"

"Well, I was ready to leave so everything would be tidy."

"Maybe you put it in something on the shelf," Estelle suggested, opening a cupboard, "or with your silverware. Where do you keep that?"

Betty snapped, "Good heavens, I don't hide money in cookie jars and coffee tins. Give me a little credit, please."

Estelle could feel her face redden. Betty's growing impatience was making her angry. She took a moment to breathe deeply. "Okay. Let's start over. You said you thought you took the ring into the kitchen."

"Yes. But now that I'm here, nothing seems right. You're the one supposed to have psychic skills. Why aren't you walking around picking up vibrations instead of just getting annoyed—"

"I'm just trying to help you to remember what you did," Estelle broke in. "Let's go through it again. Sergio was going to the car. You held the ring up like this, and you walked from the bedroom into the kitchen. Okay. Now you're standing here. What are you thinking about? Concentrate."

Betty shut her eyes for a moment. "Maybe I'm going to get a tool or something like that."

"So you must have decided where you were going to hide it." Estelle yanked open a drawer. "Maybe in here," she said, rummaging through screwdrivers, Scotch tape, assorted nails, and wads of string. "Ouch!" she yelped as a carpet tack punctured her finger.

"Be careful, dear." Betty slowly backed out of the kitchen doorway, eyes closed, as if being pulled into the living room. "I'm going to sit down for a moment. I feel funny."

Estelle began to carefully remove the contents of the drawer and sort them out on the counter. She glanced up to watch Betty settle on the couch. "Lean over and put your face into a pillow," she called out. "That'll revive you. That's right. Now, close your eyes."

Estelle watched Betty meekly fold herself over a pillow then crept over to the desk to get the checkbook. She took it to the kitchen table and was about to tear out the one thousand dollar check when she noticed the ledger stub. It was blank. She flipped back one page. Balance: $36.70. Estelle snapped. That old woman planned to con her!

Suddenly, Estelle heard a scraping noise. She wheeled around to see Betty perched on an ottoman, reaching for a candle sconce above the fireplace. Betty chuckled, "Off the wall. My little joke." She stretched to grasp the candle then toppled backward with a shriek.

Estelle flew out of the kitchen.

Betty was on the floor, struggling to get up. "My ring—"

Estelle grabbed the fireplace poker and swung it in a rage.

Betty screamed. A flow of bright red blood formed a jagged part in her white hair.

Estelle jumped onto the chair and wrenched the candle out of the wall sconce. She looked into the holder. Empty. She ran to examine the matching candlestick on the other side of the fireplace. No ring.

She stared down at the crumpled body. It looked so tiny. "You stupid woman. Why did you make me do that? And you were wrong. The ring's not even there."

Estelle lifted a knitted afghan from the back of a chair and gently rolled the body into it. She struggled, trying to pull it across the floor. Then she remembered the sheets on top of the freezer. She spread one of them on the floor, rolled the body bundle into it, knotted each end, and slowly dragged it into the pantry.

Estelle opened the freezer and scooped out a deep hole among the icy packages. She pushed the body bag against the freezer and slowly hoisted it up. Breathing heavily, she marshaled her strength into one quick burst to catapult it inside. With a loud plop, the bundle hit its mark. She carefully arranged a blanket of turkey potpies and frozen peas over it.

Estelle retraced her path back to the fireplace, toweling up drops of blood. There was a wet crimson stain by the ottoman. She readjusted a throw rug to cover it, then rearranged the furniture into Betty's symmetrical pattern. Satisfied that everything was back in the right place, she threw the towels into the freezer and pulled a cell phone from her bag.

"Ray, we hit a nice score...no, not cash but lots of jewelry...320 North Rossmore, 2B. There's an intercom. I'll buzz you in."

Estelle went directly to the jewelry box and dumped out its contents—ornate pins, costume earrings, broaches and bracelets. Something caught her eye at the bottom of the box. It was a claim ticket from the Beverly Loan Company for twenty jewelry pieces on deposit, value: thirty grand. She stared at it. Nothing left here but junk. Ray would be angry. And what would he say about that little problem in the freezer? She decided she wouldn't tell him. If Betty's neighbors didn't know her, she might not be discovered for a very long time.

Estelle went to the closet and pulled out the mink coat and evening gowns. The day wouldn't be a total loss for her. The dresses were hopelessly old-fashioned, but could be stylish prom wear. Shareen's Vintage Clothing in Venice was full of that stuff. In the back of the closet, Estelle spotted a bright blue tunic advertising a Palm Beach resort. That would fit her.

As she slipped it on, she heard the buzz of the intercom. How could Ray get here so soon? Estelle hurried over to the video intercom. A young woman with long dark hair was standing at the gate, shouting into the speaker.

"Mrs. Braddock? It's Rita Powell. You called me yesterday. We have an appointment."

Estelle noticed Betty's open daybook on a side table by the front door. An entry was scrawled in bright red ink: *Today's the day! 10 a.m. Madame Estelle; 11 a.m. Rita Powell; 3 p.m. The Psychic Connection.* So this was Betty's day for psychics. Estelle would wait until the girl left, then she and Ray would have four hours to go through the apartment.

A sudden thought intrigued her. Rita Powell would be meeting Betty for the first time; they'd only spoken on the phone. Estelle made a quick decision. She could handle this. It might even be fun. She pressed the intercom. "Come in, dear," she chirped brightly, imitating the older woman.

Estelle paced back and forth, practicing Betty's gestures and voice in an eerie stream-of-conscious monologue. "Hello, dear, I'm Betty...I would be most grateful for your help, dear...Thank you for coming...I loved to dance...Off the wall was my little joke...good heavens, I don't hide money in cookie jars...I have a check for you for one thousand dollars...which is completely *bogus* but can't we still be friends, dear..."

Rehearsed and ready, Estelle met Rita Powell in the doorway with a broad smile. "Good morning, dear. Thank you for coming."

Rita was dressed simply in a white shirt and dark pants. The outfit resembled a school uniform, and Estelle wondered how old she was. Thirty, maybe. Rita stared at her, quizzically.

"Oh, sorry it took so long to answer, dear. I was tidying up. And that's why I'm wearing this silly old shirt," Estelle explained.

"It's good to meet you, Mrs. Braddock."

"Oh please, call me Betty, dear." She steered Rita to a seat at the dining room table. As Rita pulled her chair forward, Estelle spotted her own bulky shoulder bag on the floor. She inched her foot over to slowly push it under the table.

"Actually, dear, I'm afraid I'll have to cut our session short. I just had a call that my sister is ill, and I said I would go—"

"I sense great distress in this room," Rita began. "Perhaps you have something to tell me."

Estelle swallowed and straightened up in her chair. "Yes, well, things have been difficult. I've lost my wedding ring. Say, did I tell you any of this on the phone, dear?"

Rita listened intently, not replying, but gesturing for her to continue.

"I hid it for safekeeping when I went on a cruise. Now I can't find it."

"Yes." Rita said nothing more.

Estelle took a breath and launched into Betty's history. She explained about Sergio's prediction, his admonishment about leaving the ring in the fur coat, finding the perfect hiding place for it, the shipboard romance followed by betrayal, her memory loss, and month-long search for the ring. Estelle's version was performed with such dramatic conviction that she brushed back a tear when she spoke of leaving "Cary," the handsome rogue who had recently stolen her heart and most of her money.

Rita listened without comment. Estelle looked over at her, expecting a sympathetic response to her tale.

"How long have you lived here?" Rita asked.

"Nine years. Why?"

"Funny. I see you up in the Northwest, lots of tall trees."

Estelle bit her lip. "Never been there."

She immediately flashed back to her cell at Larch Correctional Center in Washington State. She'd been stuck there for three long years, lying on her bunk, staring out at treetops. She'd done her time quietly. After a year of anger management therapy, she even stopped hating her boss, Lee Ackman, the man who'd accused her of embezzlement when he was nothing but a dirty, lying thief himself. Sure, she borrowed five hundred bucks once when she was in a jam, but he cheated customers every single day of his life. She wouldn't think about him now. She was with Ray, and he made her happy. In prison she studied astrology, tarot cards, and palm reading. She discovered that gave her a sense of power. She could silence anyone who threatened her by solemnly announcing she knew her crime and she knew her fate. It was pretty easy, actually. Everybody was there because of a bad decision; it invariably involved a man; and everybody would have plenty more trouble in the future. Estelle was so convincing, inmates began to pay her for consultations. That gave her the confidence to open a storefront business when she moved to Los Angeles and met Ray. Changing her name from Edith Hurlbert to Estelle Loren had been a good move, too.

Estelle glanced up and found Rita staring at her intently. Several minutes had passed.

"Never been there?" Rita echoed. "Well, perhaps you're

going there in the future. It's a rather strong vision. I feel it's the place you belong."

Estelle felt uneasy. She masked it by clearing her throat. *Maybe Rita actually has psychic powers*, she thought. Maybe she could even find the ring.

"So, what you want now is to find this ring?" Rita asked.

Estelle was startled. Was Rita able to read her mind, too?

Estelle composed herself, concentrating on Betty's voice. "Yes, dear, exactly. I've gone to great lengths to find it. Can you sense where it is?"

"I'd like you to describe it."

Estelle closed her eyes and imagined the million-dollar ring Elizabeth Taylor had proudly modeled in photos celebrating her engagement. Estelle graphically described a circle of small gems with one enormous diamond in the center.

Rita listened closely. "Maybe you should tell me about your husband. That might help me envision it."

"Oh yes...Richard." Estelle launched into a description of Richard Burton, his melodious voice, his pock-marked skin, his zest for life tragically cut short by a plane crash. Then she remembered that it was Mike Todd who died in an airplane. No matter. She wondered how Burton did die. Cirrhosis of the liver, perhaps.

Rita said, "I see you with a man with tattoos. Would that be Richard or Cary?"

"No," Estelle answered, thinking of Ray's muscular arms.

"Maybe you haven't met him yet. Good. Steer clear of this man."

"Why? What do you see?" she asked with concern.

"He's no good. You'd do anything for him, but he will always let you down when you need him the most."

Estelle leaned back in her chair, momentarily unsettled.

Rita stood up. "Okay. I'd like to poke around for a bit. You can go on doing what you need to do."

Estelle looked at her blankly.

"For the trip. You said you had to go to your sister's today."

"Oh, yes. Yes, I have to pack." Estelle headed to the bedroom. *That's good*, she thought. She could pack up Betty's finery.

Estelle began to sort through the pile of evening dresses on the bed and put them in a travel bag. After a moment she realized it was very quiet and wondered what Rita was doing. If she found the ring, would she pocket it and sneak out?

Estelle tiptoed to the bedroom door. The mirrors on the closet reflected a corner of the living room. Estelle saw Rita staring at the piano. Maybe the ring was inside it. Estelle crept forward to get a better view. Rita had not moved. Estelle suddenly realized that Betty's family photos were on the piano. Maybe Rita was looking at them and wondering why nobody resembled the lady she'd just met.

Rita turned suddenly. Estelle ducked back out of view and held her breath. But Rita was walking to the table and reaching for her handbag. *Good, she's leaving*, Estelle thought.

Estelle hurried over to the bed and zipped the mink into a suitcase. She didn't want Rita to come in to say goodbye and wonder why she'd take her mink to see her ailing sister. Estelle smiled at the thought. *My mink.* She'd take it wherever she damn well pleased. She thought about modeling it for Ray tonight, wearing nothing underneath. At first he might want her to sell it, but there were ways she could change this mind about that.

A noise from the kitchen jarred her. She was wrong; Rita was still out there, snooping around. Estelle flew out of the bedroom.

"What are you doing?" Estelle demanded, her voice shrill and menacing.

"I was just going to get a glass of water," Rita answered.

"Well, I really do need to be going. We can schedule

another appointment when I return. I'll write you a check for your time."

"That's not necessary," Rita said.

"Well, thank you. But I'll add today's fee to the next visit," Estelle said, walking to the front door. She stopped at the intercom screen. A burly man in a sweatshirt was looking at the directory, unaware of being watched—Ray.

She turned back to Rita, still standing at the table, "Sorry, but I really do need to go."

"Just a minute," Rita said. "I want to give you my card so you can call me." She looked through her handbag, slowly removing its contents.

"Don't bother. I know I have it."

There was a knock on the front door. Estelle wondered how Ray got through the security gate. She didn't want him to come in while Rita was there. He didn't know she was passing herself off as Betty Braddock. Everything could fall apart. Estelle went rigid, trying to figure out her next move.

Another knock, loud and insistent. Rita bounded across the room and opened the door. Two police officers stepped inside.

"What's going on?" One of the men appeared to be addressing Rita. The name on his uniform read O'NEILL.

"This woman is pretending to be Mrs. Braddock," Rita announced.

Estelle attempted a small laugh and launched into an explanation. "This has all been a big misunderstanding, Officer. I'm a friend of Betty's. She's traveling. I'm looking after things for her. I haven't done anything. You should be questioning this woman. She doesn't belong here. She doesn't know Betty!" Her words poured out in a vehement torrent.

Rita ignored her and turned to O'Neill. "You'll find Mrs. Braddock's body in the freezer."

One officer headed to the pantry as O'Neill reached for his handcuffs.

"Wait, let me explain. I just got here. Why are you listening to her?" Estelle babbled.

"We know Ms. Powell," he said. "She helped us on a missing person case last week. She just sent me a text to come here. Now, I'll need to see your ID."

Before long Estelle was walking down the corridor, flanked by policemen, her hands cuffed at her back in total surrender. Rita followed along behind them.

Estelle turned to her with a sneer. "For a minute, I thought you were the real deal. But you couldn't find the ring."

"It's not there," Rita said quietly.

"What do you mean?"

"If the story you told me was true, I imagine that Sergio came back and found it."

Estelle slumped, realizing she was probably right.

At the front gate, Estelle saw Ray leaning against his van. Their eyes connected. She smiled wanly as she was eased into the police car. *He'll follow me to the station. He will know how to get me out of this.* She turned to look through the back window as Ray climbed into the van. Estelle nodded to him. But he was already pulling away from the curb. She watched him pass and slip into the flow of traffic snaking toward the freeway.

# Little Egypt
## Georgia Jeffries

Miles of Mother Road stretched ahead, hot pavement shimmering and sashaying like a crazy asphalt goblin on crack. Thirty-nine hours since the driver crept out of downtown L.A. toward Interstate 10 in a battered, baby blue '95 Corvette with the only man she ever loved. Her bloodshot eyes were still fixed on the rearview mirror like there'd be no tomorrow. This was not the time for Mr. B's words to start banging inside her head again...

*When do you intend to claim your potential, Julia Mae?* She had stood silent under her teacher's fierce gaze, unsure in the moment what her potential was or where it might be. Perhaps it lay buried deep with some pirate treasure in a subterranean lagoon waiting to be dug up by a friendly sailor at sea? That's how she thought about life at sixteen. Mr. B knew better. His shoe-shine eyes looked at her straight and level, not up and down like the foul-mouthed boys in class. Different. He always looked at her different. Kind of the way she peered at a dead butterfly under the microscope in biology lab, curious how this wondrous creature came to such a sad state.

On the car radio, Tim McGraw crooned goodbye and good riddance to the bad girl that done him wrong. He held the low notes long and hard just so the bitch knew he meant business. Goodbye, goodbye, goodbye—

"HELLO TRAVELER! YOU ARE ENTERING LITTLE

EGYPT—HOME OF AMERICA'S ANCIENT PYRAMIDS!"

A gaudy Technicolor billboard stamped with the imprimatur of the Land of Lincoln winked at the driver speeding by. Against a far horizon the thousand-year-old Cahokia Mounds loomed big and bold, mute giants from another age with nowhere to run. Local legend speculated that the prehistoric Cahokia might have been Mayan, voyagers from another hemisphere who built the tall pyramids of dirt and rock to bury their society's elite. Relics prized by archaeologists but not by her. Not since a long ago tour guide pointed out the mound where one old chieftain's bones lay atop a bunch of shells and the remains of three hundred young females killed in ceremonial sacrifice. A steady supply of virgins for the great man's afterlife, the guide explained, no doubt the maidens were happy to be chosen.

Soon black and white highway signs began jumping in her path: CAIRO ... THEBES ... KARNAK ... HELIOPOLIS ... PALESTINE. Villages spat out of green rolling hills watered by the Mississippi, baptized by Old Testament believers over a century before. Grand monikers promising more riches than the region's soil or people could deliver.

The boot of Illinois masqueraded as the North, mendacity anybody with an ounce of sense saw through on the first visit. Most of the locals spoke slow and easy, similar to their border brethren in Kentucky, and liked their patriotic politics leaning to the right. It was no secret some pioneer families—including her own—once owned slaves and defied upstate Illinois law to raise arms for the Confederacy. Even in this century, bad blood feuds ran rampant among hard-nosed Egyptians who never forgot an injury or a slight. What the hell. She was coming home anyway. No matter how much grief her high and mighty old man threw down. Lord knows they both delivered offenses to humankind that would take seven generations to forget. Maybe here she'd be able to finally take back ownership of her Christian born name and suck in a clean breath again.

The driver jerked a sideways look at her passenger curled on his side in the shotgun seat. His eyelids quivered in a fitful sleep, skin glistening in cold sweat, breathing shallow and labored. More goddamn hurt. Hurt so bad it could make you stab somebody in the heart to make it go away.

"Hey, Ginger, give my friend, Herbie, whatever he wants." Mr. Shapiro grinned, slapping his buddy on the back before he Ubered to LAX to catch the red eye to Cancún. "On the house." Five days in a row the two of them had been behind closed doors huddling on some big deal. She watched as they sauntered downstairs from the executive offices and saw her boss slip something—a flash drive?—into his friend's pocket as he headed out. Not that it was any of her business. After she got a better look at Herbie, she decided it might be.

Ginger never wanted to disappoint her boss. Mr. Shapiro gave her a steady job in this high-class Hollywood watering hole, and she was grateful, she really was. Polite enough not to ask her about the gap of missing years on her resume, he complimented her on the fact that he'd never seen anybody, man or woman, serve up a Ramos Gin with more fizz and hired her on the spot. A family guy with manicured nails and pictures of twin granddaughters in sleek bamboo frames on his chrome glass desk, he reeked respectability. Not that she hadn't heard stories. After one too many appletinis at the Christmas party, a young waitress named Tiffany, nice kid who always pooled her tips, implied their boss's retro cocktail lounge was more than a savvy downtown investment.

"Blow," she giggled, wobbling a little in her silver-sequined peep-toes. "That's his real business. He's one of the top dogs around. We're working in a laundromat keeping his stacks of green clean." If there were facts to support such an allegation, they disappeared a week later along with Tiffany.

"She wanted me to tell you how much she'd miss every-body," Mr. Shapiro announced to his remaining staff. But when the girl's dear mother suffered a massive coronary, she had to move back to Stockton to help out. This troubled Ginger for a time because she remembered Tiffany bitching about her mom being in prison down in Chowchilla for passing bad welfare checks.

"Stupid!" the cocktail waitress said at the same Christmas party. "How stupid can a woman be?" But there was rent to pay and medicine to buy and lean times still knocking at the door, so Ginger decided "see no evil" was the best policy in questionable circumstances.

And then Mr. Shapiro's pal, Herbie the Blue Serge Suit, climbed on her bar stool, his reptilian gaze reflected in the gold-veined mirror behind them. He scooped up a fistful of Spanish pistachios, eyeing the attractive bartender with the red hair.

"We've met somewhere before."

"I don't think so."

Ginger poured the premium Chivas Regal reserved for special clientele and placed the glass on one of the recycled cocktail napkins her boss favored.

"You sure? I got a memory like a bull elephant. Never forget a face." He tapped his temple with a lascivious grin. "Or anything else. It's a gift."

"More pistachios?"

"Tasteless." He shook his head. "I like 'em salty. You?"

"Excuse me?"

"Like 'em salty?"

"Absolutely." She turned away, slicing chilled limes into perfect wedges for club sodas no one had ordered. A good safety knife, quality German steel. She'd never cut herself, not once.

"You need salty nuts. A fancy establishment like this needs to do right by its investors."

Ginger watched a cluster of tipsy singles leaving the corner banquette. Hunter green leather smooth to the touch. A comfy cradle for upscale asses after a long day. Sit, savor, spend. Mr. Shapiro knew what he was doing when he designed the place. No doubt about it, she was lucky to be here.

"You a dancer? The way you move…maybe I saw you dance someplace?"

"Not in this lifetime."

"What's that mean?"

Ginger's tight "the customer is always right" smile twitched, splintering at the edges. "Dancing is for folks with time on their hands."

She polished the Philippine mahogany bar top with a linen cloth. No scratches, her boss warned, no scratches to mar that fine finish.

"Maybe I should speak to Fred. Make sure he's not working you too hard?" Herbie licked his lips. "Anything I can do, say the word."

She'd listened to his kind before. The come-ons, the promises, the oily seductions as slick as the detritus from the Exxon Valdez. Over two decades had passed, but TV images of those dead seabirds still flickered in her mind. Smothered, the reporters said. Wings crushed, feathers blackened, so much sweet life snuffed and gone.

"I'm not complaining."

"Don't bullshit a bullshitter." He gulped down his Chivas. "Hell, who wants to be on somebody else's payroll, right? Me, all I want to do is go sit in Tahiti and knock back a couple highballs while the sun sets. How about you?"

She said nothing.

"Don't be shy, honey." He wiped his mouth with thick fingertips and leaned forward. "What would you do different if you had your life to live over?"

"Everything," Ginger blurted, her face flushing hot at the revelation.

"A girl like you?" his voice oozed more than lust. Something more dangerous. "A lot of females would kill for what Mother Nature handed you."

Did she say she wanted to *be* different? No. Be and do, two separate verbs that this son-of-a-bitch could never understand. Her grit and good looks (plus brains when she used them) had gotten her this far, which wasn't nearly far enough, true, but she wasn't throwing in the towel yet. Her son needed her.

"Hit me again, *por favor*. A double." Pulling out a monogrammed lighter, Herbie lit up a sleek Cuban and did not bother to ask if she minded.

"California law," Ginger informed him. "No smoking in bars or restaurants. Maybe you want to take that outside."

"After hours, babe." He sucked the smoke into his lungs then exhaled. "Your boss and I agree the rules don't apply."

She made no mention of her allergy to cigar smoke. Instead she flipped on the bar fan and prayed to God this would be his last drink.

They were alone now. Even the regulars had moved on to the late nightclubs or crawled home to unhappy wives. She glanced at the face of the Mickey Mouse watch on her left wrist, the one she bought when they went to Disneyland to celebrate Dante's fourth birthday. Maybe that was one day she would keep, that one perfect day when her precious child was still healthy and his daddy was still in their lives.

Fatigue swept over Ginger the way it did so often. As if she were one of those Valdez seabirds trying to swim through dark waves that sapped every ounce of strength needed to survive. As she filled his glass, he puffed on his cigar, bushy eyebrows frozen in phony consternation like two embalmed caterpillars.

"Tough life, huh?"

She turned her face away from his stinking smoke. "Did I say that?"

"Well, if you'd do everything over—"

"I'm tired of being on the short end of the stick is all. Doctors, hospital bills…"

"You look in fine shape to me."

She went silent, feeling naked and dirty in that awful way she thought was gone.

"You know how to protect your assets in these unpredictable times?" Herbie drilled Ginger with meaningful eye contact.

Only fourteen minutes until two. Fourteen minutes until Dante arrived and she could lock up.

"Diversify," he smirked, his Scotch cigar breath making her want to puke.

Knock, knock, was there a fucking brain above his Johnson? Any fool could figure out the basics of financial investment with half a chance. That was another course she could teach if she ever went back to UCLA to finish her degree. She didn't need condescension, thank you very much, all she needed was Capital with a capital "C."

"A girl with your assets deserves to be happy." He was jabbing his finger at her chest now. Crass bastard.

Happy? She didn't even remember how to spell the word. Not that there weren't nice moments now and again. But the most she could say about the last few years was hey, she showed up. A good day happened when the other shoe didn't drop. Which reminded her of that catchy commercial selling some antacid-something-or-other. (She didn't believe in over-the-counter garbage herself. Best medicine she knew was Suck-It-Up, the giant economy-size bottle. Bad day? Suck it up. Things could be worse. A lot worse. Hang around long enough, and worse was a sure thing.) How'd that old TV jingle go again? Oh yeah. "How do you spell relief?" Ginger knew. R-e-l-i-e-f was when the other shoe did not drop. That was as close as she knew to happy.

"Where're you from, Ginger? You don't look like the L.A. type to me."

"No place you ever heard of."

"Be a good girl now. Didn't Fred tell you to be nice to his best buddy?"

She hated being called a good girl. Even when she was a kid, the phrase riled her natural sensibilities.

"Illinois."

"Chicago?"

"Downstate."

"Gotcha. Some burg like Peoria."

Richard Pryor came from Peoria. She found that out the only time she saw him perform in person. A dingy club off Sunset where he did his first comeback gigs after torching half his body. He made her laugh so hard she peed her pants. It was the last time she could remember laughing like that. Laughing so hard she cried. But the crying got big and loud and out of control and she could not stop. The bouncer told her it was time to leave because she was disturbing the other patrons. Pryor went right on trash-talking while security escorted her out. She admired that kind of talent. The show must go on.

"You know what plays in Peoria, Ginger?" Herbie blew twin rings of cigar smoke out of the corner of his mouth.

"No, I can't say I do." She shifted her burning eyes from the tobacco's downwind.

"That's the joke, honey, nothing plays there. No wonder you got out of town. Who the fuck wants to die in Hicksville?"

Who the fuck wants to die in L.A., she wanted to scream, but why bother? A shithead like Herbie lacked the sensitivity to appreciate any existential point of view.

"Let's you and I have a nightcap together upstairs."

Nausea twisted her insides. She gripped the bar towel

tighter and turned away to wipe down the counter. His clammy hand slid across the slick surface and trapped hers.

"I don't drink." She slid away, glancing at her watch again. Twelve minutes until two.

"You're kidding, right?" He reached for her hand again.

She eluded his grasp. "Not even with our special customers."

"Sweetheart," his voice deepened, a harsher edge now. "I'm the man that keeps your boss in business."

"Is that right?"

"Right as rain." He gulped down half his drink and flashed a cocky grin. "Who do you think keeps the IRS from breathing down his neck?"

"Let me guess. You?"

"Now you're cooking with gas. Your boy Freddy—"

"Mr. Shapiro is not my boy."

His tongue scooped up a chunk of ice, crunching it between sharp incisors. "That's not what I hear."

Ginger could feel the short fuse she inherited from her old man sizzle and spit, hijacking good sense the way it always did.

"There ought to be a law against malicious gossip, don't you think?" Her eyes met his straight on. Fuck with me again and I'll staple your balls tight and flat, I don't care who you are.

Herbie chewed on his cigar, trying to puzzle out the answer to a different question. And then his left hand, the one with the gold wedding ring, flew through the air, slapping the bar like he'd just won an easy million in the California lottery. "October, 1995!"

There it was. Ten months she'd worked here and only one other guy had recognized her. The past was the past and that's where it belonged. She was comfortable in this place, catering the way it did to the young hip crowd who was still in grade school when her centerfold graced the newsstands.

This job she would not screw up. She promised herself and Dante that much.

"September." God hates a liar, her father used to say. As much as she despised the old man, there was no forgetting the childhood lessons of right and wrong he seared on her backside.

"Virgo the Virgin." Herbie clapped and pointed, as if she were some freak in a carnival sideshow.

Ginger winced, her breathing constricted all of a sudden. She covered with a taut curve of the mouth.

"Do me a favor, will you?"

He licked his lower lip and waited.

"Don't tell me your sign."

Guffawing, he parked his cigar and grabbed her hand between his two fat paws. "So what was it like?"

"What was what like?"

She felt him finger-fucking her right palm, the one with the orange and purple phoenix tattoo on her inside wrist. Inked deep and ragged the first time Dante was in the hospital. For years the needle took her mind off things. Different needles, different "doctors," depending on the time of day and night. All substances welcome, ingested or swallowed, she was an equal opportunity addict. Until God and the social workers took her son away. That's when she got sober. Ginger swore on her dead mother's soul she'd never lose custody of her son again.

"You know, posing in the mansion…skinny-dipping in the grotto with Hef and his pals…whatever shit you gals do."

The drunker they got, the more profane and disgusting. She stopped taking it personally a long time ago. Four minutes to go, the white-gloved Mickey Mouse hands on her left wrist promised, only four minutes.

"You mean with all those men watching?" She pulled out of his grip and removed the empty glass, taking perverse satisfaction in making him sweat. "All those bright lights on my bare tits?"

He sucked in his breath, blisters of perspiration erupting across his forehead like a bad case of teenage pimples. Pop. Pop goes the weasel. Ginger's outlaw instinct reared with a reckless vengeance. This time he would not get what he wanted.

"Well, I'll tell you. It was cold. Damned cold. My nipples stood up like little tin soldiers and my pussy hummed 'Summertime' to keep me warm—"

And then the other shoe dropped.

He jumped without warning, a middle-aged Spiderman scrambling across the bar to catch his prey. She was strong and tried to knee her attacker into oblivion, but Herbie was stronger and just as determined. Pulling her left arm free, the one with the Mickey Mouse minute hand now straight up, she grabbed a bottle of Stoli and slammed it across his jaw. Reeling, he howled like a pissed coyote too slow to corner the juicy meal he'd lined up under a full moon.

"You bitch!" He twisted her arm so far back she thought she was going to pass out.

"You goddamned bitch!"

The Stoli slipped from her grip, smashing a wall of fine spirits shelved on the mirrored display behind the bar. Shards of glass exploded into a waterfall of eighty-proof alcohol.

A scream came from somewhere. Did it belong to her? When she was in the maternity ward panting through twenty-two hours of labor, she never heard her own voice. The other mothers were moaning, wailing, pleading for painkillers. Not her, not then. When her boy was born, she closed her eyes and transported herself to another planet far, far away where there was not a weak-willed woman in sight. Another scream wrenched the air. Deeper this time. Primal.

Herbie looked over his shoulder just as the young black man attacked, pummeling his body like a speed bag at Gold's

Gym. Ginger fell back. By the time she found her balance, Dante lost his. Her son lay on the floor, his limbs jerking like a mad marionette.

The first time she saw such a sight was in Vegas, when a high roller on a winning streak suddenly jackknifed into overdrive after tipping her five hundred bucks. He whirled around like a spinning top then collapsed on the poker table. Chips sprayed across a surprised dentist from Des Moines who held a full house, but thanks to Lady Luck, was about to win big because the guy with the royal flush suffered a seizure. What were the odds?

The second time Ginger saw that same strange dance her only child almost died because she was too stoned to know what was happening. Tonight she knew. Kneeling next to Dante, she turned him over just like they taught her. Grabbed the bar towel to elevate his head. Pressed her ear to his heart to make sure he was breathing. And then she felt her hair being torn by its roots as Herbie dragged her from her son's side.

"Please," she begged. "Please!"

Herbie said something, she couldn't make out what. His voice slurred, his head bloodied, he let go of Ginger and staggered toward Dante, the jagged neck of the Stoli bottle in his fist. She lunged for the paring knife next to the limes and thrust it into his chest. He fell forward, impaled on the blade, his aorta severed.

Once Dante stopped seizing, his mother held his hand, helped him to his feet, and explained what needed to be done. Together they carried the body outside behind the brick building that housed the bar. Next to the recycling bin for plastic and empty glass, a dumpster stood ready to be filled with organic garbage. At the shadowed end of the alley, mother and son laid the corpse on top of last week's lettuce. Still weak, Dante stumbled when he climbed out of the dumpster, so she told him to go wait in the car while she finished. She would drive them home as soon as she had a little more time to think everything through.

Ginger worked quickly. Rifling through Herbie's pockets, she pulled out a wad of cash for future emergencies and dug deeper. That's when she struck gold. Her boss's flash drive, ready for the taking. Insurance better than any benefit package. Then she went back inside to sweep up the broken glass and wash down the indigo blue tile where Herbie's blood spilled. His cigar still smoldered in the ashtray next to his monogrammed butane. When she returned to the alley, she carried both, along with a brand new bottle of Chivas. One more for the road. After anointing his body head to toe with twenty-five-year-old scotch, Ginger re-ignited Herbie's last cigar, tossing it along with the lighter into the dumpster. The fire kindled, then burst into flame. Crackling. Consuming. Burning garbage and human remains together in one lovely funeral pyre.

GIDEON, 10 MILES, the highway marker announced.

Shielding her eyes from the glare of the late afternoon sun, she stared straight ahead refusing even a passing glance at the Indian burial mounds. After Ginger's mother was killed in the accident, her old man ordered her to cart the urn over one moonlit night to pepper a trail of white ashes around the ancient rocks. To appease the gods, he hiccuped through drunken sobs, so they wouldn't take his sorry soul too. The day Ginger graduated high school she headed west to college on a drama scholarship and never looked back. Until now...

In her junior year of American history when she still believed what she was told, Mr. B informed their class that the South was the only part of the United States ever occupied by a foreign power—that foreign power being Northern troops under Sherman's command. Mr. B, fifth generation Atlanta-born, knew about such things. Occupation can warp the human mind, he warned. Drain natural spirit and initiative until the defeated take for gospel any humiliation visited upon them. That's how shame takes aim at the occupied heart and never lets go.

Even as a teenager Ginger suspected personal liberation could be tricky business. With bitter years of life experience under her belt, she knew it for a fact. Nobody with the upper hand ever handed out road maps with escape routes marked in bright red pencil. This way to Freedomland, motherfucker. Still. She and her son were alive. Out of L.A. Perhaps hope was too wild a thing to be held captive after all.

She flinched at the sight of a peeling billboard shaped like a super-size piece of cherry pie—"Polly's Piece of Heaven, large enough to serve you, small enough to know you…only eight miles ahead!"—and reassured herself this was the smartest move she could make in their extreme situation.

If there was one thing she understood, it was how to hide. Even if it meant hiding in plain sight, a vision of soft curves and parted lips on a white bearskin rug. Her boss had no evidence, no trail, and no way to identify her or Dante. She was already using a phony ID so guys like Herbie wouldn't embarrass her, have mercy on his rotten ass. He had a mother too, and she regretted that he had to die on her watch. In fact, she'd already asked for the good Lord's forgiveness. Still, never having made the acquaintance of forgiveness in her "family of origin" as they said in her twelve-step meetings, how would she know the fucker if it came knocking on her front door? Not that she had a front door now. Homeless, that's what she was. Why else would her old Corvette head east of its own accord? Maybe she'd find some kind of compensation along the way for all those damn shoes dropped from a falling sky.

"Mom?" Dante stirred. His eyes drifted open, still heavy lidded with drug-like sleep. It was always this way after an episode.

She placed her hand in his. "I'm here."

A bigger cross than a lot of kids had to bear, being the way he was, with no dad to show him how to grow into manhood. Even before he got sick and fell behind in school, classmates teased him without mercy. His father's chocolate skin, her freckles and pale blue eyes—

"Shit."

He came out of nowhere, racing up her bumper like a bat out of hell. She yanked her hand from Dante's, gripping the wheel.

"What's wrong?" Her son twisted toward her.

The siren launched into its maddening whine. This stretch of road always was a speed trap, something else the old man lectured her about ad nauseam and still she managed to earn her first seventy-in-a-fifty-five-mph-zone ticket the day after she got her driver's permit. He never let her forget that one either. Shoveling chicken shit in the hen house for two months to pay him back his lousy one hundred and forty-three bucks. Pissed, she floored the foot pedal like she was running from the hounds of hell, which some might argue she'd been doing for years.

"The cops found his body—they'll put us in jail!" Dante's voice escalated to a fearsome pitch.

"Calm down!"

He started thumping on the dashboard, bug-eyed and wild, like he was about to have another fit. God, he was a sensitive plant. A Rock of Gibraltar one minute, a bowl of mint jelly the next. They were alike that way.

Up ahead the interstate turned into a two lane blacktop until Gideon, she remembered that much. Ginger made a fast exit. So did the highway patrolman, flashing his red light like he was chasing a serial killer, for Christ's sake. Usually she respected perseverance but not in this case. In this case it was her or him, and she made the decision in L.A. two nights ago that self-sacrifice was no longer an option.

Her speedometer climbed from seventy to ninety in a heartbeat. First she passed a rattletrap pickup then a clunky station wagon. Ginger was riding high. Nothing could stop her, not even the big silver semi lumbering over the crest in the opposite lane. The same lane she was now traveling in order to scoot past a kid taking his dad's Corolla out for a spin on the right, the same lane the patrolman was also speeding along, still on her tail.

"Oh my God, oh my God, oh my God!" Dante was screaming now.

The trucker did not blink. He was king of the road, even here in this land of New World pharaohs. Kings, regardless of the century, should never budge from their rightful place. That's exactly what her old man used to believe and look what happened to him.

Ginger veered out of the trucker's path back into her own lane, leaving the patrolman with two choices: collide with the kid in the Corolla or collide with the hard-nosed trucker who would give no ground. A third alternative proved more appealing. He sailed off the blacktop into Earl Hadley's cornfield and sideswiped a two-ton National Harvester at rest on the south forty.

Ginger looked at Dante, hyperventilating at her side. When she reached over, he tried to pull away. She held on, stroking his tense muscled forearm until he could breathe again. Sundown. The pyramids, behind them now, were turning purple against the butterscotch sky. Only a couple more miles to go. Up ahead she could see a half-lit neon sign advertising Polly's Piece of Heaven.

A few minutes later she crawled into a gravel parking lot in front of the pie-shaped café then circled round back. She hid the car behind a stand of weeping willows, thicker and taller than the last time she saw them. In case the patrolman called in her plates, nobody would think to search here at the end of the world. Turning off the key, she felt dizzy. It was time, whether she was ready or not. Time for her long river of regret to run into a greater sea.

She faced Dante. "You hungry?"

"No way, not in that nasty place."

"Regular meals, that's what the doctor said."

"I'll wait for Mickey D's." He stuffed a double wad of Juicy Fruit in his mouth.

The place looked deserted, not like the old days before the car crash took away her mother and left the drunk driver a bitter cripple. Ginger climbed out of her Corvette and walked up the cracked wooden steps. A tiny bell jingled like always when the door opened, but Polly did not exit the kitchen to greet her daughter. No hostess appeared to offer a menu. Johnny Cash's whiskey-throated baritone sang "Folsom Prison Blues" on the jukebox. He seemed to be the only one around.

"Anybody here?"

"We're closed!" the owner called from the kitchen.

"Then why'd you leave the door open?" She looked around, thinking that a woman's touch and a good coat of paint would do wonders.

"Lock it on the way out."

"Not leaving."

An old man in a wheelchair rolled out of the shadows, cradling a shotgun on his knee. "Don't give me any trouble."

"It's your daughter."

The old man squinted behind his bifocals, raising the gun to ward off his intruder.

"My daughter's in California."

"Not anymore."

He rolled closer, staring at the woman in front of him like she was an apparition from the Indian burial mounds.

"My God," he croaked, "Julia Mae?"

The bell jingled. She stiffened then relaxed when she saw it was Dante. They would be safe here, she reminded herself again. Safe.

"Jesus Christ," Dante whispered when he saw the old guy with the shotgun.

"Robbing the cradle now," her father snorted in disgust. "And colored to boot. This the latest no-good bum in your life?"

"No, this is your grandson."

The two men stared at each other.

Shameless! That's what the old man had hissed over the phone after her naked picture hit the magazine stands. You are a shameless woman!

He got that right. The prodigal daughter felt a wellspring of laughter deep inside threatening to break loose. How could she help but take pleasure in bringing the first man and last man in her life together? Too long coming but most miracles were. A kind of Biblical offering, her faithful mother might have called this moment, and that was good enough for her. No question her father used to be an asshole when he drank, but after he got religion to avoid the burning fires of Judgment Day he learned a thing or two about charity. He would take them in. Dante would adapt. And she would be there to protect her son as he protected her. Just because the three of them were broken didn't mean they had to stay that way. All things considered, pride proved a pretty worthless substitute for solace.

"Dante, shake hands with your grandfather."

"Not while he's holding that thing."

She stepped to her father's side, lifted the shotgun from his grip, and placed it behind the counter. He did not object. His grandson's hand grazed his grizzled claw like a soft bullet taking mercy on its mark. The old man did not pull away. The grown daughter wondered how many more pages in the book of hours she and father would suffer through together. Nobody ever knew, that was for certain. Here today, gone tomorrow. And never any warning. When Mr. B ran off with the principal's wife during Easter break, nobody saw it coming. Least of all the sad-sack principal. Before he left town, Mr. B encouraged his favorite student to join the drama club, and she was glad she took his advice.

*Julia Mae, we all got to role play life when the occasion calls for it. That's the only way to get through.*

Her fingers tightened around the flash drive in her jacket pocket, caressing it back and forth against her inked wrist. If Herbie had his life to live over, would he do things different too? A hell of a memory that bastard, up to a point. They had first met at a bachelor party in Rancho Mirage right after she landed in L.A. Three years before she won her shot at immortality with the centerfold. Funny how he remembered the airbrushed goddess—but not the teenage girl who sold her innocence on a desert night under a star-choked sky.

*A pal of mine is having a shindig over the weekend, her agent said, honchos from the business. All you have to do is smile and be friendly. Trust me, this can be a big career move.*

Julia Mae—she was still Julia Mae then—showed up as she was instructed. A curtain of smoke sucked the breath out of her lungs but she stayed. Herbie told her she was special so she stayed. He invited his friends to join the fun and still she stayed. She did not leave. She did not refuse. She did not deviate from the script she'd been given. She performed her part and they paid her for the pleasure. Herbie promised he'd remember her name the next time he lunched with his buddies at the studio. He had a great memory, he said. She had a great memory too. His Cuban cigars, the drunken cronies, their scotch-soaked hundred dollar bills. None of that mattered anymore.

She felt free now. Free as a bird.

# Thump Bump and Dump
## Wrona Gall

Stuart saluted his mirror. Makeup had transformed his young face into a wrinkled old man's. A transparent facial mask puckered spidery veins across his hands. A gray beard covered the cleft in his chin and eliminated the need for texturing a turkey neck. A lift in his left shoe created a marked limp. Mothballs scented his vintage black suit. Padding added a profile-distorting paunch.

His old man disguise was complete.

He assumed a stooped posture and walked to his garage. A spin in his Porsche would be fun, but his mission needed a nondescript vehicle like his white Chevy Nova. Adopting the annoying speed of a geriatric driver delivered him to Good Samaritan's parking lot twenty minutes later. He hung a handicapped parking card over his rearview mirror and limped to the emergency room as if he was looking for someone.

People suffering anything from hacking coughs to blood-stained appendages crowded the room. A man in a wheelchair argued with the clerk at the registration desk. An elderly woman swayed on swollen legs behind him. Not seeing a suitable candidate, Howard sat at the end of the first row of plastic chairs. He placed his straw fedora on the adjacent seat to discourage anyone germy from sitting next to him. When his elbow accidentally touched the tattered magazines strewn across the tan Formica table next to him, he cringed.

Potential patients approached the desk at random intervals. The most interesting was a gangbanger type whose swollen face lolled to one side. His arm tat of a snarling tiger stalking a lion exhibited exquisite detailing of fur and teeth when he flexed his muscle. Which was frequent.

Twenty minutes later, Howard spotted the woman he was anticipating. Large sunglasses on a dark night and her rain-coat's turned-up collar gave her away. Her furtive manner and cowed posture fortified his conviction. She clutched a pink-blanketed bundle to her chest and scurried up to the reception desk.

Howard leaned forward to eavesdrop as she spoke to the receptionist, "I'd like to see a doctor."

"Name and date of birth?"

"Nicole Wilson. June fifth, nineteen seventy-seven." She shifted the blanket to her left arm and reached into her coat pocket with her right hand. "Here's my insurance card and ID. It's my husband's insurance."

The receptionist slid the cards off the counter without looking up and tapped a brisk rhythm on her keyboard. Her fingers stopped midair. Swiveling her chair around, she made eye contact with the woman. "This is your second visit this month."

Turning back, the receptionist scanned the screen. "Actually, this will be your seventh visit in three months." She lowered her voice to a whisper. Howard leaned forward and cocked his head to listen. "Three facial contusions, broken ribs on two visits and a concussion have all been recorded. There's a note on your file from the emergency physician requesting you schedule an appointment with Family Services. Have you seen a counselor?"

Nicole jerked away from the desk. A small cry came from the pink bundle. "I meant to, but I haven't had time. Can I still see a doctor?"

"Yes, we won't deny you treatment, but *please* schedule an

appointment." The receptionist spread her hands out in a gesture of entreaty.

"I will." The woman paled and scanned the crowded room.

Howard picked up his hat and motioned her to take the seat next to him.

"Thank you." She scuttled into the plastic chair. The pink blanket twitched in her arms. She adjusted the folds and revealed a swirl of black curls. Dark eyes stared at him. Drool coated the baby's chin.

Removing a *L.A. Times* from under his arm, Howard pretended to read an article about film preservation. While turning a page, he snuck a closer look at the woman. Makeup caked her face like dried mud. Her bruises still showed in the harsh fluorescent lighting. She kept her eyes down and fingered the baby's curls. He kept his eyes focused on the paper until a nurse called "Nicole Wilson."

When she followed the nurse down a hallway, Howard wandered out to the circular drive and lit a cigarette. Smoking disgusted him, but it provided an excuse for him to loiter without attracting attention.

People trickled in and out of the hospital. Sirens and traffic provided a noisy distraction until Nicole walked out the sliding door with the baby cradled against her left shoulder. A sling supported her right arm.

Now to identify her abuser. Howard ground out his cigarette and ambled toward the street. Nicole crossed Wilshire. He followed her up 6th. The Friday night crowd concealed him as he kept her in view.

He stepped off the curb at the first cross street. Loud bangs made him jump back. Not soon enough. A skateboarder crashed into him. The pimple-faced idiot knocked him to the ground. He was about to attack him until he remembered he was supposed to be a feeble old man. He gasped for breath. "You almost killed me."

"Never saw you." The skateboarder retrieved his board and reached down to pull Howard up with his free hand. Howard accepted the gesture and creaked to his feet. After brushing his hands over his trousers, he tugged at the hem of his jacket and rubbed his face to check his wig and beard were in place. "Just watch where you're going next time." He waved a finger at the young man like an irritated teacher.

"Fuck you." The kid swerved and crossed the street in a choppy lope.

Nicole had disappeared.

The next morning Howard removed the sleeves from a threadbare shirt so he wouldn't swelter inside his broken-zippered windbreaker. Even so, rivulets of perspiration trickled down his back into his stained jeans. He knotted the ragged shoelaces of his thrift store shoes and studied his appearance in his full-length mirror. Definitely a street person to be avoided. By the time he hiked to 6th Street, he'd even reek. He added a grimy Cubs hat from his last hometown to complete his costume for the day.

Even though his movie-mogul neighbors seldom ventured out before noon, Howard studied the surveillance cameras surrounding his new home. Not a person in sight. He meandered down the street. His appearance guaranteed anonymity. People didn't notice the homeless.

Sun barely pierced the morning sky when he took up reconnaissance on the block where Nicole had disappeared. The neighborhood was gentrifying, but the litter and debris of the blighted neighborhood enabled him to blend in. Street people melted out of the trees from a vacant lot to his right. An occasional jogger passed by. Two green-scrubbed medical types joined the exodus from home to work.

Howard's face maintained the blank, mindless stare of a street person. He spied a three-legged office chair outside a chain-link fence and dragged it over to the vacant lot. After substituting a rock for the missing leg, he settled in and pulled an apple from his pocket. Sweet juice trickled down his chin.

An emaciated man hobbled out of a row of bushes and eyed the fruit. Tattered rags seemed to hold him together. "Get outta here. This is my spot." A belligerent scowl marred his face.

Howard hadn't anticipated confrontation. He raised his hand in a "stop" gesture. "Sorry. I'm not moving in on you."

"Go away. Go. Go." The man's howls were loud enough to attract the attention of a woman in a gray business suit. She looked over at the lot, hesitated, and quickened her steps.

Howard manhandled the street person into the shadow of the trees. "Listen. I have a bottle." He rummaged through his windbreaker's pouch. "And a Snickers." He shoved them at the man. "Here. Find a new place for today. Okay?"

The rheumy eyes wandered until they focused on the wine. "I gotta listen to a god-save-me talk?"

"Absolutely not. Free and clear. Just a favor for a favor."

The man clutched the bottle and hid it under his shirt. "Gimme that." He grabbed the candy, ripped off the wrapper and chewed his way toward Wilshire.

Howard returned to his surveillance. A woman in ridiculously high heels pranced down the sidewalk. An hour passed before two men in business suits exited different buildings, followed by a woman walking a retriever. He chugged from a water bottle.

When Nicole appeared in the entrance of a dilapidated three-story building, he suppressed a triumphant smile. Shoulders slumped, eyes glued to the sidewalk, she leaned on a baby stroller like it was a geriatric's walker. Her slow progress accentuated her air of despair.

Now that he had Nicole's address, he could identify her abuser. Unfortunately, hours passed, but no one else emerged from the building. Either the abuser was a lazy bum or an early riser. Concealing himself behind a row of bushes, he shed his costume and revealed running shorts and a blue Lakers T-shirt. Using tissues to wipe the dirt off his face, he slid on mirrored sunglasses.

Running like a sports freak, he arrived home forty minutes later for a well-deserved shower. Steam enveloped his marble bath by the time he felt clean. An Armani suit accessorized with white shirt and Gucci loafers transformed him into a corporate director of a management company. After adjusting his blond wavy wig, he slipped "Howard Green, Residential Consultant" business cards into his wallet and walked to the closest You Haul All.

The neighborhood deteriorated until he negotiated cracked sidewalks covered with broken glass and tattered papers. Derelict buildings outnumbered a few ramshackle houses. His destination displayed a rusted array of one-mile-from-the-junkyard vehicles.

Howard pushed open the door. The clerk leaned over the counter like he wanted to advertise his Trump comb-over. His reading glasses landed on top of a newspaper folded back to the want ads. "What can I do you?"

"I need a small truck. What are your rates?" Howard pulled his wallet out of his pocket to show he was ready to make a deal.

The clerk rubbed a scraggly eyebrow and pulled a paper smeared with coffee stains from under the counter. Howard scanned the columns. "Four hours, thirty bucks. Here's a fifty. If you throw in that big carton," he pointed to a refriger-ator sized box, "you can keep the change."

"Thanks, bro, but I gotta see a license."

Howard slid his license-of-the-day across the counter.

Comb-over copied the information onto an old scratch pad. A liver-spotted hand pocketed the money and tossed a Snoopy keyring on the counter. "Take the brown one in space six."

* * *

Howard parked on 6th Street with a clear view of Nicole's apartment. Boring hours crawled by until the sky darkened. He shifted positions on the cracked vinyl seat and alternated arm and leg stretches until Nicole appeared. A short, muscular man who shared the black curls of the infant he had seen in the emergency room, walked next to her. He barreled up to and unlocked a burglar-barred door. It banged open against the stroller. Nicole held it back with her foot and pushed the buggy inside.

Lights appeared in a second floor window a few minutes later. Approaching the entryway, Howard studied the residents' names. He buzzed Ken Wilson in Unit 2A and heard, "Who the fuck are you?"

Howard's well-rehearsed spiel rolled off his tongue. "Good evening. I'm Howard Green, Residential Consultant for the Building Management Association. I'm here at their request to conduct a satisfaction survey. All information will be kept strictly confidential. Do you wish to participate?"

Static garbled Ken's voice. "I sure as hell do. Those bastards stick their noses where they don't belong. Like a dog at a crotch." A buzzer released the lock.

Of course a bully wanted an audience. Howard smirked and stepped over the stained circulars on the lobby floor. By the time he climbed the linoleum stairs to the second floor, Ken was pacing the hall. He spoke even before Howard offered his card. "Nicole, get out here. You gotta hear this." A Mr. Personality smile slipped onto the man's face when she entered the hall. He wrapped his arm around her shoulder. She flinched.

After listening to a short tirade, Howard thanked Ken and returned to the You Haul All. He climbed into the cargo area and changed into a black polo shirt, black jeans and a brown shaggy wig. A rough scrubbing reddened his cheeks to a wind-burned flush. Large tortoise-shell glasses over a droopy moustache disguised the rest of his face.

Slouching back into the driver's seat, he settled in to wait. His phone alarm buzzed an hour later. He exited the van, strode over to his target building and palmed the buzzers. He ignored a scratchy old lady whine from 3B. The next voice brought a grin to his face. Scum 2A.

"Sorry to bother you, but you're the only guy who answered. I need a hand getting a box on a dolly. I'll give you twenty bucks if you just tilt it off the truck. Five minutes tops. On my mother's grave."

"I ain't walking down for a fuckin' twenty bucks."

"Sorry, I meant forty." Howard held his breath.

"That's more like it. I'll be down." The intercom clicked off.

Excitement flooded through Howard when Ken lumbered out the door and approached the You Haul All. He held his knock-out gloves at his side. "Want a pair? Protects the cuticles."

Ken snorted. "Hell no, but I'll take the forty."

Howard slipped on his gloves before he handed over two twenties. "It's back here." He scanned the street before hurrying around the truck and rolling up the door. "If you could just hop in and shove?"

Ken grunted and grabbed the side of the truck to climb into the cargo area. Howard raised his right hand. He slammed his fist against the abuser's head. Blood splattered in the best Pollock tradition.

Drops peppered Howard's face. He gagged, but still managed to shove Ken's body into the truck. Howard crumpled against the fender. His eyes opened to a bloody pool. The puddle repelled him. Gasping, he forced his hand against the abuser's neck. A pulse.

Damn. The knock out gloves he'd bought online had almost guaranteed a lethal punch. Howard scrubbed his face with his sleeve and clanked the door shut. His hands shook the entire half-hour drive to the abandoned lot he'd found on his way to the You Haul All.

A quick scan out the side windows and rearview mirror showed nothing but straggled trees, weeds, and trash. Running to the back of the truck, he threw open the cargo door and dragged the sticky mess onto the ground. The head made a splat when it struck a rock.

He jumped into the driver's seat and revved the engine. The truck shot backward. Tires crunched the body. The impact rocked the truck, jarring Howard against the door. He didn't mind. The noise reminded him of the pleasant *thump* when he'd smashed the abuser's skull.

He kept driving.

Three blocks east, he ran over a curb and slammed on his breaks. Pretending to be disoriented by the crash, he left the headlights on and stumbled out of the truck. A refrain of "Bump, Thump, Dump" flitted through his mind while he lurched across the lot. His steps matched the cadence.

He tripped over a rotted mattress and crashed onto the moldy cloth. Repulsion from touching the disgusting surface flashed him back to the worst night of his life. The night that made him flee Chicago and move to L.A.

The minister had called and informed him that his wife had been found on the Ladies Room floor of their church. An empty prescription bottle lay next to her body. She had left a note: *I prefer death to Howard.*

There hadn't even been much of an investigation. The note in Francine's handwriting and the ingestion of her own prescription with no evidence of external force had been conclusive. Francine's death was officially ruled a suicide.

Still, speculative looks, cancelled dinners, and unreturned phone calls from their social group seemed to accuse him of causing Francine's death. Like her depression was his fault. She had known what he expected when they married.

He wanted a trophy wife to indulge his sexual eccentricities. She wanted a Platinum Visa. It wasn't his fault she reneged. She could have left him. So she wouldn't get a dime. She'd signed the pre-nup.

Still, the social isolation had worn on him. He began to wonder if he had been overzealous in his demands. Twinges of guilt accelerated to sweat-soaked nightmares. On his third sleepless night, he put his executor in charge of his estate and took a limo to Midway Airport. He booked a ticket on the next flight and ended up in the entertainment capital of the world.

L.A. embodied a trend-setting dynamic that challenged people to do more, be more, experience everything. This vibe inspired him to reinvent himself, to overcome his melancholy by rescuing an actual victim. Not some wimp like Francine who threw a bottle of pills down her throat. Local scavengers would have boosted his rental van by now. The thieves were probably barreling down the 101, oblivious to the bloody cargo area. An abandoned house loomed in front of him. The rotted porch, a strong wind away from collapse, creaked under his footsteps. He ducked under the sagging doorframe. Testing the floor with each step kept him from crashing through the wood. After scrubbing every inch of exposed skin with antiseptic, he tossed his wig, moustache and costume onto a pile of garbage.

He smoothed the wrinkles out of his second layer of clothes, a Lakers T-shirt, cargo shorts and flip flops and dug a candle out of his pocket. He lit the wick and wedged it into his trashed belongings. In a few minutes, Howard Green would be incinerated. He'd again be Stuart Evans, L.A. cool guy.

Walking toward a glow of neon lights, he texted an Uber to take him to The Grove. This atonement stuff really made him hungry. He craved a juicy cheeseburger oozing bloody grease.

# Hired Lives
## Cyndra Gernet

*Monday Morning*

From his easy chair beside the Philco, Milton stared at the *Los Angeles Times*, his pale face sagging toward the headline, "Fifteen Million Americans out of Work."

"This should make it easy to find a couple willing to work for us, Maude. I've written an ad. What do you think?" He ran a hand through his thinning hair, and read from the tablet he held: "Wanted: Adventurous middle-aged couple for unusual long-term employment opportunity. Must be discreet and morally flexible. Library background a plus."

Maude settled her reading glasses atop her head, shifted her bulk, and peered at her husband of twenty-five years. "Mmm, is that the best you can do?"

"I thought it rather good. What would you write?"

She looked around the small living room crowded with their comfy yellow armchairs and overloaded bookshelves brought from the bigger house in Maine they'd sold six months ago. She loved the playhouse scale of the room. Like a child, she felt safer in small spaces. This eight-hundred-square-foot cottage was just right. No extra space where evil could lurk. Everything here was bright, open, simple.

"Simple, let's keep it simple," she said. "Just, middle-aged couple wanted for long-term job. When we find the two we want, we can explain it all then."

"So be it." But at the last minute, Milton retained *library experience a plus.*

The ad ran the next day in the *Los Angeles Examiner.*

### Wednesday Evening

Milton spoke around his unlit pipe. "We can't meet everyone who calls. It's just too trying—the crowds, the noise on the street. When we left the house last week, that old man swinging his cane almost broke my kneecap." Milton lifted a haunch and pulled out the newspaper he'd sat on.

Maude nodded agreement. "And the bread lines, so sad. They seem longer every time we go out."

Maude and Milton stared at each other, thoughts sluggish. Before the incident, their brains worked fast. Now they didn't.

"We could hire an answering service to field the calls, maybe do a short interview. Do they do that sort of thing?" Maude asked.

"They might if we made a list of questions. And of course they'll charge more."

"Lucky for us, that's not a problem." Maude took paper from the end table and numbered one through five. "What shall we ask?"

"Well, we have to know what they look like. They should be our general size and coloring."

Maude penciled in "Looks" beside number one.

"And we'll want to know what their previous jobs were."

Maude wrote the job question beside number two.

Milton warmed to this chore. "We could ask them to describe their lives, what they do for fun, what their likes and dislikes are."

Maude added "Interests" to the list, then said, "How about this one—do you have friends and relatives that live near you?"

"That would be good to know." Milton folded the newspaper and set it aside. "And one for me—name your favorite book and the last book you read. And that's our five. What a great idea, Maude. Now we'll only have to meet the few who sound promising. Why didn't we think of this first?"

"Why indeed?"

"I'll arrange things with the answering service." Milton took the list from Maude's hand. "In a few days, we should have several likely prospects."


*Friday Afternoon*

Maude and Milton had finished reading the packet of reports sent by the service. They both loved the interview answers of the fourth couple, Kate and Ed Kellogg, a middle-aged couple who never had children. Recently transplanted from Aurora, they had no family in the area.

Mr. Kellogg previously worked as a library assistant, but he lost that position six months ago. He now worked as a handyman. Mrs. Kellogg was employed as a part-time wait-ress, but her real love was sewing. She had asked to have a personal message attached to the file: *We get a good feeling about you from the ad and your thoughtful interview questions. I know we don't sound terribly adventurous, but we're ready for something new. Please call us. We are very interested.*

"She sounds so honest," Maude said.

"He named Sinclair's *The Jungle* as a favorite book." Milton hesitated, his brow crinkled. "They're not too good to be true, I hope?"

"They sound perfect to me. Let's call them tomorrow."

They held up crossed fingers and shared a smile.


*Monday Afternoon*

"How long shall we wait?" Milton asked. They were

seated in a red leatherette booth at the Last Drop Diner whose neon sign, a dripping coffee cup, cast a red glow on the interior. Customers sat clutching thick porcelain cups, elbows propped on table tops.

"It feels like we've been here forever, but they're only fifteen minutes late." Maude patted Milton's arm. "They'll be here."

And then they were. The pair had entered unseen through a rear door. The woman extended her hand and said, "I'm Mrs. Kellogg, and this is my husband. Sorry we're late."

The couple sat down in a whoosh of clothing. The husband was taller than Milton but not by much. His trousers were crisply pleated, held up by striped suspenders. He removed a fedora and placed it on the table in front of him. Rimless glasses covered tired, deep-set brown eyes.

Mrs. Kellogg removed her gloves and adjusted her hat. Her hands were small and freckled, the nails well kept. Maude got the impression she was vain about them. Mrs. Kellogg's face was middle-aged plain with thin arched eyebrows. Light foundation covered a good complexion starting to droop with the years, much like Maude's. She had medium brown hair cut close to her head, and waved in the current fashion curled around her small ears.

"Would you like coffee, or something to eat?" asked Milton.

A smile spread across Ed Kellogg's face. "We'd lo—" he began, then hesitated when his wife nudged him.

"Our treat," said Milton.

Kate looked at Milton. "Some coffee and biscuits would be lovely, if that's not imposing."

"Coffee and biscuits it shall be," declared Milton, waving over the waitress.

As the order was placed, Maude resumed her study of Kate Kellogg. Her outfit was handsome, evidence that she was an excellent seamstress. She wore a flared, mid-calf-length skirt, topped by a shirred blouse and belted jacket. The suit had been sewn from a Simplicity pattern, if Maude wasn't mistaken. Maude's sartorial scan was second nature after years of sewing and working in women's retail.

Kate returned Maude's scrutiny. "Why don't you tell us about the job? We're dying of curiosity."

Maude sat quiet with her thoughts. She liked how Kate gently took charge of the meeting; her voice, so reassuring.

The waitress, an older woman in a red uniform and overrun white shoes, delivered their order with a smile.

Milton stirred his coffee three times around and took a drink. "You'd be working for us, of course. Part of your job would be to give us a verbal report every evening before you went home."

Kate's eyebrows arched. She waited. When no one spoke, she said, "But what is the job? What work would we do?"

"We will get you jobs—a librarian or assistant librarian for your husband, and department store work, as a saleslady probably, would suit you, Mrs. Kellogg."

"You could get us jobs?" Ed said. "How is that possible? There are no library jobs."

Milton gestured to the basket of hot biscuits. "Why don't you finish eating, and we'll continue our discussion in a more private location. We live right down the street."

The couple exchanged a glance as they slathered butter on the rolls. Milton could tell they were weighing the wisdom of leaving the diner with two strangers. Maude saw the change in their eyes as they decided she and Milton were harmless.

"You want us to do what?" Kate asked forty-five minutes later from the comfort of the yellow chair.

"We want you to live our lives for us," Maude repeated, looking from one face to the other. The room fell silent. Maude felt her heart thump and her face grow hot.

"But why?" Kate leaned toward Maude. "Why don't you want to live your own lives?"

Ed pulled at his chin as if he'd recently worn a beard. "Are you in trouble with the law?"

Milton cleared his throat. "Nothing like that. It's complicated, and painful. We'd rather not explain if you two aren't seriously considering the job. If you would be uncomfortable impersonating us." He reached for Maude's hand.

"Would it be legal?" Kate asked.

"I hadn't considered that," Milton said. "But since we are giving you permission to live our lives, hiring you to do so, I'm not sure there would be a problem."

Ed stood up as if to leave, but circled his chair and leaned over the back. "So how would this work?"

"We'd get you the jobs using our experience and references. You'd earn those salaries, plus we'll pay you extra to report to us what goes on at work every day." Milton studied their faces.

The couple looked at each other, then at Maude and Milton.

"I really need a job. I can't wait to be earning money again, and being useful, of course." Ed beamed.

"And yet it's an unusual request." Kate looked thoughtful. "To live someone else's life. It seems a big responsibility." She looked questions at Maude and Milton.

"Can we trust them with *the incident*?" Maude asked.

"They've trusted us this far, they came here..." Milton let the words dwindle away.

Maude hesitated, then nodded consent.

"Last year we were an ordinary couple like you," Milton began. "But at nine-fifteen p.m., March twenty-third, nineteen thirty-three, everything changed." His hand tightened on Maude's. "Two men broke into our house in Maine. They had revolvers."

"Oh my God," Kate said, shooting Ed another look. "What happened?"

"One man held a gun to our heads, while the other searched for valuables." Milton's voice squeaked high, he swallowed hard. "They moved us from room to room and helped themselves to everything."

"They took my grandmother's silver and my mother's gold jewelry." Maude's face sank beneath the memory.

Ed ran his hand to-and-fro across the chair back. "Who were they? Could you see their faces?"

"No. They wore fedoras pulled low to shadow their eyes and bandanas tied over their noses." Milton pulled an initialed linen handkerchief from his pocket and patted his brow.

"What happened next?" Kate asked gently.

"They went into each room, even the bathroom, left a mess everywhere. The whole time we were afraid they were going to kill us."

"I was sure they were." Maude's voice sounded normal in her ears, but fear squeezed her throat. She imagined herself back in the bedroom again, tied to the bedposts. She had so needed to pee, but didn't dare move because if she even shifted her weight the man beside her would poke the revolver into her breast again. She had prayed that he wouldn't do anything worse. She could see the misery in Milton's eyes as the other gunman restrained him in the doorway.

She felt a soft touch on her shoulder. "Maude, Maude." Milton's face was inches from hers. "It's over, love, we're safe."

Maude wasn't sure she'd ever feel safe again. But she smiled, kissed his cheek, and rose to her feet. "If you'll all excuse me, I need to use the ladies'."

"Will your wife be all right?" Kate stood to follow her, but Milton gestured for her to sit down.

"She just needs a few moments to herself. She'll be fine."

"Are you still in danger? Are you hiding from those men?"

Worry rode Ed's words, but Kate's thoughts raced ahead of his. "Wait a minute. If you are hiding, then we'd be in danger if we assumed your identities."

Milton's face stiffened in surprise. "No, no, that's not what this is about at all. Those—" he shuddered, "—beasts didn't know or want to know who we were. To them, we were just victims to be robbed and tormented. We weren't real people with identities. And, of course, this crime happened on the East Coast. That's why we moved west."

Kate still looked doubtful. "If you're not hiding from them, what are you doing?"

"We're hiding from life. We want to live safe but small, to live by proxy. We've always led a quiet existence. Maude and I are very shy." Milton smiled. "Even before *the incident*, we interacted with the world as little as we could. We rarely went out, had groceries delivered." Milton turned from the others to look out the window, and continued talking in a lower voice. "We don't have family or friends. We never had children."

"But you had jobs?"

Ed's question pulled Milton's attention back into the room. "That was different," he said. "In a job, there's a role to play. Social interaction follows a set script. We could just manage working before the incident, but now..." Milton shrugged his shoulders, shook his head.

Maude entered the room, her hair now tidied. "Now going to a job every day is beyond us." She sat down. "That's why we need you to live the lives we can't, for a while at least." She fumbled her hands in her lap, looked up, the question in her eyes as clear as her words. "Will you live for us?"

"That went well, didn't it?" Milton asked hours later, as Maude prepared dinner. He sat in the breakfast nook shelling peas, while Maude moved back and forth between the refrigerator and sink. "I'm glad the Kelloggs agreed to work for us." The round motor atop the fridge hummed along, punctuated by peas pinging into the colander. "For a while, I had my doubts they'd sign on."

Although Maude and Milton's last house was much bigger than this bungalow, their drafty old kitchen couldn't match this compact, state-of-the-art room. The former owner had loved to cook, and designed the room herself. Square green tiles rose halfway up the walls. A tall-legged Wedgewood stove, in complementary green tones, stood beside a farmer's divided porcelain sink.

"I'm hopeful they'll work out." Maude wrestled two pork chops out of butcher's tissue and waxed paper, held them under water, then patted them dry with cheesecloth.

Milton rattled the *L.A. Times* Want Ads page. "The Los Angeles Library has an opening for an assistant librarian. With my experience on his resume, Ed looks good, but I don't think he could handle a big library. He needs something smaller. Pasadena might work." Ed held out the half-filled colander. "Is this enough?"

"More than enough. Stop shelling, or we'll be eating peas all week." Maude began slicing potatoes into rounds, and placing them in a casserole dish. "What about University of Southern California? Didn't they open a new library a couple years ago?"

"The Doheny Memorial. That would have been a good fit for the old me, but definitely not for Ed. He doesn't strike me as the academic type." Howard came up behind Maude and slipped his hands into the pockets of her bib apron, hooking his chin on her shoulder.

Maude tried to hide the familiar shudder that shook her, by twisting her body aside. Her voice was brusque. "Prepare the meat. I need to get dinner on the table."

Milton nodded, his eyes signaling an apology. Without saying a word, he took a meat mallet from the drawer and whacked the pork chops with such force the breadboard rattled.

A half-hour later, they sat across from each other on the bench seats of the nook. The gold plates looked cheerful atop the green tablecloth with corners Maude had embroidered with baskets of flowers. She shook out a matching napkin and placed it in her lap.

"Where do you think Mrs. Kellogg should apply for work?" Milton waved his empty fork around.

"There's the big stores: Buffums, Bullocks. I think a department store would be best, rather than a small specialty shop. More customers make for a busier day. I wouldn't have been able to handle the pace, but it'll suit Kate."

"Baked pork chops on potatoes." Milton took another bite. "I love your cooking."

"More peas?" Maude scooped some onto his plate. "This is a busy time in retail. Christmas is just months off. We shouldn't have any trouble getting the new Maude Norris hired."

*The Following Month*

"You'll never guess who I checked out today." Ed had been working at the Pasadena Library for three weeks. In his excitement, he sloshed coffee into the saucer he held in one hand as he gestured with the other.

The two couples were seated in front of a warm fire in the Norris's living room. As always, Kate looked put together. Ed, in his new, navy pinstripe suit, struck a professional note. The group gazed at him, waiting to hear the answer.

"Okay, nobody wants to guess, so I'll tell you." He paused, took a drink of coffee. "Upton Sinclair, *the* Upton Sinclair. He's running for governor, you know."

Milton placed his empty coffee cup on the end table. "I hope he does better in this race than he did in his bid for the senate. I'm curious, what book did he check out?"

"I knew you'd ask, so I wrote it down. Just a minute." Ed ruffled his pockets. "Did you know Sinclair lives in Monrovia? Ah, here. The book was called *The Condition of the Working Class in London,* Friedrich Engels, author."

"Interesting choice, but I thought he'd choose a book about the American working class. He is running on a socialist platform, EPIC. Stands for 'End Poverty in California.'"

"Enough politics." Maude said.

At the same time Kate said, "I've waited long enough. I've got exciting news too." Kate wore silk stockings, bought with her first paycheck, no doubt. Maude nodded her approval. Kate waited until all attention was on her. "Mae West came to the store today."

"Mae West?" Maude smiled, smoothing her skirt over her knees.

"Her chauffeur drove right up to this fancy porte cochère at the side of Bullocks so a valet could park the car. But Miss West didn't want to come into the store, so she had the salesgirls bring dresses, shoes, and hats down to her. The men had to carry down a full-length mirror. She shops from her car." Kate looked around the group, triumphant.

Maude clapped her hands. "That is so decadent, it's almost sinful."

"I'm not finished," Kate continued. "Miss West wanted to see gloves and scarves, my department, so I got to take them down to her."

"What did you show her?" Maude's free hand climbed her chest to the pearls she wore and began twisting the strand.

"Everything. I must have made fifteen trips up and back. One of the valets helped me carry, but still. I carried down calf-skinned driving gloves, black silk evening gloves, mink-lined gloves. She ordered a dozen pair of those."

"She didn't!"

"She did, and the scarves, she must have tried on every one in the store. She—" Kate stifled a giggle. "I tied a couple of shorter scarves around her neck, but they looked so small floating on her huge bosom, that we both burst out laughing."

The men smiled. Maude giggled as she pictured the scene.

"Right before the chauffeur drove her away, Miss West motioned me over." Kate mimed bending down to car level. "She gave me a big wink, and said, 'Remember, good girls go to heaven, bad girls go everywhere.'"

The women laughed. Milton rose from his chair. "You each have had an exciting day. We're pleased with your reports. Most amusing."

Minutes later, the door closed behind the departing couple. "Kate and Ed are having so much fun," Maude said.

"They do seem to be enjoying themselves." Milton reached into a pocket for his pipe.

"We'll have to do something about that."


*Later That Week*

Milton finished his call just in time. He turned on the radio to hear the opening commercial for *The Shadow*. *The Shadow*, hah. It used to be a favorite, but after the incident Milton listened with a jaded ear. There had been no daring rescue when Maude and he needed one.

Milton hauled his bulk from the chair, padded down the hall, and knocked softly on the bedroom door.

Maude opened the door a crack. From the pattern dotting the right side of her face, Milton knew she'd been napping atop the chenille bedspread. "It's getting late. Shouldn't you be making that call to Bullocks? I just got off the phone with the library."

A small charge jumped between them, lifting the corners of their mouths into naughty grins.

Maude followed her husband into the front room. Milton lowered the volume on the radio to a murmur and reseated himself facing his wife. She grabbed the phone, stretched the cord to its limit, and perched on a corner of the couch.

She dialed. "Mr. Harris, please. Yes, I'll wait."

From the radio came a low chuckle. "*I am the Shadow.*"

"Mr. Harris, hello. This is a neighbor of Kate Kellogg. She asked me to call to let you know she wouldn't be in to work this week. I should have called you this morning but I forgot." Twisting the telephone cord around her finger, Maude sent Milton a satisfied look.

With a blare of music came the words, "*Remember, don't forget to order Blue Coal, the finest Pennsylvania anthracite. Ask for it by name.*"

"Well, Kate, Mrs. Kellogg, said to say she had a family emergency."

"*Tonight as we sit here, some poor innocent...*" The dialogue coming from the radio competed with Maude's voice.

"But the truth is, she ran off with another neighbor's husband. I really don't think she'll be back at all."

In the silence following Maude's words, the radio crackled, "*No one must ever know.*"

"She did seem nice, didn't she? I could hardly believe it myself...Yes, I'm sorry too. Good luck finding her replacement."

"*The Shadow knows.*" The signature laugh sounded as Milton clicked off the radio.

He turned to his wife. "You're getting quite creative with your explanations. I just told the library Ed had accepted an out-of-state job he had to start immediately and was afraid to tell them."

"That chore is done then. So, we're ready for the final

ceremony. Are you finished in the backyard?"

Milton nodded. "I thought the stitching on this pair of ceremonial garments was particularly fine."

Maude smiled. "Do you think my choice of pink-and-blue shrouds too traditional?"


*Two Weeks Later*

Maude and Milton, propped by pillows, reclined against the headboard of their bed. Late night chill curled around the edges of Maude's newly finished crazy quilt, a swirl of color in the softly lit room.

"Did you remember to change our phone number?" asked Maude.

"I did it yesterday. You have another ad ready?"

Maude fiddled inside the drawer of the bedside table and pulled out a scrap of paper. "How does this look?"

*Wanted: Un-adventurous middle-aged couple*
*for unusual long-term employment opportunity.*
*Must be discreet and morally flexible.*
*Library background a plus.*

# Nut Job
## Sarah M. Chen

Hector Fuentes didn't want to rob his brother. All he wanted was to go inside the mini-mart that he'd been camped outside of for the past half hour and buy a Fruit Punch Gatorade. But he couldn't leave his post. His brother's big rig was due to pull into the Flying J truck stop any minute. He couldn't chicken out or screw up now.

It was all for Marisa. He promised he'd take care of her. A promise his *tia* warned him about.

"You be careful in L.A., *mijo*. Stay with your brother."

Hector didn't want to stay with his brother. He wanted to venture out on his own. When Raul left Chula Vista to haul loads for a big trucking firm in Rancho Cucamonga, Hector wanted to find a job too, but his *tia* said he was already working.

"Your job is to take care of me, *mijo*. The most important job."

Hector wasn't sure about that. He felt useless compared to his brother. The money his parents left behind wasn't going to last forever. His *tia* said it wasn't his time to leave her yet. He'd know when it was time.

Then he met Marisa. It was at a nightclub where she sang, and her voice was like hearing church bells chime. Her curves and long black hair made him want to do crazy things. Like tell her how much he loved her after their third date. Like agree to move to L.A. so she could be the next Christina Aguilera.

"It's time, *tia*," Hector insisted. It was time to leave her and be a man. Prove he could take care of his girl and his *tia*. Prove he didn't need his brother.

But it was much harder to make it in L.A. than he thought. They were already three months behind on rent. Marisa needed things like singing lessons. Money for gas because auditions were all over the place. Los Angeles was a huge city.

"Here's a job, Hector," Marisa would say. She'd circle the ad in the *Los Angeles Times*. "This is one you can do."

Hector believed her. He applied to every single job she circled and landed each one. The problem was keeping the job. At the construction site, they let him go when he refused to climb up the scaffolding. How was he supposed to know he was afraid of heights? He had to quit the gardening job when he discovered a horrible allergy to grass. The restaurant manager fired him after Hector broke more dishes than he bussed. The bartender refused to work with him because at six-foot-six and two hundred thirty pounds, Hector was much too big for a barback. He kept getting in everyone's way.

Marisa suggested he could be a bouncer, but the idea of kicking people out of a club if they got too rowdy terrified him.

He applied at a nursing home—thinking he could at least do that after years of taking care of his elderly *tia*—but they would only hire him as a janitor. The fumes from the cleaning supplies gave him violent sneezing attacks and made his eyes water so badly they told him not to come back, he was scaring the residents.

It wasn't until Marisa tossed the classifieds in front of him while he ate breakfast one morning, did he realize how bad things were. Not a single ad was circled. He looked up at her, cringing at the disappointment in her eyes as he crunched on his Frosted Flakes.

"I don't want to give up on you, Hector, but you don't make it easy. Make me not give up on you."

*Crunch, crunch.* Hector cast his eyes back down into his bowl and swallowed. Marisa sighed and left for her audition.

That was his wake-up call. He had to figure out something fast, or Marisa would leave him. But he had no clue where to start.

Maybe that's why he nodded when Celso and Florentino came over a few minutes later, asking if he wanted to smoke some weed. Normally, he said no. Marisa didn't approve. Said their neighbors were trouble. Hector usually agreed but couldn't stand the thought of moping by himself in his apartment all day.

"Hey, Hector, don't you have a brother here in L.A.?" Florentino asked, taking a hit from a joint before handing it to him. They were all sitting on the couch watching *Judge Judy*. Hector had just told them his situation with Marisa.

Hector puffed on the joint and passed it to Celso. "Yeah. Lives out in Montebello." He knew he could always move in with Raul but he didn't want to. Plus he'd lose Marisa then for sure. She'd insisted on their own place in Westlake, just east of Koreatown. Wanted to be near MacArthur Park although Hector didn't know why. The one time they went, all they encountered were homeless people and aggressive ducks.

Celso took a big hit and held it in. He lurched forward, seized by a violent coughing fit.

"Could you get a job with your brother?" Florentino continued. He glanced at Celso, and pursed his lips in irritation. "Don't take such a big hit if you can't handle it, dawg."

Hector frowned. "I did already. I didn't like it." He didn't want to admit that he'd only had one day of training with Raul, driving his big rig. Another job he couldn't hang on to. Turns out his back seized up when he drove long distances. "I don't need my brother's help."

Florentino snorted. "Your girl doesn't seem to think so."

Hector glared at him.

When Celso finally stopped hacking, he asked, "What's your brother do anyway?"

"Drives a big rig. Hauls stuff."

Celso and Florentino looked at each other. Florentino's eyebrows shot up. He grinned.

"What?" Hector asked.

"I got a guy. Julio. He can unload missing cargo if you know what I'm saying. Electronics and shit." Florentino smiled, revealing sharp little teeth. "Get us a good price."

Hector shook his head. "Raul doesn't haul stuff like that. He hauls a bunch of nuts."

At that, Florentino gave Hector his full attention.

"What?" Hector asked again.

"You know how much a bunch of nuts is worth?" Florentino asked.

Hector shrugged. He giggled. Bunch of nuts. It sounded funny. He must be stoned or something. He couldn't stop giggling.

"I'm serious, dawg," Florentino said. Then Celso started giggling. Florentino looked back and forth between them. His eyes narrowed and his mouth got all twisted.

"Bunch of nuts," Hector repeated in between his giggling fits. Celso was laughing so hard tears streamed down his face.

"Pssh." Florentino was clearly disgusted with both of them. "If you knew how much these nuts were worth, you two *pendejos* wouldn't be laughing so hard."

After they calmed down, Florentino told them. A trailer load of nuts was worth about a hundred fifty grand.

Hector was skeptical. "Naw, come on."

"Some loads are worth even more," Florentino continued. "Like pistachios are half a mil. Almonds, cashews, walnuts. They're about a hundred and fifty K."

Walnuts. Exactly what his brother hauled.

"How do you know all this?" Hector always thought his two neighbors were just a couple of dumb stoners. Boy was he wrong. Well, maybe the stoner part was true.

Florentino shrugged. "Nuts are the big thing now. Julio knows all about it. Easy to steal. Easy to unload." His bloodshot eyes fixed on Hector.

It didn't take too long to come up with the plan to rob Raul. What did take long was convincing Hector that he was the only one who could pull it off. He knew his brother's route. Knew which truck stops Raul frequented and when. He also was the only one who could drive a big rig. Hector had issue with that one though.

"I didn't do shit, man. I sat in the passenger seat the whole time."

Florentino shook his head. "Doesn't matter. You know more about it than either of us do." His eyes were sharp, not missing Hector's reluctance.

Hector sighed, feeling sick. Committing robbery was bad enough, but robbing his own brother?

"Don't feel bad," Celso said, as if reading his mind. "Your brother will be fine. Insurance pays for that shit."

"Think of Marisa, dawg," Florentino added.

That's all Hector needed to hear. Robbing Raul was the only way to keep Marisa happy. They'd be set for the rest of the year—shit, the next two years. She had to get on *The Voice* by then, right?

The sound of gears whining and grinding startled Hector from his thoughts. He sat up and looked at the parking lot entrance. The familiar big rig rumbled along, right on time, turning into the Flying J lot. It pulled up to a spot near the entrance of the mini-mart. His brother, wearing his trademark flannel shirt, leaped out of the cab and headed into the store.

Show time. Hector took a deep breath. His insides churned and his palms were sweaty. He had to keep putting the pistol down and wiping his hands on his jeans. If he sat here too long, Raul would be in and out of the mini-mart and he'd blow his chance. He'd lose Marisa forever.

Hector checked the lot. Nobody else was around. It was early morning so very little traffic came in and out since he'd been waiting here.

"*Que Dios me perdone*," Hector muttered, crossing himself. He thought of his *tia*. He was actually more worried about what she would think of him than God. "*Perdoname, tia*." He crossed himself again.

He was wasting time. Hector shoved his ski mask in one jacket pocket and his gun in the other. He leaped out of his car and quickly crossed the lot toward his brother's big rig. As he reached for the passenger door, he had a moment of panic. What if this was the one time Raul locked the door? He'd be screwed.

But thankfully, the door was unlocked. Hector hoisted himself into the cab and glanced at the ignition hoping to find the keys dangling there. Then he would save himself the misery of sticking up his brother. He could drive off with the load of walnuts and be done with it. But no keys were there.

Hector craned his neck around to look behind the seats. He spotted a portable storage unit wedged behind him. Hector remembered it held random stuff like jackets and tools. A mini-fridge was tucked behind the driver's seat. Behind all that was the sleeper compartment but instead of a nice mattress with a blanket, there were discarded fast food wrappers, empty water bottles, a hammer, a soccer ball, a couple of hangers, and two pairs of work boots.

Raul clearly didn't use the sleeper cab for anything but storage. Made sense since he rarely made cross country trips. Mostly just back and forth between San Pedro and Bob Olson's Walnut Farm in Tulare. Hector cursed himself for not remembering this.

He tried his best to shove everything to the floor. Luckily, beneath the mess was a sleeping bag. He figured he might as well tuck himself into it or else his brother could just glance in the rearview and spot him lying there like an idiot. Hector wormed his way inside the sleeping bag, but it wasn't easy. He finally contorted himself into a kind of extreme fetal position. Then remembered his ski mask.

"Shit."

He sat up and dug around in his jacket pocket for the mask. Remembered his gun in the other pocket. He pulled the mask over his face and went back to his uncomfortable fetal position inside the sleeping bag. He held the gun in his right hand, tucked underneath his chin, hunkering down as low as he could. He was grateful for the lack of sunlight. At six a.m., it was dark enough for the lot to be shrouded in shadow.

He fidgeted, unable to get comfortable. His folded legs were wedged tightly behind the portable storage unit. The top of his head pressed against something hard. Craning his neck around, he saw he was smashed up against a small square window, like half the size of an airplane window. Just as he was about to sit up and re-adjust himself all over again, the driver's side door opened.

His brother stepped inside the truck and settled himself behind the wheel. Hector saw him place a large Styrofoam coffee cup in the cup holder. A paper bag rustled, most likely Raul's breakfast burrito. The scent of beans and cheese proved him correct. Hector prayed his stomach didn't growl because Raul would surely hear it. He could hear chomping and then a loud burp.

*Come on, come on, start the engine.*

Hector had Raul's schedule timed perfectly. His brother's next stop would be just north of Magic Mountain, in the small town of Castaic. About an hour and a half south from where they were now. Raul would have to take a piss from the large coffee he just bought, and his favorite truck stop was there. The one with the clean bathrooms and the pizza rolls he liked. As soon as the truck slowed to exit for the truck stop, Hector would leap up from the sleeper cab and stick the gun into his brother's neck. He'd say in his best Clint Eastwood impression, "Get out of the truck or I'll shoot." He'd leave Raul on the freeway shoulder and haul ass down to San Pedro to meet Julio. Exchange the walnuts for a hundred and fifty grand. After splitting the money with Celso and Florentino, Hector would be left with fifty K. He'd be able to buy Marisa her own recording studio if she wanted.

Castaic was a perfect place for the hold-up because it was a quiet rural town in the northwestern part of Los Angeles County. Mostly a passing point for travelers and truckers along the I5. Raul would have a tougher time finding help down there than say, the San Fernando Valley or downtown L.A. At least that's what Hector hoped.

It was starting to get stuffy and hot in the sleeper cab. The extra insulated sleeping bag plus Hector's jacket plus the ski mask with no mouth hole didn't allow much ventilation. Sweat dampened his upper lip and underneath his arms.

The engine roared—thank God—and after a few seconds, the truck crept forward, turning right. Hector tried to settle into the sleeper compartment as much he could, but between the fear of making too much noise and having no room to do anything but shove his head further into the tiny window, he was stuck.

The tractor cruised along what Hector knew was Highway 99 and then soon Raul would merge onto the 5, headed south for Los Angeles. His brother burped every few minutes and slurped from his coffee cup. Otherwise, it was a fairly dull ride.

After about an hour and a half, the truck slowed and Raul put his blinker on. Hector knew that was his cue. Only problem was his right leg had fallen asleep. He tried to stretch it out but didn't have enough room. Wriggling around, he tried to wake it up but nothing was working. He pressed his head into the window so his chin practically tucked inside his neck. This gave him enough space to stretch out his leg just a bit f-u-r-t-h-e-r and ah, yes, he felt the blood rush through his calf and right foot. All the way to his toes.

Then the pins and needles hit and *oh Dios mio!* He hated the pins and needles. *Oh Dios mio! Oh Dios mio!*

Hector didn't know if he screamed this out loud or what, but suddenly Raul whirled around and stared right at him. A strangled cry. Hector wasn't sure if it came from Raul or himself. The tractor brakes shrieked and Hector's head slammed into the mini fridge. He struggled to lift himself upright just in time to see his brother grab something from a compartment above the rearview mirror and point it at him. Holy shit, it was a gun.

Raul fired and Hector screamed. Was he hit? He couldn't tell.

"Raul, it's me!" His voice was muffled thanks to the ski mask. He tried to yank it off but the stupid sleeping bag had him all tangled up. Like a strait jacket.

The truck lurched to the left. Hector thrashed around in the sleeping bag. His pistol fell to the floor.

Raul spotted it and his eyes widened. He fired again.

"Raul, wait!" Hector felt a sharp pain in his ear. He shrieked. "Shop shooting at me!" He finally freed one of his hands and yanked the ski mask off. Fresh air hit him and he breathed in deeply.

Raul's mouth fell open. Hector had never seen him look so freaked out before.

"Hector, you stupid *pendejo*. What the fuck are you doing back there?" Raul swiveled back around and shifted the gears again. The truck lurched to a stop.

Hector put his hand up to his right ear and felt sticky wet stuff.

"Oh shit." Raul clambered over the gear shifts to Hector. He moved Hector's hand and inspected the side of his head.

"I think the bullet just grazed your ear. You're lucky I'm a horrible shot. You gonna be fine."

Hector tried to sit up. Raul pushed him down. "Lie down. I'll get help." Raul's face darkened and his voice turned sharp. "What the hell were you doing, you stupid *cabron*?" He whacked Hector on the side of the head and Hector yelped. "What'd you have a gun for, huh? You planning on killing me?"

"No, no," Hector said. "It wasn't even loaded."

Raul shook his head, made a noise out of the side of his mouth. "I'm gonna call nine-one-one, okay?"

Hector nodded. He thought of something. "Why'd *you* have a gun?"

Raul pulled out his phone. "We've been having so many cargo thefts lately. Kern County Sheriff formed a task force and everything." He shrugged. "So I got me a gun just in case." He glared at Hector. "Didn't think first time I used it, it'd be on my little brother." He snorted. "Stupid *pendejo*." Raul tore his flannel shirt off and pressed it against Hector's ear. "Here, hold that down, okay? We need to stop the bleeding."

Hector did what Raul told him. He pressed the flannel against the side of his head. Part of the shirt flopped over his face. He breathed it in. It was soft and warm. Smelled like Raul. He heard Raul talking to someone. Hopefully 9-1-1.

Hector closed his eyes. The pain in his ear had dulled somewhat but he noticed that it became more and more difficult to breathe. Like he couldn't get enough air into his lungs. Hector gasped and choked. Maybe he was actually shot in the lungs. Raul re-appeared over him, concerned.

"The paramedics are on their way. Hector, you okay? What's wrong? You don't look so good."

Hector moved his hands to his throat. "I—can't— breathe." His breaths came out in little rasps.

"You were doing fine a second ago. Now your lips are blue. What the hell did you do?"

Hector clutched his chest. It felt like someone was sitting on it, pressing down hard. He felt Raul's hands all over his torso. "Why can't you breathe, man?"

Hector shook his head. *How the hell was he supposed to know?*

Raul's expression changed. Like he knew what was going on. "Oh shit. This happened to *tia* when we were kids."

*What? What?*

"The nuts, man. You two have the same allergy. She couldn't breathe. Just like this. Where's your EpiPen, Hector? Gimme your EpiPen."

Hector didn't know what an EpiPen was. He shook his head but that made everything blurry. He felt woozy. "But—I—didn't—eat—nuts." It was a struggle to talk.

Raul snatched his shirt from Hector's grip. "My shirt, man. The one I always wear at the nut factory. It's covered in nut dust." He threw it on the floor.

Nut dust. Now that was funny. Nut dust. Hector giggled but all that came out was a strangled wheeze.

Nut dust. Celso would sure appreciate that one.

Hector would have laughed too if only everything would stop spinning. And if he could get some air into his lungs.

# Crime Drama/Do Not Cross
## Melinda Loomis

"I can't eat, I can't sleep, I feel sick all the time. He keeps leaving messages on my voice mail. Not outright threatening, but just enough to make me uncomfortable. And text messages, and I had to lock up my Facebook account…"

We'd already had this conversation. Chloe had a tendency to repeat herself, as if she doesn't think you realize the gravity of this situation. But it was all in my file, which contained the novel-length emails she'd sent me with every minute-by-minute detail of her relationship with Charlie Brendan, from the sickeningly sweet, cute meet, to her discovery that he cheated on her with just about anything with a pulse and two X chromosomes, and had been doing it for quite some time.

"I'll contact him by phone first," I explained to her as she sniffled over coffee I'd insisted on ordering. We had to order something. You can't just show up at a coffee shop and take up room without ordering something. Plus, I'd been on a major bender as of late and needed caffeine to get through this conversation. Chloe just needed something to do with her hands while explaining the sad state of affairs.

While she fiddled with her coffee mug, I told her, "A lot of times, just knowing that someone is investigating them is enough of a wakeup call to get them to back down. If that doesn't work, I'll show up at his house and have a friendly chat with him. Next up is his place of work and he won't want that, so that should be the end of it." She nodded along.

We were getting up to leave when I remembered one last thing. "Do me a favor, Chloe. You have got to resist the urge to respond to his messages. Just don't do it. You need to go radio silent while I handle this. Engage, and you're playing his game. Can you do that for me?" She nodded some more. It didn't strike me as particularly emphatic. I wondered how long she'd hold out.

I handed Chloe my card, which she clasped delicately between her forefinger and thumb while wiping away a tear with the back of her hand. *Alexandra Jones*, read the card. *Private Investigator*. But Chloe already knew that. She had tracked me down, sought me out to help her with her problem: a typical jerk ex-boyfriend making empty threats. In my experience, exes are big talkers, but unless they were abusive in the first place—in which case I send the client straight to the police—my experience has been that it's just a truckload of hot air. Little big men mouthing off because they can. Personally, I blame the Internet for creating a generation of keyboard and smartphone idiots who think they can say anything and get away with it as long as they're not doing it face-to-face. The vast majority back down when actually confronted by a real person and not a computer screen.

Then she thanked me so pathetically it made me think of an abused puppy. She gave me a sad smile. "You have no idea how much I appreciate you being able to do this."

I shook her hand firmly, and with my other hand parked my trademark fedora firmly on my head. Despite my still pounding headache, I looked her right in the eye and gave her my go-to slogan: "Consider it done."


Sixteen years went by so fast.

This will be the final season of the first and now last remaining version of the *PI*s—you know, the *PI: Private Investigator* shows. After hearing the news, I went on a self-medicating bender to ease the pain. There went my chance to be on the show of my dreams. How did it go by so fast?

My Hollywood dream was going as planned when I hit town in 2001. Why does that number feel so archaic? It doesn't feel like it was all that long ago that 2001 was downright futuristic. Straight outta Phoenix, not that far really in terms of distance. I didn't even have to get on a plane, just got in the car and didn't stop until I saw the Hollywood sign. But it was like I'd arrived on another planet. I found an apartment on a side street off Hollywood Boulevard, a little hole-in-the-wall place, more like a hotel room with a kitchen, but it was right in the thick of it. Sort of. Back then the Hollywood renaissance was still under construction. They were still working on the subway and Hollywood & Highland hadn't opened yet. In fact that part of town was considered kind of a dump. I didn't care. It was Hollywood and it was where I wanted to be. I reveled in my Hollywood address.

Prior to my move, when I was finishing up what my family and friends all considered a worthless drama degree, a new show debuted. It was a mid-season afterthought that nobody expected anything from. Nobody at the network, anyway, but *PI: Private Investigators* was an instant hit with a lot of people. About twenty-five million people per week, in fact, including yours truly. I was a huge fan. If I'd had any doubts about pursuing an acting career, which I didn't, that show would have put any remaining concerns to rest. It was so popular that in the next few years it produced two spinoffs.

Its richly diverse cast of characters was headed by former LAPD homicide detective Stephanie "Stevie" Armstrong, champion of those whom the system had failed and who needed someone to pursue justice on their behalf. Like every good hero, Stevie had a personal philosophy that guided her passion for her work: "Everyone deserves justice." Stevie said it all the time, to anyone who would listen, repeated it like a mantra. She left no one behind.

The original show was set in L.A., and over the years I often saw them filming around town, especially when they were doing a Hollywood-based episode. Some of the ones I actually saw being shot were "Director's Cut" (Season 2, Episode 20), "Famous Idiots" (Season 5, Episode 12), "Shot on Location" (The Season 7 finale/cliffhanger), "$#I! My Costar Says" (Season 10, Episode 14), and "Neither This Noir That" (Season 13, Episode 9). Bunch of others too, but those were some of my favorites. And as I learned my way around the City of Angels, playing "Spot That Location" became more and more a part of my obsessive *PI* viewing experience.

And now it's all ending. And I never got to be a part of it. I'd been drinking pretty much nonstop since I heard the awful news.


By the time I got home from my meet-up with Chloe, my head and stomach felt a bit better and I realized I was going to have to be sober long enough to get through this case. I figured it would only take a couple of days. Then I could get back to mourning the loss of *PI*.

I sent Charlie Brendan his first warning, using the email address Chloe had provided. You would think it would have tipped her off that he probably wasn't the monogamous type:

*To: goodtimecharlie69@aol.com*
*From: ZanJonesPI@yahoo.com*
*Re: Chloe Bale*
*Dear Mr. Brendan:*
*I have been retained by Chloe Bale in regards to your ongoing harassment of her.*
*She has provided me with copies of emails and social media messages you have sent her, as well as transcripts of voice mail messages you have left for her. After reviewing*

these messages, I agree with Ms. Bale that they are harassing in nature. At the least, they are causing my client physical and emotional stress. At worst, they could be construed as potentially threatening.

This is an official notice requesting that you immediately and permanently suspend any contact with Ms. Bale, in person, via email, telephone, social media or any other avenues of interaction.

This is the only "request" you will receive. Your harassment of my client is actionable, and if you refuse this polite request, action will be taken.

Please respond to this email within 48 hours to confirm that you will no longer be contacting or harassing Chloe Bale.

Thank you,

Alexandra Jones

Private Investigator

He didn't have to know I'm not former LAPD like Stevie Armstrong. He also didn't need to know that in actuality, my real-life private investigator cases were few and far between, and pretty benign in nature. Life isn't like television, you know, and this wasn't my first choice of career. In a situation like this, usually just the suggestion that this could become a legal problem is enough to get a person to back off. Pretty simple stuff, actually.

I couldn't figure out why I wasn't breaking in. I could get agents but couldn't keep them. I went on auditions but couldn't get a callback. The one big break I had was a national cookie commercial. National spots are big bucks, and I lived off that one for over a year. And yet, even with all that free time to devote to my career, nothing happened.

My agent advised me to stick to commercials. He thought he could get me some work, but I didn't want to hawk cookies or anything else. I didn't even want to be myself. I wanted to be Alexandra "Zan" Jones, PI to the unfortunate and downtrodden of Los Angeles, alongside Stevie and the team, and if not them, at least alongside brooding, justice-obsessed Winston Cole of *PI: Chicago,* or former marine Zack Miller and the dedicated team of *PI: Dallas.* But preferably the mothership.

I created Zan for myself when I decided to do the PI thing for real. It was about eight years ago. I had ordered new checks through the mail but they never arrived. They had mysteriously vanished somewhere between the bank and my apartment. But whoever took them cleaned out my bank account. Once I figured out what had happened, the bank reversed all the transactions, but there were a couple days where I was freaking out. Then I got a call that solved the mystery. It was about one of my checks that had been returned, a check that the thief used to try and make a car payment. I explained to them that my checks had been stolen and that I hadn't written the check at all. They were kind enough to let me know who owned the car and where she lived.

Her name was Donna Hagen and she lived in my apartment building. At last I was going to have that big gotcha moment, just like on crime shows. In retrospect, it was probably a bad idea because I had no idea if she could get violent, but I went to her door and rapped on it with the same officious urgency that Stevie Armstrong always uses to let the person of interest on the other side know that she might be a woman, but she was a formidable woman in charge of the situation. In this case a formidable woman who was going to cheerfully introduce herself, ask for the rest of her checks, and enjoy the resulting deer in the headlights expression when Donna Hagen realized she was busted. I was a human smoking gun.

You would have thought she would have been cautious

about opening her door to a stranger, given that she was ripping off someone who lived just one floor and a couple doors away. Maybe she was expecting someone, because she swung the door wide open and looked at me expectantly. It was a moment of absolute euphoria.

I gave her a dazzling smile and introduced myself. "So, Donna. The thing is you have my checks and I want them back."

She almost pulled it off and, as an actress myself, I had to give her at least some grudging credit for that. But before the poker face could slam into place there was a split second jolt when Donna realized I was on to her. I loved it.

"So, if you'd go get the checks, that would be great." I was giving a hell of a performance myself.

She shook her head insistently. "You're looking for my roommate. She split a couple weeks ago." Then she slammed the door in my face.

"Riiiiight," I bellowed at the door.

It turned out that Donna had been ripping off several people, both in our building and elsewhere. She feigned innocence and blamed it all on her non-existent roommate. Months later we got to testify against her in court. But for me that moment at her door was the high point of her getting busted. I had solved the crime and it felt fantastic.

"Everyone deserves justice," I announced as I turned away from Donna's door. I had just gotten mine, and it was so, so sweet.

The only thing missing from the experience was not having a badge or some sort of accreditation to wave in her face, like they do on TV. Nonetheless it was a high that lasted for days, and I decided I could see myself doing that kind of work in real life, at least until I could get the acting career in gear.

So I became Zan.

A crapload of paperwork (part of which—the prior experience requirement, I fudged), background check, and one state exam later, I had my PI license. No one questioned that I was changing my name at the same time. I concocted the story that I was an actress trying to remake myself to try and jumpstart my comatose career, and that was the end of that conversation. Apparently I wasn't the only one who thought Alexandra "Zan" Jones was a lot catchier and more dramatic than Susan Cooper. I bought my first fedora and started wearing it twenty-four-seven, and gave myself a catchphrase for good measure. I figured it would all come in handy when I finally got on the show.

Because, you see, it was also a calculated career move. I hoped that in addition to getting to be Zan, eventually I could solve a high enough profile case to make the news. My plan was that the novelty of casting an actress who was a real-life PI on a show about PIs would prove irresistible to the *PI: Private Investigators* producers and network, and I would be in.

If I was being perfectly honest, I didn't really want to deal with Chloe, who has texted me twice and left a voice mail to boot despite my telling her she'd hear from me in a couple of days. You'd think she would know how annoying it is to be hounded like that. Maybe they deserved each other. Charlie and Chloe, how sweet. Bet Chloe thought it was adorbs back when things were still all kissy-face between them. I wondered if they'd have given all their kids "C" names just to be cute if things had worked out differently.

I'd much rather be cracking cases with Stevie and the team than dealing with Charlie and Chloe and their crap. The loss of this show was killing me. I'd come to the realization much earlier that I prefer that reality, that life, even if it only exists in my imagination, to my own. And now it was going to vanish forever. Stupid network. With both Chicago and Dallas cancelled last season, that world was now gone forever. A world I just wanted to immerse myself in, the Los Angeles world of *PI: Private Investigators*.

\* \* \*

Guess who didn't respond to my email.

It wasn't hard to find Charlie's house in Pasadena. Chloe's directions were good, it was just off Lake Street, one of the main drags through town. Nice house, too. Family money, according to Chloe, and she had begged me not to let him buy me off. Chloe didn't come from money and would be making payments.

Given how big the house was, I was half-expecting a butler to answer the door. But no, it was Charlie himself, looking just like he did in the picture Chloe had given me. He didn't seem unhappy to see me. I got the impression that he wouldn't be unhappy to see anything remotely female show up at his door, and that quite possibly he was used to it.

I was pretending to flip through my file on him when the door swung open. When it did, I quickly closed the file and waved the wallet that held my official PI license and my not-so-official National Private Investigators badge (thirty-nine dollars on Amazon). I also made a point of shrugging my jacket so he could get an eyeful of my sort of realish-looking sidearm (actually a starters gun that only fires paper caps, twenty-five bucks on eBay).

"Hi, Charlie," I said, because Stevie was always telling the team that calling someone by their first name makes the exchange seem more casual and therefore comfortable, and also might lull them into a false sense of security. "I'm sorry to bother you at home, but you didn't respond to my email, so I thought it might be more effective to discuss this situation face-to-face."

He didn't say anything, but looked amused by the whole thing. In fact, he invited me in and offered me a drink. It made me wonder if this guy didn't watch even more television than I did. He was right on script. Nice and cordial.

I accepted cautiously and followed him into the kitchen.

He didn't know my gun was useless, but I was all too aware of it. As we entered the kitchen, I did a quick visual sweep of the room, all cop-like, then positioned myself against the counter, a fully loaded knife block just behind me, well within reach if things got ugly.

"So you're the private investigator." It was more of a statement than question. "I don't mix drinks at home," he added as he pulled a half-empty bottle of wine out of the fridge, then reached up to a cupboard for glasses.

I wanted to keep things low-key. "It's not a big deal, Charlie. Kid's stuff, when you think about it. Things didn't work out between you and Chloe, and she wants to move on. You don't even have to do anything for her, just stop doing what you're doing. Stop hounding her and move on. Pretty simple, actually."

Charlie handed me a drink I had no interest in, then gave me a big smile and informed me, "You're trespassing."

Weak. "Not even close, Charlie." I shook my head, as if saddened that he wasn't a worthier opponent. "You invited me in."

"But I didn't invite you *over*," he explained. "I didn't give you my email address either, so your contacting me that way was also unwelcome."

So Charlie wanted to play the semantics game. No problem. I could do that all day long.

Then he took a step toward me. It wasn't exactly a threatening gesture, more like a power play. I leaned back against the counter so that my jacket fell open, just a friendly reminder that as far as he knew, I was armed to the teeth and licensed to use any firepower I deemed necessary. That's when he unexpectedly backhanded me across the face. And he did it hard. I saw stars.

Chloe never mentioned anything about physical abuse, even when I specifically asked if he was prone to violence. She had insisted she'd never seen any sign of it. Guess she was lucky all he did was leave her a ton of annoying messages.

While I was trying to recover from the shock, Charlie went for my gun. I wasn't sure if this was a good thing or bad thing. If he found out it wasn't a real firearm, he couldn't shoot me and claim I had broken in, but it would also expose me as less than the authority figure I needed to be to make this work.

But he wasn't trying to shoot me. He got the gun and threw it across the kitchen floor, then turned back to me, laughing and leering. That's when I realized how *Good-TimeCharlie69*, the insatiable womanizer, was going to deal with this particular problem.

I was still leaning back against the counter. I reached behind me and pulled the out the biggest knife in the block and waved it at him.

He kept laughing. "Oh, you wanna play rough? I can play rough." Such a cliché. I don't know how he gets women with lines like that. Must be the money. He seemed to think he was hilarious.

He isn't laughing now.

Stabbings are messy, but self-defense is a right. I'm no good to my client or my team dead. If I had to fight to the death, so be it. Charlie brought this on himself. After all these years I don't think there's anyone on the team who hasn't had to take a life in the line of duty, either to protect a client or one of our own. Poor Stevie even had to shoot the mayor in "L.A. Coincidental" (Season 4, Episode 8).

Turned out the hard part of stabbing him was puncturing the skin. Then the knife just slid right in. I got him on his right side, just under the ribs. I'm not sure what I hit, but it was a gusher. Good Time Charlie shrieked like a girl, and I think that's what freaked me out the most.

I was fixated on the blood that was starting to coat my hands while we struggled. It was warm and sticky and made my stomach churn, but for some reason I couldn't let go of the knife. And Charlie wouldn't stop making that awful high-pitched sound, and his struggling with me was just making the wound worse. I needed to get the situation under control.

And then I thought about what Stevie would do in that situation, and suddenly I had this incredible sense of calm. I let go of the knife and Charlie slipped to the floor, where he quieted to dull moans. I had acted in self-defense, so there was no reason for me to panic. Charlie had acted in a menacing fashion. If necessary, it would be my word against his, and I wasn't the one whose actions were making my ex sick and frightened. Stevie would have my back on this.

His cell phone was on the counter by the fridge. I tossed it at him.

"Call nine-one-one. And stop harassing women."

He gaped at me. He probably still didn't think he'd done anything wrong.

I left Charlie to his own devices. I'm no doctor, so I have no idea if his injury was life-threatening. If he called 9-1-1 he'd probably be okay. If not, I really didn't care. All he had to do was act like a man and stop hassling his ex-girlfriend. It's wasn't brain surgery.

But it was a lot of blood.

I called Chloe from the 210 freeway. She answered with a timid, "Hello?"

"Chloe, this is Zan Jones. I'm calling to let you know that Charlie Brendan isn't going to bother you anymore."

"Are you sure? Like I told you, he doesn't know when to quit."

"The threat has been neutralized," I advised her in my best *PI: Private Investigators* delivery. "You don't need to worry about him."

There was an awkward moment of silence, and I thought about wrapping the call by telling her I'd invoice her and she could make payments as she's able to, but it felt sordid to mention money. Stevie never does because it isn't about the money. It's about justice for our clients.

It was like Chloe couldn't believe her good luck, because she asked again, "Are you *really* sure?"

"Very sure, Chloe."

She sounded dazzled. "How did you pull that off?"

"I can be very persuasive."

This prompted a burst of giggles that sounded like a welcome sigh of relief. "You sound like someone out of a movie," she laughed.

I was extremely pleased to hear that. Someone needed to do a *PI* movie.


As I sat parked in the unholier than usual Highland Avenue traffic, I rehearsed how I would explain myself to my boss. The blood on my hands was drying and felt kind of scratchy, but would be impressively dramatic when I handed off the Charlie Brendan file to Stevie. My blouse and jacket were probably shot, though. Blood's hard to get out.

I wasn't the least bit surprised when I discovered why traffic was worse than usual. *PI* was back in Tinseltown, filming in front of the Chinese Theatre. I drove past the legendary courtyard, made a right on the next street, and just parked it right there, just like we do on the show. What I had to do was too important to worry about things like finding an actual parking spot.

I pushed my way through the Hollywood Boulevard looky-loos and marched up to Stevie and, with the respect and deferment that she has always elicited from her team, I handed her the red-smudged file and told her, "Stevie, the Charlie Brendan situation has been handled."

She seemed distracted and somewhat surprised at the sight of me. Probably the blood. She was worried that I'd been hurt, that it was my blood. It was odd to see her speechless. That just doesn't happen to Stevie Armstrong.

I was trying to give her the details, but someone started yelling about security and I was surrounded by uniforms and hustled away. I guessed maybe they found Charlie. I wasn't all that concerned. Stevie never abandoned anyone. I was certain she'd have my back until things could be sorted out and it's ruled self-defense, and we could all get back to bringing justice to the fine citizens of Los Angeles.

# On Call for Murder
## Paula Bernstein

I will never get used to the sound of a beeper going off at two in the morning. I'd collapsed on the bed in the intern's on-call room at Los Angeles Memorial Hospital, and had drifted into that state of REM sleep in which my body was still tense for instant action.

"Doctor Kline, please call two-three-one-one stat. Two-three-one-one stat," the electronic voice demanded.

I groaned and knocked the beeper to the floor, fumbling for my cell phone so I could return the call.

"Two West," said the cheery voice of the ward clerk.

"It's Doctor Hannah Kline. You paged me?"

"Yes Doctor. Nina Petrov, patient of Doctor Avery, says she can't breathe. She had a cesarean section this morning."

"I'll be right there," I said.

I slid out of bed and speed-walked to the nursing station. At least I didn't have to get dressed. I was wearing wrinkled scrubs. Sometimes I wondered what the patients thought about being accosted in the middle of the night by an apparition in messy green pajamas, wielding a stethoscope.

I remembered Nina well. I'd assisted on her surgery that morning, a perfectly routine cesarean for a breech baby. The surgery had proceeded flawlessly. I wondered what had gone wrong.

When I entered the room, a nurse was hovering over the patient. Nina was sitting as far up as the hospital bed would allow, and she was holding on to an oxygen mask.

"Nina, it's Doctor Kline," I said. "What's wrong?"

Nina's eyes focused on my face and she reached for my hand. "Chest hurts," she whispered. "Can't breathe."

"How long has this been going on?" I asked.

"I was in here at eleven and took vital signs. She seemed fine then. She rang for help just a few minutes ago," the nurse said.

Nina was clearly in trouble. I counted about forty breaths per minute and there was an unhealthy blue cast to her lips.

"Can I listen to your lungs?" I asked, reaching for my stethoscope. She bent forward.

I drew a blood gas, and ordered a stat portable chest x-ray and an EKG. Nina was in so much distress that she didn't even wince when I stuck the needle into her artery. I mentally ticked off the most likely possibilities: pulmonary embolus, aspiration pneumonia or amniotic fluid embolus.

I leaned over and took her hand.

"Nina, I'm arranging for you to go to the ICU so we can help you breathe, and I'm going to call Doctor Avery." She nodded.

I left the room, went to the nursing station, and called the post-surgical ICU. Nina needed to be put on a respirator, and I was seriously concerned that she might wind up dead. Once I had everything organized I called Doctor Avery.

I'd heard about Charles Avery from the other residents but had only met him yesterday morning. Avery was too slick, too glib, and too Gucci for my taste, and I could tell that he didn't like women doctors.

"Doctor Avery, I'm calling about Nina Petrov. She's in respiratory distress. I've arranged for her to go to the ICU and ordered all the routine bloods and imaging. It looks as if she'll need to be intubated."

There was silence on the other end.

Finally, he said, "Call me back when you have all the lab

results. I'll arrange for a pulmonary consult."

"Yes, Doctor," I said, wondering why he wasn't coming in himself to evaluate her. According to my fellow residents, Nina Petrov was rather atypical for an Avery patient. Maybe he only came in at night for celebrities.

I had really liked Nina. She was an attractive young woman with broad Slavic features, light blue eyes, straight blonde hair, and a cheerful smile. I had met her yesterday morning.

"Are you Russian?" I'd asked. Los Angeles has a large émigré population.

She nodded. "I was born there. My parents came here when I was very young."

Her English was without an accent. I smiled at her. "Have you picked out a name yet for your baby?"

She shook her head. "I'm giving him up for adoption."

I felt embarrassed. That explained why there was no father in the room.

"Sorry, I didn't know. We'll be taking you back to the operating room in a few moments," I said as I made an awkward exit.

I learned a bit more from Charles Avery as we were scrubbing. "Nina is a surrogate," he said, lathering his immaculate hands with Betadine.

"Oh," I said, noncommittally.

"The baby is the biological child of one of my infertile couples," he said. "We used the husband's sperm. The wife's eggs were past their prime."

So, Nina was a walking baby factory. I'd wondered how much she was being paid and how she felt about giving up a baby that was half hers. I could think of easier ways to make money.

\* \* \*

225

I was six months into my internship at Los Angeles County Hospital and was doing a short rotation at Los Angeles Memorial, the city's most prestigious private facility, just east of Beverly Hills. Our residency program wanted us to see how the other half lived. It was quite an eye opener.

Whereas obstetrical patients at the County lay in cubicles, divided by curtains, each Memorial patient had a beautifully furnished room where she could labor, deliver, and recover without moving. Most patients opted for epidural anesthesia, and spent their time painlessly watching a flat screen TV.

If I ever decided to get pregnant, I definitely wanted to deliver at Memorial. However, delivering at the best hospital in town was no guarantee of protection from bad complications. I was very worried.

An X-ray tech arrived in Nina's room with a portable machine, followed by the EKG tech. The gurney arrived shortly after with its defibrillator and oxygen tank. Two strong guys transferred Nina and her IV to the gurney. I walked with them to the ICU.

The post-surgical ICU was staffed twenty-four-seven by full-time hospital faculty, trained in intensive care medicine. I felt superfluous.

By the time we arrived, all the results were back. I showed them to the ICU attending physician and moved out of the way. He had Nina sign a consent form, sedated her, and placed a tube into her main bronchus. A nurse attached her to a respirator.

"What now?" I asked.

"I'm ordering a scan to see if she has a pulmonary embolus," he said. A definitive diagnosis was badly needed. I was astonished at how quickly she had deteriorated, and at a loss for an explanation.

I took a few minutes to complete my detailed note. Then, dreading the conversation, I called Doctor Avery back with an update.

\* \* \*

I didn't get any more sleep that night. The next morning, I took a short break and retreated to the women's locker room to shower, put on clean scrubs, and brush my hair. Before returning to the ICU, I went downstairs to the coffee shop for a quick latte and a scone, one of the perks of a rotation at Memorial.

By seven a.m. I was back in the ICU, just moments before Charles Avery arrived. His face looked drawn. There was faint stubble on his cheeks and a hint of puffiness around his eyes. He noticed me, nodded, and raised his eyebrows.

"How is she doing?" he asked.

"Not well."

Just then, a strikingly beautiful woman walked toward us. She appeared agitated.

"Charles, what is going on? Last night she was perfectly fine. This morning I stopped by to say hello before going to the nursery, and I find her in the ICU looking totally moribund. What happened?"

Avery sighed. "I wish I knew. Grace, this is Doctor Kline, the resident taking care of Nina. Grace Clavell and her husband Keith are the baby's parents."

Grace was thin, blonde, about forty, and dressed like the ostentatiously rich women I'd gotten used to seeing in Beverly Hills. Her straight hair, not a strand out of place, brushed her shoulders. Her eyes matched the color of her blue silk suit. There were tight lines around her thin, perfectly pink-lipped mouth. She glanced at me without interest.

"It looks as if Nina has some sort of embolus," Avery continued. "I don't understand why it should have happened. We're doing everything we can for her."

"Will she be all right?"

"I hope so," he said.

"Will she be able to sign the final papers?" Grace asked.

"There are no final papers," Avery said. "The legal agreement was signed before she became your surrogate, and your husband is the biological father."

Grace's face relaxed. I could tell that Nina's well-being was not her priority.

"In that case," she said. "I'll head down to the nursery."


There is something about the ICU that reminds me of a silent movie. The phone rings, the monitors beep, and everyone whispers. It would be major sacrilege to say anything out loud.

It was late afternoon, and Nina's condition was getting worse. The final diagnosis was an amniotic fluid embolism, but something about the picture was wrong. I'd seen one before: an acute change in the middle of surgery, accompanying the sudden separation of the placenta from the uterine wall. Symptoms never appeared twenty-four hours after a routine cesarean section.

The nurse came in and hung a bag of steroids.

"Doctor Kline, shall I administer the RhoGAM?"

"I suppose so." I had a hunch it wouldn't matter. I wrote the order.

Nina looked half-dead. The respirator tube protruded from the side of her mouth where it was carefully taped. Spittle ran out the other side. She was asleep from the morphine that had been used to sedate her. On one hundred percent oxygen, she was barely holding her own.

"You'll need to talk to Doctor Kline, sir. She's taking care of the patient."

I looked around. The ICU receptionist was escorting a couple in my direction. The man was tall and gray-haired with a mustache and an air of authority. The woman was Grace.

"Doctor Kline, I'm Keith Clavell, and you've met my wife.

We're here to see Miss Petrov. Can you tell us how she's doing?"

"I'm not permitted to discuss her condition with anyone who isn't a family member, sir, but if you would like to see her, you may visit one at a time for five minutes," I said.

Mr. Clavell nodded and went in the direction of Nina's door.

"Such a tragedy," said Grace. I nodded.

Mr. Clavell came out of Nina's room and joined us. He appeared visibly distraught.

"Doctor, is there anything at all I can do to help? I'd be happy to give blood. I'm a universal donor."

"That's thoughtful of you. Nina doesn't need a transfusion now, but your offer is appreciated."

He nodded. "Let's go. There's nothing else we can do." Grace followed him out.

I looked at my watch. It was almost time for turnover rounds. I could sign Nina out to the on-call resident and finally go home and get some sleep. I could barely keep my eyes open.

Going home was no trivial matter. It involved driving through the downtown interchange at rush hour, desperately trying to stay alert enough to avoid getting killed. I thought nostalgically of the New York subway, where, if I got a seat, I could doze.

I was a New Yorker, born and bred in Brooklyn, and a graduate of Vassar. I'd gone to medical school at Harvard. My Los Angeles residency was an unwelcome side effect of my recent marriage. My husband, Ben, is an architect, and was offered the job of his dreams in L.A. I'd assumed we would be staying on the East Coast, and had interviewed with all the best New York and Boston programs. I didn't have the heart to tell Ben to turn the job down, and I didn't want us to be living on opposite coasts, so I scrambled at the last minute to find a Los Angeles residency. I wound up at County, not my first choice. I was trying to make the best of it.

We were renting a bungalow in Pasadena, an easy commute to downtown, but an agonizing daily drive to Memorial Hospital. It was dark when I pulled into our driveway.

Ben greeted me at the door. I collapsed into his arms.

"I made you dinner," he said. "Can you stay awake long enough to eat it?"

I followed him into the kitchen. "Chicken soup and ice cream," he said. "I bought the chicken soup at the deli." Cooking was not Ben's forte, but it was the thought that counted.

I sat down and listened to the whir of the microwave. The scent of chicken wafted in my direction.

"Bad day?" Ben asked.

"The worst," I said. "I think my patient is going to die."


I woke to the alarm at six a.m., still exhausted. I pried open my eyes and splashed my face with ice cold water, dreading my return to the hospital.

When I got to the ICU, it was clear that Nina was worse. It broke my heart to look at her. She was in a coma and unresponsive to all but the most painful stimuli.

"Pardon me, are you Doctor Kline?"

I turned to see a stocky young man with Slavic features and thinning sandy hair.

"I'm Alexander Markovic, Nina's boyfriend. Can you tell me how she's doing?"

"Not well, I'm afraid, Mr. Markovic. We're doing all we can."

"That bastard," he hissed under his breath. "May I see her?"

"She's in room five," I told him.

When he emerged his eyes were damp and his fists clenched. "Where's Avery?"

"Doctor Avery hasn't come in yet this morning."

"Give him a message. Tell him that if she dies, I'll kill him." His voice quivered, and his eyes were moist. He walked out before I could see him cry.

I stared after him, shaken, wondering if I should repeat his threat.

I began reviewing the chart again, not that I expected to learn anything new. There had been something on my mind all morning, just out of reach, and as I skimmed through yesterday's labs, I caught it.

They had given her RhoGAM, the antibody injected into Rh negative mothers after the birth of a Rh positive baby to prevent problems in future pregnancies. But Nina's baby shouldn't have been Rh positive, not if Keith Clavell was the father. Hadn't he just told me he was O-negative, the blood type of the universal donor?

I picked up the phone and called the blood bank to verify the baby's type.

"A-positive, Doctor."

I was puzzled. I wondered whose child Nina had borne, and if Keith Clavell knew the baby wasn't his, or for that matter, if Charles Avery knew. I poured myself a cup of bitter ICU coffee and as I gulped it down, Avery walked in.

"Good morning, Doctor Kline. Any change in Nina's condition?"

"She seems to be deteriorating, Doctor," I said. I told him the results of the most recent imaging and blood gases. He listened perfunctorily and stared at the respirator settings.

"Better call in a neurology consult. See if she's brain dead," he said.

"Yes, Doctor. Do you know a man named Alexander Markovic?"

Avery nodded. "I believe so. He used to date Nina when

she worked as a medical assistant in my office. She dropped him just after she became pregnant. Was he here?"

"Here and very angry. He threatened to kill you if Nina didn't get better."

Avery blanched. "She's not going to get better."

"Do you think you should notify the police?"

He shrugged. "They aren't going to do anything about it."

"One other thing, Doctor Avery. Nina's blood type is O-negative, and the baby is A-positive.

"So?"

"Mr. Clavell mentioned he was a universal donor, also O-negative. If that's true then he's not the biological father."

"You must be mistaken. You didn't mention this to anyone, did you?"

"Of course not," I said.

"I wouldn't worry about it, and I certainly wouldn't upset the Clavells at this difficult time. Do we understand one another?" he said.

"Yes, Doctor Avery."

"Good girl." He walked out of the ICU and I exhaled. *Good girl* indeed. I did not like Charles Avery.

I finished my notes and headed out the door in the direction of the outpatient clinic. I'd just gotten to the elevator when my beeper went off.

"SICU stat. SICU stat."

A moment later I heard the Code Blue alarm over the loud speaker.

I sprinted for the door. There already a crowd in Nina's room. The EKG monitor was a flat line, and a heavy-set nurse with large biceps was pumping her chest.

"Everyone, step back." It was the ICU physician.

"You," he pointed to the nearest nurse. "Push two amps of bicarbonate and get me the paddles."

He applied the electrodes to Nina's chest.

"Stand clear."

Nina's body gave a convulsive jerk. The heart monitor stayed flat.

"Again."

Out of the corner of my eye, I saw Doctor Avery elbowing his way into the room. His face looked almost as blue as Nina's. She jerked again as the electric current jolted her. No heartbeat.

"What time is it?" he asked.

"Ten-forty, Doctor Avery."

"I'm calling the code." The nurse stopped pumping. Someone disconnected the respirator. It was over.

I sat down in a corner and started to shake all over. It was the first time someone I had operated on had died. I couldn't imagine that the day could possibly get any worse.


Maria D'Anuncio was in charge of the night cleaning crew in the medical building on North Bedford Drive in Beverly Hills. On Wednesday at ten o'clock at night, Maria was busy cleaning the suite of Doctor Charles Avery.

She emptied the trash, vacuumed the rug, sprayed the glass, and polished the door knobs. Then she opened the door to the doctor's consult room and began to scream.

The doctor was sprawled across his desk. There was a neat, round bullet hole in the middle of his forehead. He was quite dead.


I was hiding out in the hospital coffee shop with a mug of coffee and a side of bacon. I hadn't gotten much sleep the night before, wondering if there had been anything at all I could have done that would have made a difference for Nina. I knew it wasn't my fault, but it didn't make me feel any better.

At this early morning hour the coffee shop was almost

empty, with only a few, bleary-eyed physicians reading their email at widely scattered tables. As I looked up, I noticed a middle-aged man with a shaven head, wearing a rumpled gray suit jacket barely closed over a substantial paunch. He headed in the direction of my table. I looked down at my phone, hoping that avoiding eye contact would encourage him to sit far away. The last thing I needed this morning was a friendly chat with a stranger.

"Doctor Hannah Kline?" I looked up. The stranger reached into his pocket and pulled out a badge. "I'm Beverly Hills Police Detective Max Morgan."

I put down my mug with a splash that sent coffee onto my bacon. "Police?" I said. "What's this about?"

"Mind if I sit down?" He pulled up a chair without waiting for my assent. "It's about Doctor Charles Avery." I waited for him to go on. "Doctor Avery was found shot last night in his office."

My face must have shown my shock. I was speechless.

"One of the ICU nurses overheard a conversation between you and a man visiting patient Nina Petrov. She said the man threatened to kill Doctor Avery. Is that true?"

I nodded. "He said he was Nina's boyfriend, and he was very distraught when he saw her condition. His exact words were 'tell him if she doesn't get better, I'll kill him.'"

"Did you believe him?"

I paused and thought about it. "Not really."

"Why not?"

"He was so upset. I could see the tears in his eyes. It was like a child having a tantrum and threatening a parent. I didn't get the sense he really meant it."

"Did you tell anyone?" the detective asked.

"I told Doctor Avery," I said.

"What was his reaction?"

"He seemed shaken, but when I asked him if he was going to notify the police, he just shrugged it off."

"Did the boyfriend tell you his name?" Morgan asked.

"Alexander Markovic," I said. He wrote it down in a small notebook.

"I understand that Nina Petrov died yesterday. Was there malpractice on Doctor Avery's part?"

I shook my head. "It was a routine C-section for a breech baby. Doctor Avery was a very skilled surgeon. I didn't see anything wrong, and I assisted him."

"Then why did she die?" Morgan asked.

"She developed an embolism from amniotic fluid that went to her lungs. It's a rare complication and often fatal," I said.

Detective Morgan chewed thoughtfully on his lower lip. "Tell me about Doctor Avery. Was he the kind of man to make enemies?"

"I only met him two days ago. All I know about him is what I've heard from other residents."

"And that is?"

"Doctor Avery had a very high-class celebrity practice. He was very successful."

"Was he well liked, or was he the kind of man who pissed people off?" Morgan asked.

"You'll have to ask the other residents," I said. "As I told you, I just met him."

I wasn't about to gossip with the police. It wouldn't take them long to find out how pompous Avery was.

"One more question, Doctor Kline," the detective said. "Tell me about Miss Petrov's baby. What's the story?"

"Nina Petrov was paid to be a surrogate for Keith and Grace Clavell. Mrs. Clavell was infertile so Nina was having the husband's child."

"Any issues over that between the doctor and the couple?" he asked.

I shrugged. "Not that I know of." The child clearly wasn't Keith Clavell's, but revealing that information was a violation of patient privacy.

"Thank you, Doctor. If you think of anything else I should know, call me." He rose and handed me his card.

"I will," I said. I put the card in my lab coat pocket and attempted to finish my coffee, but it was already cold. Just then, my beeper went off. The nursery wanted me to circumcise Baby Clavell. I signaled the waitress for my check and thought about what I should do next.

Doctor Avery had clearly not wanted me to say anything to the Clavells about the blood type discrepancy, but Doctor Avery was dead, and if he had done something fraudulent the couple had the right to know. I wasn't interested in being a party to something unethical. I paid my bill and headed for the elevator.

Circumcision is my least favorite surgical procedure. Even though I use an effective local anesthetic block, I always feel guilty at the possibility of causing even the slightest pain. When I'm done, I always cuddle the babies before wheeling them out to their anxious parents. Fortunately, the parents rarely wish to be present while I'm operating.

Grace was waiting for me in the patient lounge.

"All done," I said. "He didn't cry at all."

Grace glanced over at the baby, who was sleeping, and turned to me.

"Thank you, Doctor Kline. I'll be taking him home later today. I can't believe that Doctor Avery has died. The nurses are all talking about it. Did you know?"

"I heard," I said. "Is Mr. Clavell here?"

"He had a meeting this morning," she said. "He'll be here later."

I was surprised. I would have thought that taking home one's son would have been a higher priority than a business meeting.

"I have a question," I said. "When you were in the ICU,

your husband offered to donate blood and said he was a universal donor. That means he's blood type O-negative. Is that correct?"

Grace nodded. "Keith donates blood frequently. The Red Cross is always calling him."

I decided to sit down. "Mrs. Clavell, there's something you need to know. Both Nina and your husband are O-negative, but the baby's blood type is A-positive. Your husband can't be the father. Two Rh-negative parents always have an Rh-negative child. It's possible that Doctor Avery lied to you."

She shot me a look of fury. "You fool. I know Keith isn't the father. My husband is sterile."

"Then why?" I asked.

She sighed. "My husband was desperate for a son, and we didn't conceive. I was pretty sure I wasn't the problem."

"So you consulted Doctor Avery?"

"Yes. Avery told me Keith was sterile, and I told him to tell Keith that the infertility was my fault. I didn't think he could handle the news, and I was afraid it would destroy our marriage."

"Why not adopt?" I asked.

"Keith was obsessed with having a biological child. I suggested to my husband that we use a surrogate with his sperm, and I asked Doctor Avery to use a sperm bank specimen instead. He agreed."

"How did you find Nina?" I asked.

"Nina was working for Avery and was happy to oblige. Everything was fine until she died, and now Charles is dead too." She looked as if she might break into tears at any moment. "If you tell my husband, the news will devastate him."

"I understand. There's no need for me to say anything. Enjoy your new son." I left the room and headed in the direction of Labor and Delivery.

* * *

I made the rounds of the labor rooms and retreated to the nursing station. As I was writing notes, my cell phone rang. It was the hospital operator.

"There's an outside call from a Mr. Alexander Markovic. Should I put it through?"

Nina's boyfriend. I would have imagined he'd be in an interview room at the Beverly Hills police station by now. Why was he calling me?

"Yes, please," I said.

"Doctor Kline, I just called the ICU to ask about Nina, and they told me she died yesterday. Would you be willing to talk to me? I'm only five minutes away from the hospital."

My curiosity warred with my common sense. "I can meet you in the coffee shop in fifteen minutes," I said.

Mr. Markovic was waiting for me at a corner table. He was nursing a cup of tea. I sat down across from him.

"I'm so sorry about Nina," I said. "We did everything possible, but her lungs gave out."

"I really loved her," he said. "I wanted to marry her. If she hadn't let Avery talk her into being a surrogate, she'd still be alive." His lower lip trembled, and I could tell he was fighting for control.

"Why do you think Nina chose to be a surrogate?" I asked.

"She wanted the money. The Clavells offered her a large sum, more than she could have earned in years of working." He fidgeted with his napkin, tearing it into small shreds. I waited.

"I've been trying to think of a tactful way to say this, but I haven't come up with one, so I'm just going to tell you what's on my mind. I hope you don't think I'm crazy," he said.

"Why would I think that?"

"Because, I believe that Nina was murdered and that Avery was responsible."

"Why are you telling me this?" I asked.

"You were there, at her surgery, and you took care of her afterwards. I need to know if there was anything at all that appeared suspicious to you."

"That's a pretty strong statement, Mr. Markovic. Perhaps you'd better tell me why you think her death wasn't natural."

He hesitated. I could see him scrutinizing my face, trying to decide whether to trust me any further. Finally, he spoke.

"I didn't find out about Nina's decision to be a surrogate until it was too late to talk her out of it. She told me she was pregnant and didn't want to see me again. I was devastated. I didn't hear from her for months, and then, a few weeks ago, she called me. She said she was frightened and needed my help."

"Frightened of what?"

"Of Charles Avery. She thought he was going to kill her. The baby wasn't Keith Clavell's. He was sterile. The baby was mine."

"Are you saying that Avery knew that?"

"Oh, yes. The two of them put one over on Clavell and that prissy wife of his. Nina was afraid that Avery would try to get rid of her after the birth to make sure Clavell didn't find out. She wanted me to stay near her in the hospital and take her away afterwards."

This wasn't making sense to me, but I needed to hear the rest. He was staring at me like a whipped puppy.

"I can't imagine what you must have felt, learning that Nina was giving away your child," I said.

"Oh, but she wouldn't have. We agreed to go away together with the baby."

"What are you planning to do now?" I asked.

"I've already done it. I saw a lawyer days ago. I'm demanding a paternity test and fighting for custody."

As I faced Alexander Markovic, I found myself at a loss for words. I had never considered that Nina's death had been anything but an obstetrical catastrophe. Yet, all along, it bothered me. If her death was murder, Avery was hardly the only suspect. There was a highly protective and jealous wife, as well as a rejected lover who had more than adequate motives.

I chose my words carefully.

"You may be right. There is nothing I can think of at the moment that would be helpful to you, but I've also been troubled by her death. I can review the chart again. Perhaps something will suggest itself."

"Thank you," he said.

"Have you considered talking to the police?" I couldn't imagine why they hadn't brought him in for questioning yet.

He shook his head. "They wouldn't believe me. Avery is a hotshot doctor. I'm just a grieving boyfriend. You won't say anything to Avery, will you?"

I stared at him. "Say anything? Doctor Avery is dead. He was found in his office this morning."

Markovic looked genuinely surprised. "I'm not enough of a hypocrite to say I'm sorry. Heart attack?"

"Bullet. He was murdered."

This time he really looked stunned. Before he could ask me any more questions, I was saved by my beeper.

"Sorry, gotta go," I said, and fled the coffee shop.


Late that afternoon I descended on Medical Records. Nina's chart was thicker than I remembered. I took it to a cubicle and carefully read all those sections most doctors don't bother with.

It took me only twenty minutes to find it. Nina Petrov had been murdered, and I thought I knew how it was done and who was responsible. I reached into my lab coat pocket and pulled out a card. It was time to call Detective Max Morgan.

The detective agreed to meet me in the hospital lobby at six-thirty p.m., immediately after sign-out rounds. I escorted him to the Doctor's Lounge and described my encounter with Alexander Markovic, as well as my conviction that he was correct about Nina's death. Detective Morgan gave me a skeptical look.

"You think she was murdered? How?"

I took a breath. "Nina died as a result of a rare complication of pregnancy called an amniotic fluid embolism."

"Never heard of it," Morgan said.

"No reason you would have," I replied. "Here's how it works. At the time the placenta separates, amniotic fluid gets into the maternal blood vessels and goes to the lungs. It sets up an inflammatory reaction that interferes with breathing. It's often fatal."

"Why do you suspect murder?" he asked.

"What confused me was the timing. Usually symptoms appear very soon after birth, but in Nina's case, she was operated on at seven-thirty in the morning and didn't begin to have difficulty breathing until after midnight."

"Couldn't there be some medical explanation for that?"

"Perhaps," I said, "but according to the nurses' notes, Doctor Avery went into her room at eleven-thirty p.m. It's a very unusual time to make rounds."

"What are you implying he did?"

"Bear with me. Nina had her C-section at thirty-eight weeks. Hospital rules mandate that if you deliver someone before thirty-nine weeks, you must prove lung maturity. That is done by removing amniotic fluid with a syringe and sending it to the lab."

"Did he do that?"

"The history says he did, but there was no lab slip corroborating it. I called the hospital lab and the private lab his practice uses. Neither of them had any record of receiving the fluid sample."

Morgan scratched his head and wrinkled his nose. I could tell he wasn't following my reasoning. "Exactly what are you suggesting?"

"I think he saved that sample of amniotic fluid and put it into Nina's IV when he went to her room. That would explain the sudden late onset of symptoms."

"What would motivate Doctor Avery to kill his patient?"

"If Markovic told the truth, Doctor Avery had passed off a surrogate who was already pregnant as the bearer of Keith Clavell's biologic baby. That's pretty shady unethical behavior, even if Mrs. Clavell knew her husband was sterile."

"Wait a second. She knew what?"

This resulted in my needing to recap the conversation with Grace Clavell, as well as the blood type results.

"Didn't you interview Alexander Markovic?" I asked.

"We did."

"Did he tell you he was the father of Nina's baby?"

Morgan shook his head. "Markovic just gave us his alibi for the time frame of the murder, and it was unshakeable. He's a cameraman. He was working on a TV show and has multiple witnesses to account for his whereabouts during the time Doctor Avery was shot. We let him go."

"It might be a good idea to find out who the father of that baby is," I suggested. "Nina could have lied to her boyfriend to get him to help her. Doctor Avery could have used a sperm bank specimen." Morgan nodded.

"Your theory is very interesting. We should be able to figure out paternity."

"If his death is connected to Nina's," I said, "you might want to talk to Grace Clavell. She sounded pretty protective about keeping her husband in the dark."

Morgan smiled at me. "You've given this a good deal of thought. I appreciate your help."

"Anytime," I said.

I was on duty again that night, and was hopeful that it would be uneventful. Labor and Delivery was quiet, so I retreated to an on-call room in the hope of catching a few hours of sleep.

I closed my eyes and tried to lull myself into a state of relaxation. My head was crammed with more information than I knew what to do with. There were two murders, a very ingenious murder method for one, and an unknown killer for the other. I wondered if Detective Morgan had followed up on any of my suggestions. There was one other thing that was bothering me. Two people who knew about the Clavell baby had been murdered. Was I next on the list?

I spent the next few days looking over my shoulder and making sure I wasn't alone anywhere in the hospital. I imagined that in a while my paranoia would wear off. Late one afternoon I received a call from Detective Morgan.

"I thought you might like to know that your hunch was correct," he said.

"What hunch was that?"

"You said that Markovic might not be the father of the baby. We got a DNA sample from him and ran it against DNA we obtained from the placenta. His paternity test was negative."

"So Avery did use a sperm bank sample, as he and Mrs. Clavell agreed?"

"It's simpler than that," Morgan said. "He used his own sperm."

It took me a moment to process that statement. "He could

have lost his license for inseminating a surrogate with his own sperm," I said.

"He may have inseminated her the old fashioned way," Morgan said.

"If he used his own sperm for the Clavell baby, I wonder if he didn't use it on other surrogates, or even his patients. That would certainly expand the number of people who might have a motive to murder him," I suggested.

"It would indeed," Morgan said.

"What about Mrs. Clavell? Have you spoken to her?"

"We interviewed her today. She claims she was home all night with her new baby and a baby nurse when Avery was killed. We're checking her alibi now."

"Let me know if there is anything else I can do to be helpful. I'm happy to answer any medical questions."

"Thanks," Morgan said.


I was relieved when the day was over. Ben was at some architecture conference, so I had no need to fight the rush hour traffic home. Instead, I pointed my car in the direction of Beverly Hills. I parked in a lot on Beverly Drive and window-shopped at a leisurely pace. I found a fabulous art bookstore, and spent a while browsing. As I came out and glanced up, I saw Keith and Grace Clavell, wheeling a baby carriage in my direction. She spotted me and waved, so it was too late to duck back into the store.

"Doctor Kline." Her smile seemed pasted on. I suspected she was no more interested in seeing me than I was in chatting with her.

I smiled back. "I hope parenthood is treating you well." Just then, the son and heir let out a scream. Grace took a sniff, identifying the problem.

"Oh, dear. He and I need to make a stop in the bathroom at Nate 'n Al's," she said.

"I'll wait for you here," her husband said. "We live just up the block." He pointed north toward the fancy residential part of Beverly Hills.

"Well, nice to see you again," I said, looking at my watch.

It was time to head home. I moved quickly away from him and toward the parking lot elevator. Just as the elevator door was closing, a well-shod foot stopped it, and Keith Clavell joined me. He grabbed my arm, digging his fingers into my biceps.

"I want to know what Nina told you about Alexander Markovic," he said.

I grabbed his wrist, twisted it off my arm, and stepped back.

"Nothing," I said.

"She didn't tell you he was the father of her baby?" The elevator was moving down toward level 3P.

"I only talked to her for five minutes before I assisted on her surgery." The door opened.

I stepped out, and he followed. My car was in a far corner of the garage, and I didn't see anyone nearby. I stayed put, where the security camera could see me and where, hopefully, others would soon exit the elevator.

"Markovic is suing us for custody. He claims he's the real father," Clavell said.

"If you had doubts about paternity, why did you take the baby home?" I countered.

"That baby was bought and paid for. Avery and his bitch got one hundred grand apiece," he said.

"Why didn't you ask Nina who the father was?" I asked.

"I couldn't. She was dead when I got the papers."

"You could have asked Avery."

"I did. He's a lying son-of-a-bitch. No one makes a fool of me, you included," he said.

"I have nothing to do with this."

"You told my wife there was a problem with the blood type," he said. "I think you'd better come with me, Doctor Busybody." He grabbed my arm again.

"Let go of me," I screamed.

"Let go of her," said a young woman who had just walked out of the stairwell. She was wearing jeans, an L.A. Lakers sweatshirt, and a baseball cap.

"Mind your own business," Clavell said.

The woman pulled a gun. "This is my business. Beverly Hills PD. Let go of her."

I took the opportunity to aim a well-placed kick at Clavell's nether parts, and he let go. I retreated out of range.

"On the ground, hands behind your back," the cop said. Two minutes later a police car raced into the parking garage, and two muscular guys cuffed Clavell and shoved him into the back of the patrol car.

"I want a lawyer," he shouted.

I felt myself shaking. I couldn't remember ever having been so frightened. I took a few deep breaths, regained a measure of control, and turned to the young cop. She looked like a teenager with her freckles and blonde ponytail. "Thanks, Officer. Perfect timing."

She grinned. "You can thank Detective Morgan. He's had a tail on you all day. He was worried about your safety."

"I was worried about it too," I said. "I was afraid I knew too much information that someone was desperate to keep quiet."

"We found the murder weapon this afternoon," she said. "A forty-five, registered to Keith Clavell with his prints on it. It was in a storm drain on Bedford Drive. We're booking him for the murder of Charles Avery."

"Thank Detective Morgan for me," I said. "I owe you guys. I shudder to think of what Clavell might have done if you hadn't been here."

"You impressed Max. He said you had the makings of a good detective," she said. She walked me to my car. I opened the door and slid, with relief, into the driver's seat.

"I appreciate the thought," I said as I turned on the engine, "but I'm hoping I never get this close to a murder again."

# Seth's Big Move
## Stephen Buehler

When Seth woke up that morning, oversleeping like he usually did, he had no idea this would be his worst day ever. His alarm went off at seven, then seven-thirty, and then the pounding at the door pulled him from a dream of winning the Oscar at three minutes after eight. He wiped the sleep from his eyes, threw on a pair of boxers, and dragged himself to the door.

"Who is it?" he yelled.

"Movers," the gruff voice said.

Shit. Today was the day he was moving in with his girlfriend, Emily. He was supposed to have all his belongings in boxes but he only finished loading up two containers before he fell asleep in front of his new Sony seventy-five-inch flatscreen. In the last couple days, he bought a Playstation 4, an X-Box One, an iPad Pro, and a two-in-one laptop/tablet with the hundred-thousand-dollar inheritance his parents left him after they perished in a car accident.

"Are you going to open up or what?" said the impatient voice.

"Yes, yes, sorry," Seth said. He unlocked the flimsy door.

Three short, muscular, Hispanic men walked in. "Not done packing?" the one who seemed to be in charge said.

"I was working on my role," Seth said. "I'm in a play in two weeks and I have this long soliloquy."

"We'll finish the packing. Better if you not here," the same guy said.

Seth was super relieved. He hated stuff like packing, moving boxes, hauling anything heavy. He'd only enjoy it if his character did it in a movie.

At that moment he couldn't believe his luck. He had only been in L.A. for a month and already landed two soap opera appearances. On the second one he actually delivered a line while opening the hotel door, "Right this way." Not fair it was cut before airing. His mother would have been so proud of him.

Remembering his mother numbed him for a moment. She was his biggest fan. She continually told him to follow his dream, even when people told him he had no talent.

Seth grew up in Indiana but there weren't enough juicy roles for him there so he moved to New York, which was also a bust. Nobody would hire him. L.A. was his last chance to make it big. In Hollywood, if you want something bad enough, you get it, right?

Seth dressed and checked his phone for the time. If he worked it right, he could "accidentally" bump into a casting director who bought a chai latte at the same time every day at Grind It Up, the local industry coffee hangout.

"I'll meet you guys at two o'clock, right?" Seth said to the head mover.

The guy cocked his head for a moment. "*Si*," he said. "We meet you there." The other two guys chuckled. They probably laughed because they wouldn't make it there by two because of the all the work Seth left with them. Oh well, chances were he'd be late too.

Seth missed the casting director, but he did run into Gary, a fellow actor in his Stanislavski workshop. Seth insisted on paying for their drinks. They chose a table with a clear view to the door, just in case any VIPs might walk in.

"So you're really going through with it?" Gary said.

"You've only known her for a month."

"Met her the day I arrived in L.A. Nothing like her in the Big Apple." Seth sighed with the satisfaction of finding the perfect girl. "She's the best. She has a stable job, makes good money, and likes to take care of me." A quality he always looked for in a woman.

"She's your sugar mama," Gary said.

"Are you forgetting the hundred grand I inherited? I'm a player with cash." Seth grinned.

"What does she do?"

"Something in finance. It sounds too complicated so I tune it out. She'd be more involved with our move but her offices are moving today as well. She was in charge of finding her company a penthouse suite," Seth said.

"So she left the move up to you?" Gary said.

"What can I say, she trusts me. Actually she hired the movers and set everything up. I just have to meet them later at two. Can't screw that up, can I?"

"She really doesn't know you, does she?"

Seth rolled his eyes.

"How are the new digs?" Gary said.

"I dunno. I let her pick it out. She insisted she handle everything. She wanted to let me work on my role for the play, you know, so I could kill it opening night. We're moving to the west side, so we'll be living large."

"You have some life. You know that, right?" Gary said.

"What can I say? When you got it, you got it." Seth said.

They continued gossiping and decided they had enough time to see a film. They left the theater talking about how they would have been better than the actors that played the leads.

Seth checked his phone for the time, three o'clock. Shit. He was late. The movers would be waiting for him. He didn't want Emily to find out.

Before getting into his car, he looked at his scribbled notes to check the address Emily recited to him. His writing looked like chicken scratches but he finally figured it out: *1122 Gayley Ave. Apt 109.*

He used his phone's GPS while driving over in his clunker of a car, a 2001 Cavalier. Next week they planned to go car shopping. He wanted something German. *Ja.*

Switching on the radio, he tuned to the all-day talk sports station. The sportscaster couldn't believe that North Carolina lost the NCAA championship. Seth winced, he couldn't either. He bet big on NC, seventy thousand dollars big. It was a lock, a sure way to double what was left of the inheritance. He'd have to stop at the bank before Emily got home to withdraw what he owed Rudy. *You don't want to get on Rudy's bad side,* he thought. He'd heard stories of people disappearing. Seth didn't usually use Rudy's service but he was the only bookie giving two-to-one odds on the game.

All the street parking was taken in front of his new apartment complex, but he snagged a spot on a side street.

*Wow,* he thought, *the apartments look huge. This will be some move up.* Good thing Emily made money big time, since he had lost all of his on the bet. She never got mad at him. Anyway, he'd be paying his fair share soon.

No moving truck out front. Maybe they were putting the boxes away for him. That would be sweet.

As he walked into the foyer, he dug the slip of paper out of his pocket. Man, he needed to work on his penmanship, but was finally able to read "Apt 109."

Shit, he didn't have a key. He hoped the movers were still there with the door open. He repeated to himself, *109, 109,* trying to remember it. If it was a line in a play he'd have it, no problem.

Ah, the door to 109 was open. His lucky day. He pushed on it, revealing a massive living room. It even had a fireplace. He couldn't wait to see how big the bedroom was; the one he just left could barely fit his bed.

Two steps in, he stopped. Wait a minute. Where were the boxes? The place should be overflowing with his boxes, all his new electronics, his clothes. Emily told him the furniture from her apartment was going to be delivered, too. She would be pissed when she found out how incompetent her movers were. He should call them; straighten them out.

Seth fished his cell out of his tight jeans' pocket and stared at it. Who were the movers? Emily had handled all that too. He'd have to call her and ask her the name of the company.

Oh well, she seemed to be the forgiving type. He pushed speed dial and got her voice mail. "We're sorry, that number is no longer in service." What? That can't be. How stupid, he must have hit the wrong button. He was careful on the next try. Same recording. *Shiiiiiiiiiit! What was going on?* He tried again, same thing.

Her work—he'd call her there. After hitting that number, the phone rang and rang, not even a voice mail. This couldn't be happening. He replayed all of her instructions in his head. Meet the movers at two o'clock and start unpacking in the new apartment. Emily would try to get away by five but with her new job she might be late.

He'd have to drive over to her office and confess how he screwed up. But wait. Her firm was moving today. Where to? Century City? He was up shit's creek. He had screwed up before but never as bad as this.

A new idea crept into Seth's mind. *No way.* He pushed it back down.

The only thing to do was to wait at Grind It Up until five, then come back here and meet his girlfriend. Before closing the door, he unlocked it in case he arrived before Emily, who surely must have a key.

A perky blonde stood outside the door. "Thinking about moving in? It's a great apartment. Even has a fireplace."

"What? No, my girlfriend and I rented it last week. We're

settling in today, but I think there's been a mix up with the moving company."

"No," she said. "I know for a fact that apartment isn't rented. Manager stopped by earlier. Told me she wanted to rent it out soon. Seemed desperate. She was behind on her quota of filled apartments."

"I'm sure you're mixed up," Seth said. "Emily, my girl-friend, signed the papers last week. She even showed them to me."

"And you read them?"

"Well, no, not all the way. But I do remember the move-in date as today," he said triumphantly.

"Maybe I'm wrong," said the blonde. She walked away whispering under her breath, "But I'm not."

This moving in thing was not working out. Maybe he should have listened to Gary. Seth had only known Emily for a month, right around the time he got his inheritance. Every-thing happened at the same time. The thought he had pushed down earlier wormed its way back up into Seth's mind.

Could she be a con man, er, woman? His Emily? The one that said she'd take care of him, the move, their joint checking account?

He tried her cell again and received the same message: *not in service*. How to find her? He didn't even know where she worked, and had never been to her apartment. She claimed it was always too messy.

Seth had seen *Ocean's Eleven*, *The Sting*, *The Grifters*, and *House of Games* plus plenty of other con men movies. He loved the genre and claimed to be an expert. Con man is short for confidence man—they gain your confidence; you com-pletely trust them; hell, you even think they're doing you a favor, and then *wham*! They steal everything you own.

Not everything. He still had his inheritance. Wait, he just opened a joint checking account with Emily. He needed that money. His life depended on that money.

He sped over to his Bank of America. In line, he asked every person if he could go ahead of them, there was an emergency.

He finally made it to the teller, and slipped his ID under the window. "I'd like a cashier's check for this account."

"How much?" the pixie behind the window said.

"All of it. Should be around seventy-one thousand dollars," he said.

She hit a few buttons. "I'm sorry, sir, but there is no money in this account. A cashier's check was issued for seventy-thousand dollars yesterday. It's been closed, though we had to leave some money in the account to offset any upcoming fees or checks. The remainder will be returned to you in a month."

"My name's Seth Gramble. Maybe it's under a new account, a joint account with Emily Jones." Jones. The name smacked him upside the head. He had even made fun of it to Emily. "Jones, what a common name. You must have six billion relatives."

"I don't see anything," the teller said.

"Let me talk to the manager," Seth said.

"Just a moment." She picked up the phone, but he couldn't hear her conversation.

"Excuse me, Mr. Gramble," said a portly older man. "We can talk in my office. Maybe we can figure out what's going on."

Mr. Rodriquez tapped his keyboard. Yesterday, Seth's personal account had been changed into a joint account. Right after that a withdrawal of seventy thousand dollars was made. Then the account was closed, all by a Ms. Emily Jones. She had not set up a new account with BofA.

"You don't understand," Seth said, desperation gripping him.

"I'm sure there's some kind of mix up," Mr. Rodriquez said. "Why don't you call Ms. Jones? She should have the cashier's check, and will be able to clear this up for you."

"I did. She doesn't answer. I called her work number, they don't answer. We moved in an apartment today, but all my stuff is missing. I've been conned. I demand my money back." He slammed the desk.

"Mr. Gramble, control yourself."

"Control myself?" Seth stood up. "You gave her my money."

"Because she was on the account." Rodriquez looked at the monitor. "We have both of your signatures."

"What?" Seth remembered signing a bunch of paperwork, some of it to do with the bank.

"Mr. Gramble, if you suspect you've been taken advantage of, I suggest you report it immediately to the police."

Seth's phone beeped. Not quite a ring. He took it out and read an alert he had set: *Rudy Valentine, 4pm.* This couldn't be happening. His gambling debt. On top of losing everything, he still owed Rudy seventy thousand dollars. There was no way he could pay him back that day. Or maybe ever.

"Mr. Rodriquez, I need the money, right now. Can you give me a loan?" Seth said.

The bank officer shook his head.

Desperate, Seth slapped both hands on the desk. "Give. Me. My. Money," he said, enunciating each word.

Two firm hands grabbed him from behind.

"Excuse me, sir," said the beefy security guard. "I think it's time for you to leave. You can either walk out, or I can detain you and call the authorities."

"Someone took my money," he said into the guard's non-caring face.

The large man didn't move a muscle.

"Okay, okay, I'm going," Seth said. He shrugged off the restraining hands and stormed out of the stupid bank.

Where to now? He called Gary and told him to meet him at Grind It Up.

They got a table outside.

"Seriously? She played you this whole time?" Gary said.

"Looks that way. I don't know what I'm going to do. I'm losing my mind. I haven't even told you the worst part."

Gary stared over Seth's shoulder as a large shadow covered the table. The shadow of a giant.

"What?" Seth said, turning around. He wished he hadn't. Behind him, Rudy Valentine's intimidating figure blocked out the sun. Behind Rudy was an even bigger man who made the six-foot, three-inch Rudy look tiny.

Rudy acknowledged Gary with a nod. "Would you excuse us," he said. "Mr. Gramble and I have business to discuss."

Gary shot up out of his seat and scurried back inside the coffee shop.

"Where's my money?" Rudy said. "I know you have it, you showed me your bank statement before the bet. You have over seventy grand in your account."

"You're not going to believe this—"

"Then don't tell me," Rudy said. "Tell me what I will believe."

Seth gulped a sizeable amount of air. "My girlfriend stole it. She wiped me out. Took everything."

"I said tell me what I *will* believe."

"It's the truth. I swear. The only things I have left are the clothes on my back and my shitty car."

"Mr. Gramble. I know you call yourself an actor but today's not your best performance." Rudy paused, looked Seth up and down. "Contrary to what you've heard, I'm not a monster. Tell you what I'm going to do. I will give you until noon tomorrow to bring me my money. Bring it here, to this table. Do you think that's fair, Mr. Gramble?"

Seth did not think it was fair. He should be off the hook because he was the one who was robbed. There was no way he could get together seventy grand by tomorrow. Seth did not express these thoughts. "Yes, I think that is fair," he said with his best self-assured voice.

Rudy put his hand out to shake. Seth put his hand out, and Rudy grabbed it and pulled Seth out of his seat. Rudy shoved Seth's hand over to the ogre who wrapped his massive hand around Seth's little finger and snapped it back.

The crack of the bone and cartilage could be heard inside the shop. But it wasn't nearly as loud as Seth's scream. The ogre didn't let go and kept pressing back on the finger.

"Mr. Gramble," Rudy said. "This is just a sample of what could happen to you if you don't bring me what's mine. Do you understand?"

Seth sucked in a boatload of air. "Yes, yes, make him stop. Please."

Rudy gave a slight nod to his assistant. The ogre snapped Seth's finger back into position and released it. The thugs left without another word.

Gary ran out of the coffee shop. "Whoa, man. What was that about?"

"Get me some ice," Seth said through his teeth.

They sat in the Cavalier while Seth wrapped a paper bagel bag filled with ice around his finger.

"I don't mean to sound like a pessimist, but you've got nothing left. If you don't show up with the money that guy's going to break every bone in your body," Gary said.

"Thank you, Captain Obvious," Seth said.

"I can loan you a couple of hundred but that's nowhere near what you need."

A small giggle escaped from Seth. "I don't even have enough gas to leave town. I'm totally screwed. I might as well show up tomorrow and say, 'Break away, fellows.'"

"It's not like the bank can give you a loan," Gary said.

"The bank." Seth remembered how they let Emily take his money and then threw him out. He hated that bank. The bank was the cause of all of his problems. "Get out," Seth said.

"Why?"

"No offense, Gary, but it's my problem."

"What? Maybe I can help."

"No, you can't. I really don't want you involved with this. Please go."

"Okay, bro," Gary said, slowly sliding out of the car.

Seth had stopped off at the playhouse to get the costume of a seventy-year-old grandfather, a role he was preparing for. He realigned his gray wig and looked at himself in his rear-view mirror. He really looked like a septuagenarian. He bet the bank would think so too. Grimacing, he unwound the bandage around his hand. His pinky was twice its normal size, but now he had to act like it didn't hurt.

The plan was simple but dumb. Seth knew it. He was at the end of his rope. He had nowhere to turn. Robbing the bank that screwed him and threw him out like garbage was the best he could come up with. Yes, he couldn't get the seventy grand with one try. If he left the bank with ten grand, that might hold Rudy off for another day. Then another bank or two. Might even make the papers as the Grandfather Bandit. Bank robbers usually were apprehended, but maybe, just maybe, Seth's acting ability would be Tony-worthy and they'd never know it was him. He'd make enough money to pay Rudy, then stop his crime spree and disappear.

Show time! The security guard strolled outside to keep an eye out for any shady characters hanging around the outdoor ATMs.

Seth's old man character had a degenerated hip and couldn't afford a replacement. He limped into the bank using a cane, and stood in the maze of lines like cattle waiting to be slaughtered. He pushed his gold-rimmed glasses up his nose several times and gummed his lips because the old man's dentures didn't fit correctly. He glanced at the security camera on his left; they were getting his good side.

The same pixie teller he had before nodded at him. It felt like opening night. He took a deep breath to calm the jitters. Staying in character, he slowly made his way to her and, with an old man's shaking hand, slipped a piece of paper under the window. *Give me everything in your drawer. Grab the money out of the drawers on your left and right. No silent alarms. No dye packs or people will die. I'm not alone.* Seth suppressed a smile because of his clever word play with "dye" and "die." Perhaps that could be the Grandfather Bandit's trademark, amusing, stick up notes.

The pixie froze. She blinked several times before pushing all her cash under the window. Seth stuffed the money into a Ralph's recyclable bag. The frightened cashier then grabbed the teller's money on her left and shoved that through the window. Seth put that money in the bag, and daintily wiped the sweat off his brow, careful not to smudge the makeup. The teller on the right pushed her drawer closed. Her narrowed eyes told him, *You're not getting my money, old man.*

Seth shrugged and walked out of the bank with his newfound cash. He continued his grandfather persona until he turned the corner behind the bank and stopped to look around. No one in sight. There he whipped off the wig, the long coat, and then wiped the makeup off his face. He stuffed everything into a backpack he had stashed there earlier, and walked away as Seth Gramble, a twenty-seven-year-old actor who had escaped from Indiana.

Sirens wailed as he continued his innocent jaunt to his car. The best place to hide? The empty apartment Emily had tricked him into believing would be theirs. Nobody but her knew about it.

Walking down the hallway like he was a resident, he opened the door to 109. Good thing he left it unlocked. He entered and turned the dead bolt. He did it, he robbed a bank. He twirled around once, stopped, and took in the empty living room. He felt elated and sick at the same time. Yesterday he had the world by the balls. Today he was a full-on bank robber who was glad his mother didn't see him play his latest role.

Taking off the backpack, he slid down the wall into a sitting position. It wasn't right but he didn't have a choice. His back was literally against the wall, and he smiled at the irony.

The door burst open. In charged three policemen wearing full body armor and pointing guns. He complied with their every command. Maybe he wasn't such a good actor after all.

As he was escorted out into the hallway, the door to 104 opened. Out stepped Emily.

Her mouth gaped as she did a double take. "Seth," she said. "What's going on? What are you guys doing?"

"Stop," Seth yelled. Pointing with his shoulder at his girlfriend. "She robbed me first. It's her fault. She took everything from me."

The police pushed him outside.

"Please," Emily pleaded. "Let me talk to him."

One sympathetic cop said, "By the car. Only for a minute."

"What did you do?" Emily said.

"What did I do? It's what you did. You stole my furniture, my inheritance, and my Hollywood future."

"I don't understand," she said.

"Don't play me for a fool. How do you explain that there's nothing in our supposed apartment?"

"What are you talking about? Everything's there."

"Apartment 109 is empty!" Seth said, tired of her games.

"But I told you we were in apartment 104, not 109. Don't you remember?"

"In my pocket, there's a piece of paper," he said.

"May I?" she asked the officer. He shook his head then reached into Seth's pocket and fished out the note. The policeman looked it over before giving it to her.

Emily read it. "104. Look." She held it in front of Seth's eyes.

He was sure he had written 109. He looked closely at it. Then he saw what happened. The way he scribbled the four, it looked like a nine.

"What about my inheritance?" he said.

"It's safe and sound in our new account at Citibank. Remember me telling you how I hated the service at BofA? They treat you like it's their money. I closed the account last night, and opened a new one first thing this morning."

"Your phone," Seth said, more and more desperate. "It says the number is no longer in service."

"Work gave us new phones and new numbers. They wanted all of us to have local area codes. Our office phones were out of order for most of the afternoon, switchboard problems. And I wanted to call you all day, but this move had one problem after another. I've had the worst day ever," she said.

"Okay, that's enough," the officer said. He put his hand on Seth's head and guided it into the car.

*She had the worst day ever? That was nothing compared to mine*, Seth said to himself. His chance to make it in Hollywood was dashed. Maybe there was an actor's workshop in prison.

# BIOGRAPHIES

## *EDITORS*

**MATT COYLE'S** debut novel, *Yesterday's Echo*, won the Anthony Award for Best First Novel, the San Diego Book Award for Best Mystery, and the Ben Franklin Award for Best New Voice in Fiction. His second book, *Night Tremors*, was a Bookreporter.com Reviewers' Favorite Book of 2015 and was nominated for an Anthony Award, a Shamus Award, and a Lefty Award. Matt's third book, *Dark Fissures*, was released in December 2016. Matt lives in San Diego with his yellow Lab, Angus, where he his writing the fourth Rick Cahill crime novel.

**MARY MARKS** is a native Angelino and, with the exception of her teenage years, has lived most of her life in Southern California. The first book in her award winning Quilting Mystery series was published the year Marks celebrated her seventieth birthday. These cozy mysteries take place in the San Fernando Valley and feature Martha Rose, a zaftig, fifty-something divorced Jewish quilter. The fourth book in the series, *Something's Knot Kosher*, was published in June 2016. Marks lives in Camarillo, CA, with her loyal dog Ginger, orange cat Louie, and dozens of unfinished quilts.

**PATRICIA SMILEY** is the *Los Angeles Times* bestselling author of four mystery novels featuring amateur sleuth Tucker Sinclair. *Pacific Homicide* is the first in a new series about LAPD homicide detective Davie Richards. Patty's short fiction has appeared in *Ellery Queen Mystery Magazine* and *Two of the Deadliest*, an anthology edited by Elizabeth George. She has taught writing at various writers' conferences in the U.S.

and Canada, and has served on the board of directors for the Southern California chapter of Mystery Writers of America and as president of Sisters in Crime/Los Angeles. For more information, visit PatriciaSmiley.com.

# CONTRIBUTORS

**AVRIL ADAMS** lives in the Inland Empire. She writes crime fiction, often in the noir genre. Her story "The Lowriders" was included in *Last Exit to Murder.* She has had several other short stories published. In addition to crime fiction Avril writes science fiction with a humanist twist, and children's stories. She is working on a novel starring an African-American female PI. Her animals are an inspiration for her fiction.

**PAULA BERNSTEIN** is the author of the Hannah Kline Mystery Series. A native New Yorker, she migrated to Los Angeles to obtain a PhD in chemistry at Caltech. After receiving her degree, she did research and then attended medical school at the University of Miami. She returned to Los Angeles for internship and residency and, like her character Hannah Kline, has spent her professional career as a practicing obstetrician gynecologist.

**LYNNE BRONSTEIN** spent many years in the Santa Monica-Venice area and supported herself as a journalist while contributing to the literary community with four books, poems and short stories in numerous magazines, readings, and organizing poetry events. She has been nominated for the Pushcart Prize and the Best of the Net Awards and her short story "Why Me?" won a prize in the poeticdiversity Short Fiction Contest.

**STEPHEN BUEHLER'S** short fiction has been published in numerous on-line publications including Akashic Books. "Not My Day" appeared in the *Last Exit to Murder* anthology and "A Job's a Job" in the *Believe Me or Not—An Unreliable Anthology.* He's expanding his novella, *The Mindreading Murders,* about a magician, into a novel and shopping around his mystery/comedy PI novel *Detective Rules.* On top of all that he's a script consultant, magician, and dog owner. Visit him online at StephenBuehler.com.

**SARAH M. CHEN** juggles several jobs including indie book-seller, transcriber, and insurance adjuster. Her crime fiction short stories were accepted for publication online and in various anthologies, including *All Due Respect, Plan B,* Shotgun Honey, *Crime Factory,* Out of the Gutter, *Betty Fedora,* and *Dead Guns Press. Cleaning Up Finn,* her first book, is available now from All Due Respect Books. Visit her online at SarahMChen.com.

**ANNE DAVID** lives in Pasadena with her husband, John. She retired from a lifetime spent in elementary education with the intention of beginning a new career writing children's books. Somehow she deviated from that plan and turned to murder and mayhem with an eBook, *The Accidental Benefactor,* followed with another murder in "The Best LAid Plans." She has a BA in English, a MA in Reading Instruction, and a PhD in Literacy and Language Arts.

**GAY DEGANI** has had three flash pieces nominated for Pushcart consideration, and won the 11th Glass Woman Prize. Pure Slush Books published her collection *Rattle of Want* in 2015 and her suspense novel *What Came Before* was republished by Truth Serum Press in August 2016. She blogs at Words in Place http://wordsinplace.blogspot.com/.

**L.H. DILLMAN** lives in Southern California. "Lead Us Not into Temptation" marks the third appearance in print of Carolina Roundtree, the ever-resourceful and oft-underestimated housekeeper with a unique sense of justice. "Thicker Than Water," another Carolina Roundtree story, can be found in the 2015 Sisters in Crime/LA anthology, *LAdies Night*. The author is currently writing a novel about a father-daughter legal team trying to free a former Black Panther framed for murder.

**WRONA GALL** writes suspense novels that highlight action with intriguing characters. Moving from hometown Chicago to the creative haven of Ojai, California, she writes and paints while enjoying friends, husband Jim, and daughter Vanessa. She won the Malice Domestic Unpublished Writer's Award, has another published short story and has written articles for *Chicago Life* and *Fire to Fly* magazines. Her paintings have been exhibited in numerous museums and are included in major corporate and private collections.

**CYNDRA GERNET**, writer and speech pathologist, leads a quiet, bookish life with her husband, Mike. Cyndra and Mike often joke about finding someone to handle the annoying business of modern life for them; hence, the inspiration for "Hired Lives." Ms. Gernet thanks Jerrilyn Farmer and the Friday morning writing group for many years of support and inspiration. "Good Grief," Cyndra Gernet's comic short story, was published in SinC/LA's 2015 anthology, *LAdies Night*.

**GEORGIA JEFFRIES** sold her UCLA graduate thesis to *The Smithsonian* then figured it was time to learn how to write. After working as journalist for *American Film*, she cracked TV's glass ceiling to become a writer-producer of an Emmy-winning drama. She created original pilots for HBO, ABC,

CBS, NBC, Showtime and is adapting the bestseller *72 Hour Hold.* A professor at USC's School of Cinematic Arts, she is completing a supernatural thriller based on the true story behind her aunt's murder in the Illinois heartland.

**MELINDA LOOMIS** was born and raised in Southern California. She has at times been an office drone (working in everything from insurance to post production), culinary student, and unemployed bum. *LAst Resort* is her first time as a published author. She got the awesome news that she was accepted as a contributor on her birthday. Melinda lives in Marina del Rey, CA, with her extremely photogenic cat Sophie. Visit her website at MelindaLoomis.com.

A former private detective and once a reporter for a small weekly newspaper, **G.B. POOL** writes the Johnny Casino Casebook Series and the Gin Caulfield P.I. Mysteries. She also wrote the SPYGAME Trilogy, *Caverns, Eddie Buick's Last Case, The Santa Claus Singer, Bearnard's Christmas,* and *The Santa Claus Machine.* She teaches writing classes: "Anatomy of a Short Story," "How to Write Convincing Dialogue," and "How to Write a Killer Opening." Visit her online at GBPool.com.

**LAURIE STEVENS** is the author of the Gabriel McRay psychological thrillers. The series garnered twelve awards, among them *Kirkus Reviews* Best of 2011, the 2014 silver IPPY for Best Mystery/Thriller, and *Library Journal's* 2015 Self-E Award. Laurie is a "hybrid" author, having first self-published her books, then signing with an agent and selling her books to Random House, Germany. Laurie is a second-generation L.A. native and enjoys setting her stories in L.A. and the Santa Monica Mountains near her home. For information, visit LaurieStevensBooks.com.

**WENDALL THOMAS** has worked in L.A. as a development executive, entertainment reporter, script consultant, and screenwriter, developing projects for Warner Brothers, NBC, Disney, Showtime, PBS, and A&E. She has taught in the UCLA Graduate Film School since 1997, consults in the U.K., Europe, Australia, and New Zealand, oversees Screen Queensland's program for emerging filmmakers, and lectures annually at the Melbourne International Film Festival. Her short story "Loser Friend" appeared in the SinC/LA anthology *LAdies Night* (2015).

**MAE WOODS** wrote three episodes of HBO's *Tales from the Crypt,* and produced USA Network's *When Danger Follows You Home.* Her feature film credits include posts as an associate producer and development executive. She co-edited SinC/LA's *Murder by 13* and was published in *Murder on Sunset Blvd.* Mae has written for MGM Home Entertainment, Digital City, Mysterynet, and Abdo & Daughters Press. She currently works as an oral historian for the Academy of Motion Picture Arts and Sciences.

OTHER TITLES FROM DOWN AND OUT BOOKS

*See www.DownAndOutBooks.com for complete list*

By J.L. Abramo
*Chasing Charlie Chan*
*Circling the Runway*
*Brooklyn Justice*
*Coney Island Avenue* (*)

By Trey R. Barker
*Exit Blood*
*Death is Not Forever*
*No Harder Prison*

By Eric Beetner (editor)
*Unloaded*

By Eric Beetner
and Frank Zafiro
*The Backlist*
*The Shortlist*

By G.J. Brown
*Falling*

By Angel Luis Colón
*No Happy Endings*
*Meat City on Fire* (*)

By Shawn Corridan
and Gary Waid
*Gitmo* (*)

By Frank De Blase
*Pine Box for a Pin-Up*
*Busted Valentines*
*A Cougar's Kiss*

By Les Edgerton
*The Genuine, Imitation,*
*Plastic Kidnapping*
*Lagniappe* (*)
*Just Like That* (*)

By Danny Gardner
*A Negro and an Ofay* (*)

By Jack Getze
*Big Mojo*
*Big Shoes*
*Colonel Maggie & the Black Kachina*

By Richard Godwin
*Wrong Crowd*
*Buffalo and Sour Mash*
*Crystal on Electric Acetate* (*)

By Jeffery Hess
*Beachhead*
*Cold War Canoe Club* (*)

By Matt Hilton
*Rules of Honor*
*The Lawless Kind*
*The Devil's Anvil*
*No Safe Place*

By Lawrence Kelter
and Frank Zafiro
*The Last Collar*

By Lawrence Kelter
*Back to Brooklyn* (*)

*(*)—Coming Soon*

46988734R00172

Made in the USA
San Bernardino, CA
20 March 2017